# A
# Dirty Woman

## AJOY GHOSH

authorHOUSE®

*AuthorHouse™*
*1663 Liberty Drive*
*Bloomington, IN 47403*
*www.authorhouse.com*
*Phone: 1-800-839-8640*

*Published by AuthorHouse 10/15/2014*

*ISBN: 978-1-4969-4737-6 (sc)*
*ISBN: 978-1-4969-4738-3 (e)*

# Author's Note

Dedicated to those innocent & helpless girls who are the victims of Human Trafficking.

It's a naked fact that every year, thousands of innocent girls are trafficked by the Beasts of our society and sold like an animal in Human Flesh market. I saw many incidents when worked in rural India. The helpless teenage girls were sold to the hands of the animals who were looked and dressed like human. I saw the tears of those girls as a silent observer.

This is a story of one such girl who was victim of human trafficking and sold like an animal several times. After many years, that girl returned to her village one day and started her final journey to save thousands of helpless women who were victims of human trafficking and social injustices like her.

World will change one day and trading of human flesh will be stopped one day, I firmly believe.

The name of the characters and the places used in this novel have no resemblances with the actual names and places. If anyone finds any resemblance, it is nothing but a coincidence.

Ajoy Ghosh
Brownsville, Texas 78520
2014

# *Chapter-1*

Morning is cold today. It is September month, not winter time. Today is oddly cold. Temperature has fallen down like winter months. Viswanath gets up early. He has lot of works in the morning. Today, Madam is going to Kolkata. Viswanath exactly does not know why Madam is going. He has heard from Nitish Babu that Chief Minister will confer one award on Madam. Nitish Babu is the Manager of Madam's office. Viswanath has been working for last two years at Madam's house. He has been given the charge of maintenance of garden. Madam loves flowers, rose particularly. Viswanath has planted varieties of rose plants in the garden.

The total area of house and garden will be more than an acre. House is two storied and the flower garden is in front of the house. There is also a large space behind the house. When Viswanath first came, the area was vacant. Viswanath has planted fruit trees of mango, guava, jackfruit, litchi, and berries there. He grows seasonal vegetables also. The garage is built at the backyard. The entire area is protected by boundary wall so that no trespasser can enter in the garden and house.

Viswanath is busy to pluck fresh vegetables for Madam's breakfast. Madam likes fresh vegetables. Madam also likes fresh cucumber & carrot in salad. Viswanath picks a few cucumbers & carrots. He has made one flower bouquet for Madam. Madam is going to meet the Chief Minister in Kolkata. She will stay there for one week.

Viswanath is busy. He wants to finish his morning works quickly. It is already seven morning. Madam will start within an hour. Nitish Babu is going with Madam. He will be more than fifty years old. He takes all care of Madam like his sister. In the house, there are six more staffs who help in cooking and maintaining of the house. Madam has no kid. Viswanath could not guess her actual age. She may be forty or more. Viswanath also does not know whether Madam is married or not. He dares to ask anybody. Although Madam always speaks with all of them and cares for everybody who are in her house. Madam has pleasant personality. Viswanath never saw her angry. Madam always wears white color sari.

Viswanath gives the vegetables to Gita who is the cook. Gita is busy too. She will cook vegetables and make chapattis for Madam. Madam likes vegetable dishes with chapattis. Madam eats vegetarian dishes only.

Pintu, the driver of Madam has come early. He has parked the car in front of the gate and is busy in cleaning the car. He is checking the engines, break oil etc. The distance from Berhampore to Kolkata is about 200 miles and it will take 4 to 5 hours to reach in Kolkata.

Nitish Babu has come early today. He is busy in office and advising of the urgent works to Samar Pal who is Accountant. Madam and Nitish Babu will be out of office for one week.

Madam comes out at eight o'clock after breakfast. Pintu opens the door of the car. Viswanath gives the flower bouquet to Madam. Madam receives the bouquet. Gita, Samar, Narayan, and all staffs have gathered to say good bye. Madam talks to each one. She says Pintu to drive carefully and takes a halt at Krishnanagar which will come midway of the travel. Nitish Babu takes the front seat beside Pintu. Madam enters in the car's back door. Nitish Babu already has put Madam's and his luggage inside the dickey of the car. Pintu starts engine and the car leaves slowly.

Madam is going to Kolkata, the capital of West Bengal state in India. The Chief Minister of the state will confer one Civilian Award on Madam tomorrow for her contribution in social work. The award has been announced a few weeks ago.

In the press conference, the Minister, who announced the name of Madam, said, "the state feels proud to confer its highest Civilian Award on Salma Roy for her relentless fights against the evils of the society and bringing a section of women of our society to the normal life from their dark and ill-fated life. Salma Roy, throughout her life, has uplifted hundreds of women in the villages of Murshidabad and other districts who had been living a distressful life and were victims of society. Salma Roy has formed more than 500 Self-Help groups comprising of only women members particularly who are neglected and helpless in all respect. She gave them self-employment. Now under her leadership, all the Self-Help groups are earning sufficient incomes which are being shared by those women members and they are living a modest life today."

It was published in all leading newspapers and telecasted in television channels. After that, all TV channels were busy to telecast her interview. One TV channel has made one documentary on her life. Salma Roy is a well known figure in the State as well as National news channel. State has also recommended her name for National Civilian award in the next Republican day.

Salma is going to Kolkata to receive the award from the hands of Chief Minister. The car is moving at a medium speed. Glass windows are open. Gentle breeze is passing through the open windows. Weather is not cold now like early morning.

Salma feels empty all of a sudden. Aninda is appearing before her eyes continuously. Salma closes her eyes. Lot of tears are coming out. Salma wants to cry today.

All her past memories are appearing before her eyes one by one. As if, it happened yesterday. Salma feels presence of Aninda sitting beside her in the car.

Salma remembers everything from the day one when she first met Aninda. Aninda came to her village, Nayanpur, perhaps 25 years ago. The year was possibly late eighties.

———ɯɯ·ɔɘɤɔ·ɢɤɘ·ɔɘ·ɯɯ———

Aninda Roy, a bright young officer, was transferred to the bank at Nayanpur. What would be his age? Early twenties or mid twenties, Salma didn't know his age correctly. Tall, handsome, and fair complexion, his eyes were deep and it seemed that he thought everything deeply. Pleasant behavior he had. Salma never saw him angry. How was Salma introduced to Aninda? That was a story indeed.

Salma's father, Javed Ali Sarkar, was running a *Tanga* (horse cart) in the village. Javed's income was not certain. Every morning, Javed went to the village bus stand for passengers. Passengers were not good numbers every day. The bus came from Berhampore, the head quarter of Murshidabad district. The distance was about 40 miles and the same bus plied 4 times each day. Javed waited at the bus stand for passengers who would go to nearby villages. Javed was not the only *Tanga* rider. There was severe competition. When Javed bought the *Tanga*, he was the only *Tanga* rider at the bus stand. At the beginning, he was getting good number of passengers and his income was good. But, his luck was not good. The number of *Tangas* was increased to ten at the same bus stand. Number of *Tangas* were more, but flow of passengers was not increased. Obviously, it affected the daily income of Javed. It happened in many days that Javed did not get any passenger and returned home empty hands.

Salma's mother, Ruksana, took house maid job in one Hindu family of Nayanpur. Salma was their elder daughter. She had one sister and 2 brothers. Family was big but income was not sufficient. Javed didn't have any agricultural land. His income was from Tanga only.

Nayanpur was a small village. It was located at the border of India and Bangladesh. The great river *Padma* was passing by the side of Nayanpur. The river was considered as demarcation line between India and Bangladesh. There was a Border Security Camp at the village. Nayanpur had population of both Hindus and Muslims. Unlike other border areas, Nayanpur was exceptionally calm. Muslims resided at the Eastern part of Nayanpur, locally they said "Purba Nayanpur" and all Hindus resided at Western part, locally said "Paschim Nayanpur". There was a big field in between *Purba* and *Paschim* Nayanpur. The boys and girls of Nayanpur and the adjacent villages played on the field. On Durga Puja time, Hindus made a big stage and celebrated Durga Puja there. Salma every year went to see the Durga Puja with her brothers and sister. There were one primary and one Secondary school at Nayanpur. One bank opened branch in the village. The staffs of the bank came from Kolkata. Salma knew that Kolkata is a big city and Capital of their State, West Bengal. There was one Post Office in the village. The bus stand was located outside Nayanpur. Her father Javed every day morning went to that bus stand and waited for passengers.

Javed took a loan from the bank for purchase of horse and *Tanga*. The loan was given to him under Integrated Rural Development Programme (IRDP). He got subsidy from Government and Bank Manager told him to repay loan with interest within three years. Bank Manager gave him a pass book and told the amount of monthly installment, he had to pay every month. Javed's happiness was no limit the day he got approval of loan. At last he got his own horse and *Tanga*.

On the day his loan was approved, one member of the local *Panchayat*, Tahasin Sheikh came to his house at the evening time. Javed welcomed him. Tahasin told Javed that he had a private talk and wanted to say secretly. Javed invited him to his bedroom. He locked the door.

"Javed Bhai, we are happy that your loan is approved by bank," Tahasin said. "We requested the Bank Manager for your loan and told that Javed is a poor man. If one *Tange* loan is given to him, his family will be benefited. He has no income and no agricultural land."

"I am really grateful to bank and all *Panchayat* members. In fact, I have no words to express my gratitude," Javed replied.

"You know, Javed, it was very difficult to convince the Manager of the Bank," Tahasin continued. "He didn't agree to give you loan. He asked security and guarantee. I told that Javed has no land. Only he has a small house. Please give him loan without any security. You know, I requested the Manager that we are taking the responsibility of his loan payment. Then Manager agreed to give you loan. But...?"

"What happened? You want to say something?" Javed asked.

Tahasin lowered his voice and almost whispered.

"Manager asked five hundred rupees for your loan," Tahasin said. "You know, Javed, I requested him a lot. But he didn't agree. I promised him that I am taking the responsibility to collect the money from Javed. Javed will pay when the loan will be given to him."

"Five hundred rupees? Where shall I get the money? It's a big amount to me. You know, Tahasin Bhai, my financial condition. I am a labor now and I have no fixed daily income. I have six members in my family. How can I manage five hundred?" Javed left a long breath.

"That I do not know. You have to pay five hundred. Manager will not give you the loan if you do not give him five hundred."

"Tahasin Bhai, you know all. Tell me how can I arrange money?" Javed asked.

"Javed Bhai, I have one idea. You can manage the amount. Manager will give you the full loan in cash. Keep five hundred separately and buy one horse and *Tanga* by rest four thousand five hundred. We shall manage a cash memo for full amount of loan. You will get money and give it to me. I shall give to Manager," Tahasin advised.

"Ok, I shall do what you told. Please request Manager to give me loan amount within a week. I got information of one good horse and *Tanga* from Durgapur a day before. The owner has agreed to sell by five thousand rupees. I shall request him to take four thousand five hundred and give his horse and *Tange*. I shall repay rest five hundred slowly from my income. I hope he will agree."

Tahasin left saying good night.

Javed sat like a statue. Ruksana asked him, "what happened? You look disturbed."

Javed could not tell her. He was in a happy mood before Tahasin came. He knew what difficulty he faced for getting the loan under IRDP from Bank.

He met the *Pradhan* of the Nayanpur Gram *Panchayat*, Gumani Hussain about six months before. That time, Javed was a daily labor and worked in the agricultural fields of others. He had not got works regularly. He got jobs only during crop sowing season and harvesting time. He had to sit idle without any work in most of the months in the year. During off season, he often went to Berhampore and worked at a private ware house. The ware house owner knew him and gave him job of loading and unloading of rice grain bags in trucks.

Javed stayed during that time at Berhampore and came to Nayanpur only once in a month. He brought food grains, cloths, grocery items from Berhampore for his family. His daughters and sons were waiting when Javed would come. They didn't have any good dress. Ruksana worked as a maid servant in other's house.

One day, Javed got information of the IRDP loan from one of his co-workers at Berhampore. He knew that one bank was opened at Nayanpur. Next time, when he came to Nayanpur, he went to bank for loan. That was a memorable day to Javed.

It was his first occasion in life, he went to any bank. The bank was located at *Paschim* Nayanpur area and was opened at the house of Bara Babu. Bara Babu once was the land lord of the village. Bara Babu was his nick name. His actual name was Surapati Mondal. His age would be 60 years. Earlier he was the *Pradhan* of Nayanpur *Panchayat* when Congress Party was ruling the state. Currently, *Panchayat* was captured by ruling Left Front and Bara Babu was no longer the *Panchayat* Head. Present *Pradhan*, Gumani Hussain, Tahasin Sheikh, and all other members belonged to Left parties.

When Javed reached bank, there were many customers in the bank. He asked where Manager was sitting. One staff showed to the Manager's chamber. Javed with lot of hesitation entered inside the chamber. He forgot that before entering, he had to take permission. In fact, he didn't know all that formalities. He straightway entered.

"Sir, I want a loan. I am very poor. I have a big family. Sir, please give me a loan," Javed said.

Manager was busy in his works. He raised his eyebrows and looked at Javed.

"Who are you?" Manager asked.

"Sir, I ... am... Javed Ali... Sarkar," Javed was fumbling. All his words chocked at this mouth.

"I am not here to donate money. Go to *Panchayat* and bring their recommendation," Manager's voice was loud with full of irritation.

"Sir, I am very poor. *Panchayat* may not give any recommendation. Please help me. Please give me a loan. I promise I shall repay your loan within time what you say. Sir, I have 2 sons and 2 daughters. They do not get food daily. My wife works 2 houses as maid servant. I do not have daily work here. I work temporarily at Berhampore," Javed tried to speak.

Manager asked him to sit on the chair. Javed was hesitant. He never sat before such a big man like Bank Manager. He was hesitant to sit. Manager again asked him to sit. Manager called one gentleman and briefly said why Javed came to bank. He also told to take an interview and proceeded if Javed was eligible for any loan under IRDP.

That gentleman told Javed to follow him. Javed came to the main hall of the bank. He found many bank staffs working there. He saw one cabin which was partitioned by iron grill and glass. One person was working there. There was a small queue before that particular counter. That person was receiving cash from the customers. He might be the Cashier, Javed thought.

That gentleman came to his place and asked Javed to sit on a chair.

"What type of loan do you want?" he asked Javed.

Javed didn't have any knowledge of type of loan. He could not reply. Only he told, "Sir, I want loan?"

"Ok, I want to know what will you do with the loan?" that guy again asked.

"I do not know. Please tell me what shall I do with the loan?" Javed asked.

That gentleman laughed and asked, "Javed Bhai, you should think what business you will do. It is the system of bank's loan that the applicant should request loan for a particular business or project and based on his experience, bank approves loan. Please tell me if you have any experience of any business," he asked.

"Sir, I did not do any business in life. I am a poor man and daily labor. I have no steady income. I want to do any business in Nayanpur with the help of bank loan. Please tell me what type of business will be good for me?" Javed asked.

That officer possibly understood what Javed wanted to speak. He was in the bank for last 2 years and knew that most of the rural people could not express what actually they wanted. He saw innocent face of Javed, the poor rural man, who had no steady income at all. Every day, he handled many rural customers. They did not have education and no regular income. He told Javed to come next day and would think a suitable business for him.

Before leaving, Javed asked politely, "Sir, what's your name?"

"I am Aninda Roy. I am Loan Officer of this bank," that officer replied.

# Chapter-2

Javed returned home with cheerful mood. He said everything of his visit to Ruksana. Salma was present there. Salma was quite matured and understood what her father said. Javed appreciated a lot about that Loan Officer, Aninda Roy.

Next day, Javed reached to bank before opening of the bank. He waited at the main gate. Bank opened at 10 o'clock. All the staffs and officers came on time. Aninda Roy and Manager came almost at the same time. Aninda saw Javed waiting outside bank. He called Javed and told him to wait for a few minutes as the bank just opened and they needed to do some daily formalities. After about half an hour, Aninda called Javed to his loan section. Javed was eager to hear what Aninda would tell him. Aninda asked him to sit on a chair.

"Javed Bhai, I thought about your case. You have no past experience of doing any business. I suggest not to do any business like grocery or garments shop or any food items with the bank loan. You could not manage and might suffer loss due to no past experience," Aninda said.

"Yes Sir, I have no experience at all. Please tell me what should I do? I want to repay loan to bank within time but I do not find where shall I use the bank loan?" Javed asked.

"Do you know driving?" Aninda asked.

"No Sir, I do not know," Javed replied.

"It's a problem. It is a village and scope of viable activities are less. What shall I suggest you? "Aninda's voice became lower.

"Sir, I have an idea," Javed said.

"Tell me, what is your idea?" Aninda asked.

"If I buy agricultural land with the loan, I can cultivate rice and vegetables. I am sure that I can do best with the loan and can repay loan," Javed said.

"No, Javed Bhai, it is not permitted to buy land out of bank's loan. We have no such scheme. I am thinking about a good project which will suit you and I can propose the project under Integrated Rural Development Programme(IRDP). If it is considered under IRDP, you will get at least 25% subsidy from Government and your loan burden will be less," Aninda said.

"Sir, please think and I shall do whatever you will suggest," Javed said.

"Yes, I got one," Aninda's face became bright.

"Please tell, Sir," Javed said.

"You know that bus stand of Nayanpur is located outside the village. The passengers who come by bus, have to walk to Nayanpur or adjacent villages. Many times, we face problems when we have luggage. If any alternative vehicle is available at bus stand, it will be helpful for all passengers," Aninda said.

"Yes Sir, you are right. The distance from bus stand to Nayanpur is about one mile and all passengers have no other alternative but to walk," Javed added.

"I think, Javed Bhai, if any horse cart which you call *Tanga*, is available at bus stand, it will help all passengers to reach to their destination comfortably particularly those have luggage," Aninda said.

"You are correct, Sir," Javed added.

"Javed Bhai, If we give you a loan for purchase of one horse and cart (*Tanga*), can you not start this business? I am sure it will be the best project for you."

"Sir, I have no knowledge of Horse cart (*Tanga*) riding. Can I do it?" Javed was hesitant.

"No problem, Javed Bhai. You work at Berhampore. I saw many *Tangas* at Berhampore Central Bus stand. You request any of them that you want to learn *Tanga* riding. It is not car or bus that you need a driving license. It is very easy. If you try for one week, you can learn."

"Sir, I must learn. Please give me one week time. I shall come again," Javed said.

"No problem, take your time. When you will be ready, please come to me directly. I shall make your application ready for approval."

Javed was happy. He came home almost running. Ruksana and Salma were waiting for him. He said everything what Aninda told him and his proposed new business. Javed was so happy that he told Aninda's name at least hundreds time. He had not seen such a person, so sympathetic. It's unbelievable.

Next day morning, Javed went to Berhampore by the first morning bus from Nayanpur. When he reached the Ware House, work was not started. His employer, Susanta Babu just arrived.

"How are you Javed Bhai?" he asked Javed. "How was your holidays? How are Salma Beti and your sons?" He Knew Salma. Salma once came to his ware house when Javed fell sick about 6 months before.

"Sir, all are fine," Javed replied.

"Did you finish your breakfast? You have come early. Come and take something from my packet," Susanta Babu said.

Susanta Babu liked Javed. Javed knew that Susanta Babu always tried to give him extra hours of works so that Javed could earn more. He knew Javed's family condition.

"Sir, I have one request today. I want your advice. I shall do what you say. You are my God. My family is surviving with your mercy," Javed said.

"Javed Bhai, don't say so. Who am I to see your family? Everything is done by the God," Susanta Babu said.

Javed knew that Susanta Babu was religious minded.

"Tell me what is your question?" Susanta Babu asked.

"Sir, you know my family condition and my income. My Salma is now marriageable. My two sons and younger daughter are also growing. I could not give them proper food. My wife works at two houses as maid servant. I want to do a business."

"Business? Javed Bhai, it's a good idea. But how can you do without money? Who will give you?"

"Sir, I went to Nayanpur bank two days ago. I met Manager and Loan Officer. They will give me loan for *Tanga* business. They told me to practice *Tanga* riding before approval of loan. Sir, I want your help. If you please help me in practicing *Tanga* riding, I can get the loan."

"Very good, Javed Bhai. It's a wonderful idea. I must help you. So if you get loan, you will leave me."

"Sir, I shall not forget your help. I know my family is surviving only due to your help. How can I forget your help, sub?" Javed said.

Susanta Babu thought a while. "Javed Bhai, I have one friend at Khagra *Bazaar* who has one private *Tanga* for use of his own. I shall request him to help you so that you can practice *Tanga* riding. It's easy to learn. If you practice one day, you will learn. Only thing is that I shall miss you when you will start your business at Nayanpur. Do not forget me. And do not hesitate if you need any more help from me."

Susanta Babu was kind and went to his friend's house that day. His friend agreed as requested by Susanta Babu. His friend's *Tanga* was operated by one Salim Haque. His friend told Salim to help Javed so that he could learn *Tanga* riding.

Javed met Salim Haque. Every morning, he went to Salim Bhai and practiced *Tanga* riding. Javed was sincere and within a week time, he was fully confident in *Tanga* riding. It was not at all difficult.

"Javed Bhai, one thing you should always remember," Salim said.

"What is that?"

"Always take care of the horse like you family member. Give food at fixed time daily. If your horse is healthy and ok, it would give wonderful service."

"Salim Bhai, your horse is very obedient,"

"You see, my horse has become my son's like. Horse is very loyal and can sacrifice life even for its master," Salim said.

Javed thanked Salim Bhai a lot. He took permission from Susanta Babu for leaving. Susanta Babu gave him a tips of fifty rupees for his good and loyal service. He reminded Javed not to forget him if Javed needed any help.

Javed was a simple and innocent man. He worked hard. Everybody in the ware house liked him.

Javed returned to Nayanpur. He said everything to Ruksana and Salma. His two sons were junior to his daughters. After Salma, his second daughter was born. He had given her name Tashlima. After Tashlima, his 2 sons were born a year's gap. His son's names were Danish and Nassir. They are now only 8 to 10 years old. Tashlima might be 12 years. Salma was the eldest and she would cross 16 in next winter. Salma was marriageable. In his society, all girls were married early before 16 years. Javed had no savings. How could he arrange marriage? Even, there was no system of dowry in his society and groom gave money to the bride as per custom, still, he had to spend a good amount of money for receptions and other expenses. It's not easy to arrange marriage without spending a minimum amount which Javed had not saved. Javed thought if he could save extra money from his *Tanga*, he would arrange marriage of Salma in next year. By that time Salma would be seventeen.

Javed was happy. Ruksana, Salma, Tashlima, Danish & Nassir were happy too. They could not remember when all members of their family were happy together.

Javed had one uncle, Mozammel Sarkar, who lived nearer to his house. Mozammel had one grocery shop at *Paschim* Nayanpur Hindu areas. Javed didn't have any other relative at Nayanpur. Javed's father died long before when he was only 10 years old. His mother also died after his father. Javed had no other brother and sister. His uncle, Mozammel Saheb took care of him after his parent's death. Javed did not get any chance to go to School. When he was only 12 or 13 years, his uncle asked him to work as field labor at the houses of Hindu families. The Hindu families were considered rich in the village and all of them resided at *Paschim* Nayanpur. Javed and all other Muslim families lived at *Purba* Nayanpur, Eastern part of Nayanpur. Most of the Muslim families were poor and worked in the agricultural fields of Hindus. But the work was seasonal and they could manage work only 5 to 6 months in a year. Rest of the months were painful when they had no work. Javed and other Muslim youths went to Berhampore that period for earnings. At least 100 Muslim families lived at *Purba* Nayanpur. Most of the villages in Nayanpur *Panchayat* were Muslim dominated. Hindu population was not significant. Only 50 Hindu families lived in *Paschim* Nayanpur.

*Paschim* Nayanpur was better developed than *Purba* Nayanpur. Bank, School, Post Office, hotel and all shops were located at *Paschim* Nayanpur. Electricity was also available there. But supply of power was erratic. Only 4 to 6 hours, power was available in a day. The road from bus stand to Nayanpur was built up recently by concrete. Earlier, it was a mud road and during rainy season, villagers faced lot of difficulty to walk. That road had been extended up to the river of Char Gopinathpur. The name of the river was *Bhairav*. *Bhairav* was a small branch of *Padma* and it was passing around Char Gopinathpur.

The river became dry during summer time. But in rainy reason, it became full and many times, flood was seen. The river was not wide. Ferry service was available at Char Gopinathpur. There were at least 25 villages in Nayanpur *Panchayat* area. Only Nayanpur was having concrete road, electricity and transport facility. All the people of other villages had to come to Nayanpur to catch bus for going to Berhampore. In Nayanpur, local cultivators brought their vegetables for sale twice in a week. All vegetable venders gathered at the market place of *Paschim* Nayanpur. Local *Panchayat* had built one shopping area for vegetable venders. *Panchayat* office was also located there. Gumani Hussain was the *Pradhan* who hailed from Pirajpur village which was the next village of Nayanpur.

When Javed was young, he saw construction of the main connecting road from Nayanpur to Berhampore. Soon, buses started to ply on that road. There were 2 towns located on the way to Berhampore. Those towns were Sheikhpara and Islampur. Islampur was the head quarter of the block, Raninagar. The distance from Nayanpur to Islampur was about 20 miles. Islampur was a small town. One hospital and one college were there. Villagers of Nayanpur *Panchayat* came to Islampur for shopping and medical treatments. There were many good doctors also. The school of Nayanpur was up to 10th Standard only. The students of Nayanpur *Panchayat* took admission at Islampur college for higher study. They commuted daily by bus.

Javed didn't get any chance to go to school. His desire was that at least his sons should get education. There was no culture of his society to send girls to school. Girls were born for household works at their parents family before marriage and husbands family after marriage. Javed wanted to send Salma to school. He asked permission from his uncle, Mozammel Saheb. His uncle onwards sought permission from Imam of the local *Masjid* but Imam did not allow to send Salma to school. Salma wanted to go to school. But Javed had to follow the instructions of Imam. It was about 10 years before. Salma was then only 5 to 6 years old. Situation had been changed a lot. Muslim girls were going to School like boys and they were also going to Islampur College after school.

Lot of changes Javed saw in his life. Javed could not read and write. Even, he did not know what was his actual age. Only he could remember, when he married Ruksana, his uncle told Ruksana's father that Javed was 20 years old. Javed could remember those days. That was the year when Bangladesh Liberation war against Pakistan started. He saw thousands of Bangladeshi people came to Nayanpur areas for shelters. Javed that year married Ruksana. Ruksana was only 16 years old, his uncle told.

That was really a horrible time. The war in Bangladesh continued several months. Government opened relief camps for refugees and Javed worked there as volunteer. One day, Bangladesh got freedom. All refugees retuned back to Bangladesh. Government closed all camps. Many years passed after that. It might be more than 20 years. Javed could not remember correctly.

After marriage, Javed was serious to earn more. His uncle was a good friend of Bara Babu, Surapati Mondal. At his request, Javed got job at Surapati Mondal's firm. His duty was from morning seven to evening six. Surapati Babu gave him breakfast and lunch. Wage was less. But it was good for two members. Ruksana every day at the evening time waited for Javed. They were happy. Four years after their marriage, their first child Salma was born. After Salma, Tashlima and two sons were born.

Family size was increased but not income. Days were passing. Pains and sufferings were part of their life. Javed sincerely wanted to start new venture for his family.

Next day, Javed reached to the bank to meet Aninda Roy, the Loan Officer. When he reached, bank was opened already and all the staffs were busy at their desks. Many customers were there for depositing cash and other banking transactions. Javed went to Aninda. Aninda was busy with another customer. Seeing Javed, Aninda said to wait for a few minutes. When he was free, called Javed.

"What happened? Are you now ready to do *Tanga* business?" Aninda asked.

"Yes Sir, I learnt *Tanga* riding at Berhampore. I can do. No problem now," Javed replied.

"Very good. Let's start the application process. Javed Bhai, I want to tell you that it will take at least 3 to 4 months time to complete the entire process and get your loan. You may ask me why does it take so many months? I am explaining. Your loan application will be considered under IRDP where you will get subsidy from Government at 25 % or more. Your application will be prepared and recommended by the local *Panchayat Pradhan*, Gumani Saheb and after that it will go to Block Office at Islampur. Block Development Officer will verify the loan application and your income certificate given by *Panchayat* and will recommend to our Bank for approval and disbursement of loan. It takes total 3 to 4 months period to complete all steps and process."

"Sir, 4 months? I have already left my job at Berhampore. What shall I do now? I have no savings at all. I have big family. How can I manage?" Javed was disappointed.

"Javed Bhai, it's a normal process. It will take. I understand your condition. I can assure you that I shall follow up at each step for early disposal. But there are certain things which are not in my hand. Today, I am initiating the process and I shall personally tell your name to *Pradhan* Saheb, Gumani Hussain. He will come to our bank today as we have one meeting. By the by, are you free at evening time? It is the norms that before sponsoring any IRDP proposal, bank should inspect the case and visit the residence of the applicant. If you are free, I can do that work today."

"Yes Sir, I am totally free. You can come to my house anytime. It's our luck that you will pay visit to my small house."

"No Problem, I shall go today."

"Shall I need to talk to Manager regarding my loan application?"

"Not required, I shall tell him. When your loan application will be forwarded to our bank from BDO Office, Manager generally calls all applicants for one formal interview. It is not required now to meet the Manager."

"Ok, Sir. I shall wait for you today."

"One more thing, Javed Bhai. I already told you that you have to wait for a few months. I suggest you to return to Berhampore and do your job. Tell your Master about this and I am sure he will re-employ you. Next time, when you will come to Nayanpur, come to me. I shall tell you the progress," Aninda said.

Javed left hurriedly as he had to inform Salma about the visit of Aninda Roy. Ruksana was not in house. She was working at her Master's house. Javed was hesitant. He had no good furniture. There was no good place also in his house where he would invite Aninda to sit. His house was small, only 2 rooms and one kitchen. One double bed was there, no other furniture.

On returning home, he told everything to Salma. She was as well worried how to welcome Aninda Roy. No big man came to their house so far. Salma was a wise girl. "Don't worry, Abba," She said. "I shall manage everything."

It was afternoon time. Salma told Javed to take bath and finish lunch.

Salma arranged everything within an hour. She went to Mozammel Saheb's house and brought one good chair. She also borrowed one good tea cup, plate and, one good bed cover. Salma was expert in all house works. Very soon, she changed the room. She placed chair at the room and covered the dirty bed with the bed cover. She bought biscuits from *Paschim* Nayanpur. She arranged everything for tea preparation. Javed saw that Salma made everything ready. He was happy. The distance between *Purba* and *Paschim* Nayanpur was only a quarter mile. It took 10 minutes to reach. Javed, Salma, and all were waiting for Aninda Roy. Ruksana came from her work. Danish and Nassir came back from school. Tashlima was helping Salma to give final touch. Everybody was sweating.

Aninda came at evening time. Javed greeted and welcomed to his house. Javed invited him to his small bed room. He introduced Salma to Aninda. Ruksana, Tashlima, Danish and Nassir were scared to come in front of Aninda. Aninda sat on the chair which was brought and decorated specially for him. He was possibly the most important guest who first time came to Javed's house. Javed was busy and asked Salma to bring tea and other things to Aninda.

"Javed Bhai, don't be busy. I don't want to take tea now."

"Sir, my daughter, Salma arranges tea for you. Please do not say no."

Aninda smiled and told Salma to make one cup of tea without milk.

Salma first time saw Aninda, tall, young, and handsome Bank Officer. His complexion was fair. Hairs were long. Possibly, he did not cut hairs for several months. Dress was simple, not like a big man. Eyes were deep and bright as if he was thinking something intensely. Very calm and pleasant look, mid twenties might be. Javed sat on the floor. Salma brought tea cup and cookies for Aninda. Aninda took the tea cup and made a long sip.

"Javed Bhai, you know, it is the norms of bank when bank receives any loan application, bank visits the residence of the applicant and verify the applicant's documents. It is formal and don't be worried. I want to send one inspection report to Block Office. Your application will be prepared and signed by the *Panchayat*. Tomorrow, you will go to the *Panchayat* Office and meet *Pradhan*, Gumani Hussain and Gani Bhai. Gani Bhai is the *Pnachayat* Assistant. You are lucky, today both Gumani Saheb and Gain Bhai came to our bank. I told everything about your case and requested them to recommend for *Tanga* loan for you. They know you well and told me to help you. Do not worry. Tomorrow you will go to *Panchayat* and they will make your application ready," Aninda said.

"What documents shall I bring to *Panchayat* Office?" Javed asked.

"Do you have ration cards?"

"Yes Sir, I have ration cards for all members of my family. I do not have any other documents," Javed replied.

"No other document or certificate is required. Only we need ration cards. Please bring your ration cards. I want to see," Aninda said.

Javed asked Salma to bring the ration cards. Salma brought all the ration cards. Aninda requested Salma to bring the lamp nearer to him as there was dark covered in the room. Aninda verified all ration cards and said everything was good.

"Javed Bhai, your total loan amount will be Rs.5000 for one horse and one cart(*Tanga*). It is the present project cost for *Tanga* loan in Murshidabad district. *Panchayat* will recommend for Rs.5000. I have told Gumani Saheb. You will get subsidy from Government of Rs.1500. Therefore, your loan amount will be Rs.3500. This subsidy is free and Government will give you for your business. You will pay Rs.3500 with interest within 3 years. We shall fix monthly installments and you will pay every month of your installment. We shall not ask you to pay during first 3 months. What you will earn in first 3 months, keep it separately and use for maintenance and other expenses. Please do not fail to repay the monthly installment. It is a good scheme. I know, you are hard working man and will not default in loan repayment," Aninda said.

"Sir, I promise, I shall repay your loan before time. I am poor, Sir. I have no words to express my feelings to you. You are my God. Who cares of the poor nowadays? You have given me time and taking all pain for my loan. I shall not forget you, Sir," Javed's eyes were full of tears. Salma silently was hearing the talks of Aninda and her father.

"Don't say so. It is my duty to grant loans to the poor people of the villages. Our bank has hired me for the job. I am not giving anything to you. You deserve this type of loan due to your poor financial condition," Aninda said.

"But Sir, you have given me time and personally taken initiative for my loan. You are exceptional. I shall never forget," Javed said.

"Javed Bhai, how many children you have?" Aninda asked.

"Sir, I have 2 daughters and 2 sons. Salma is the eldest. She is 16 years old. I am looking a groom for her. If I can save extra from *Tanga* business, I shall arrange Salma's marriage next year," Javed said.

"Why are you busy for Salma's marriage? She is too young still," Aninda looked at Salma. Salma's face became red.

"No Sir, It's my big burden. I cannot sleep properly. My second daughter is 12 years and 2 sons are 10 and 8 years old. My wife also works as a housemaid in 2 houses," Javed said.

"Do not worry, Javed Bhai. Everything will be good."

"Sir, where are you living? How many years you are in bank?" Javed asked.

"I am living at Jangli Saha's house at *Paschim* Nayanpur nearer to my bank. I have taken one room at his house on rent. I am in this bank for last 2 years. After joining the bank, I have been posted first here," Aninda replied.

"Who are in your family?" Javed asked. Aninda smiled. "I am alone. My parents are in Kolkata. I am their only son."

"Javed Bhai, I have one request. Please keep it within you," Aninda said.

"Please tell me Sir."

"You know, all *Panchayat* members are not good. It is a rumor that one *Panchayat* member asks money for IRDP loan from the applicants. I know Gumani Hussain, and Gani Bhai. They are honest. But if anybody asks money for your loan in our Manager's name or my name, please do not pay anything. You know, in rural areas, it happens often. I am alerting you in advance. If somebody asks, tell me his name," Aninda said.

"Ok, Sir, I shall tell you. I am illiterate and this is the first time, I am going to take loan. Thank you for your help, Sir," Javed replied.

"Ok, Javed Bhai. I am leaving. Next time when you will come from Berhampore, contact me at my office. If there is any development, I shall tell you," Aninda said.

Javed asked Salma to show light to Aninda on the road as there was total dark all where. Salma came out with kerosene lamp to show light to Aninda. When Aninda reached to the road, he told Salma to go back. He could go to his residence.

Salma stood for a few minutes and watched the footsteps of Aninda.

*Chaptar-3*

Javed reached at the *Panchayat* Office early morning. Gumani Hussain and Gani already came. Gumani Hussain was the Assistant Head Master of local High School of Nayanpur. Every week day, he came to *Panchayat* Office first before going to school. It was his daily routine. Gani was full time Assistant of *Panchayat* Office. Gani lived at Molladanga village which was located in same Nayanpur *Panchayat*. Gani was a hard working guy aged 30 and Gumani Saheb liked him. There were nine *Panchayat* members elected in Gram *Panchayat*. All belonged to Left parties. Prior to the present *Panchayat* board, it was ruled by Congress party and Bara Babu, Surapati Mondal was the *Pradhan*. In last election, Surapati was defeated by Tahasin Sheikh. Surapati Mondal was the head of *Panchayat* for several years. Javed, during monsoon time, worked at Surapati Mondal's firm.

Gumani Hussain was busy with some office works. Seeing Javed, he called him at his office.

"Javed, Loan Officer, Aninda Roy told me about your loan case," he told softly. "Gani was with me when I went to bank yesterday. Go and meet Gani. He will prepare your loan application. Give answers to the questions and information correctly so that Gani can fill it up. Did you bring your ration cards?" Gumani Saheb asked.

"Yes, *Pradhan* Saheb, I brought all ration cards," Javed replied.

"Good, now go to Gani and do your work. When it will be ready, bring it to me for signature."

"*Pradhan* Saheb, how many days it will take to get loan?"

"Javed, you know, your loan will be granted under Government Rural Development Programme. After my signature, your loan application will go to Islampur Block Office for B.D.O's approval. You know there are 20 Gram *Panchayats* under the same Block Office. Only one person is there to process the IRDP loan cases. Hundreds of loan applications reach daily. It will take a few months say 3 to 4 months. Sometimes, it takes 6 months."

Javed sat on the floor. He bent his head on his knees. He could not speak any more.

Gumani Saheb noticed that. "Don't worry, I have one meeting in the next month with B.D.O. Aninda Roy will also go to attend the meeting. It is our quarterly review meeting. I shall tell your case to B.D.O for early process and send back to bank for loan disbursement. Now, go to Gani and complete the application," Gumani Hussain said.

Javed came to Gani who was busy with a few villagers in his room. Gani told Javed to wait for half an hour. Gani called Javed when he was free. Gani brought one loan application and started to fill it up.

"Javed Bhai, tell me full name of all members of your family & date of birth," Gani asked.

It was difficult to say correct date of birth. Javed did not know when he was born.

"Gani Bhai, I do not know what is my age now."

Gani was not at all surprised. He knew that in Nayanpur, most of the villagers didn't have any birth certificate. They didn't have any record or information of their ages.

"Javed Bhai, try to remember something of your past so that I can estimate you and your wife's age."

Javed could only remember when he married Ruksana, his uncle Mozammel Saheb told the bride's family that Javed was 20 years old.

Ruksana was 16 years when married. His marriage happened when Bangladesh Liberation war started.

Gani thought a while and remembered that Bangladesh liberation war was started in the year 1971. It was about 20 years ago.

Gani calculated age of Javed as 40 years and Ruksana as 36 years as per information given to him. Javed could remember that 4 years after his marriage, Salma was born and second daughter 4 years after Salma. His sons were Junior. Danish was born 2 years after Tashlima and Nassir 1 year after Danish. Gani calculated their ages accordingly.

"Javed Bhai, do you have one copy photo? I want it which will be pasted on your loan application."

"I don't have any photo."

"No problem, go to Islampur. There is a photo studio which delivers photo on the same day."

"What is the name of the studio?"

"Sorry, I forgot the name. It is located on the bus stand of Islampur. Ask any one there."

"I am going now."

"Wait, let me complete your application and get it signed by *Pradhan* right now. Give your photo today evening. I shall send your application with photo tomorrow to Block office."

Gani was busy in fill up. Within an hour, it was ready. Gani brought the application to Gumani Saheb for signature. Gumani told him to send to Islampur Block Office through the *Panchayat's* runner.

Javed again met Gumani Hussain and thanked him a lot. He also thanked Gani Bhai for his support.

Javed went to Isalmpur without delay. He got the photo at the evening. He returned back to Nayanpur by the last bus and from bus stand, he straight went to Gani Bhai's house to deliver the photo. Gani took the photo. "Ok, Javed Bhai, I shall certainly forward your application tomorrow," Gani said.

When Javed reached home, it was about 9 o'clock night. Ruksana and Salma were waiting outside house. Javed told everything of that day's development. He had to wait for final approval of Block Office. He told Salma and Ruksana that he would not wait for the loan approval. It's wise to join the duty at Berhampore and when he would get news of loan approval, he would leave the job finally. He was certain that his master, Susanta Babu would re-employ him.

Javed was terribly tired due to lot of hectic activities throughout the day. He took dinner and went asleep.

Next day, Javed went to Berhampore and told everything to Susanta Babu. Susanta Babu was happy to see Javed again.

"Javed Bhai, do work here as long as you want," he told Javed. "I know, why do you want the loan? What I pay to you, is not sufficient for you and your family. You are maintaining two establishments. You are here and your family is at Nayanpur. Please understand my situation. My business is going dull nowadays. You know, there are lot of risks in food grain business now," Susanta Babu suddenly was silent for a while.

"You can remember, once 25 labors were working in my warehouse. Now only 10 labors are working. I am sorry that I could not pay more. You start your own business and I am sure that you will be able to earn good. My blessing will always be with you," Susanta Babu said.

"Sir, I regard you as my elder brother. You gave me the job when I was in need. I could not forget you."

Javed joined the work at the Warehouse with other labors.

Days were going. Javed came to Nayanpur after two months. He went to bank and met Aninda.

"Javed Bhai, there is no news of your loan case. It had not come from Block Office."

"How many days more it will take, Sir?"

"I am not sure when it will come. You know, we had a meeting with Block Office last month. Myself and Gumani Saheb requested Block Officer to consider your loan application early. But it would take time. Block Office is busy nowadays."

"When shall I come next?"

"You need not come to bank. One letter will go to your address when it will be granted by Block Office. By the by, Javed Bhai, buy one five rupee Non Judicial stamp paper which will be required at the time of signing of loan documents."

Javed told everything to Salma and Ruksana of the development.

Javed returned back to Berhampore at his work next day.

It was summer time. Holy *Ramjan* month started. All Muslims were in fast for one full month. Javed also observed *Rojas*. He thought that he would go to Nayanpur during *Eid*. Javed was religious minded and observed *Rojas*. There was a *Masjid* near warehouse where Javed worked. Susanta Babu allowed one hour break to all his Muslim workers during *Namaz* time. Every year, Susanta Babu arranged special *Ramjan* dinner a week before *Eid*. He invited his Muslim guests and all workers to the special dinner, *If tar.*

Javed took one week leave during *Eid* and came to Nayanpur. Susanta Babu gave him two hundred rupees as tips for purchase of new cloths for all his family members. He gave a new sari and told Javed to give it to Salma. Sasanta Babu loved Salma like his daughter. His only daughter died untimely. If alive, would be at the same age of Salma. Susanta Babu saw the shadow of his late daughter in Salma.

Javed spent entire money for purchase of new cloths for all. He reached home one day before *Eid*. Everybody was waiting for him.

When Javed reached home, Salma came to him dancing. Her face was full of smile. Javed asked what happened.

"Abba, bank sent one letter two days before."

"What is written in the letter?" Javed asked.

Salma didn't read and write. She went to bank and met Aninda. Aninda told her that Block Office granted the loan and subsidy to Javed. Aninda also told to communicate Javed as early as possible so that Javed could sign the loan documents. All were well. Everybody was happy. Javed celebrated *Eid* with lot of joy and happiness.

Bank was closed for *Eid* holiday. Javed already bought one five rupee stamp paper for loan documents. After *Eid* holiday, Javed went to bank early morning before bank opened. Aninda seeing him at the bank's main gate, called inside the bank and told him to wait for a few minutes. Manager, Aninda and other staffs were busy to complete the opening formalities of the bank.

It was a rural branch of People Bank. People Bank had one branch at Berhampore and Islampore also. It was a big Public Sector bank. Nayanpur branch was opened a few years ago. Only 10 to 12 staffs worked at the branch. Aninda was posted as Loan Officer.

Aninda called Javed to his desk. Aninda took out Javed's loan proposal from the file and was busy to prepare loan documents. He took half an hour to fill in up of the documents. He took the non Judicial stamp from Javed and attached with the loan documents.

"Javed Bhai, now sign the documents."

"Sir, I cannot sign." Javed was illiterate.

"Ok, no problem, I am taking your thumb impression."

His left thumb impression was taken on each page of the loan documents. There were many pages and Javed put his thumb impression. Aninda made everything ready and made one loan passbook.

He told Javed how much was monthly loan installment and what was the rate of interest. He explained everything about loan documents and what was written in the documents. Aninda thereafter brought loan documents and pass book to Manager for signature.

"Sir, Javed's Loan documents are ready. Please check and sign it," Aninda said to the Manager.

Manager welcomed Javed and asked to sit.

Manager handed over the Loan Passbook to Javed. "Javed, Mr.Roy has already told you the monthly installment, interest, repayment period, etc. I want to advise you that you should not forget to deposit monthly installment. If you could not arrange for full monthly pay in any month, pay whatever amount you could manage. There is no hard and fast rule that you will pay entire amount of monthly installment at a time.

"I promise, Sir, I shall never delay in payment," Javed's eyes were full of tears.

"Javed, I wish you best of luck in your new business."

"Sir, when shall I get money?"

"Come tomorrow. You know, we have to finish all works relating to your loan case and it would take hours time," Aninda told.

Javed came home. His joys had no limit. He told everything to Salma. It was a golden day for Javed and his family.

At the evening, Tahasin Sheikh, the *Panchayat* member of Nayanpur came to his house.

Javed was shocked to hear what Tahasin demanded from him. He could not believe that Manager had asked money from him. He was in a fix and could not decide what he should do. If he paid Rs.500, how could he buy the horse and cart? All of a sudden, he remembered Aninda who told him not to pay any amount to any *Panchayat* member if he was asked to pay in the name of Manager of the Bank. Javed went to Aninda's house that night. Salma asked him to finish dinner. Javed didn't reply to her.

Javed knew Aninda's residence. Aninda took the residence on rent at Jangli Saha's house at *Paschim* Nayanpur. Distance was less than a quarter mile. When Javed reached, Aninda was about to leave for dinner. Seeing Javed, Aninda was surprised.

"What Happened Javed Bhai?" he asked. "You are here at this odd hours."

"Sir...," Javed was fumbling and could not find words.

Aninda guessed something happened wrong.

"Javed Bhai, please tell me what happened?" he said. "Do not fear. You can tell me safely."

"Sir, Tahasin Sheikh came to me. He told....," again Javed was fumbling.

"What he told, Javed Bhai? Please tell me. I want to know. Do not fear. I shall keep everything secret," Aninda wanted to know.

Javed told everything. Aninda's face became changed. He was furious but could not express before Javed.

"Javed Bhai, I heard lot of allegations against Tahasin Bhai. I know he collected money from the borrowers in the name of Manager and also my name. You are not his first pray," Aninda said.

"What shall I do now?" Javed asked.

"Do not pay a single rupee to Tahasin. Come to the bank tomorrow and I shall disburse your loan. You will buy your horse and cart as early as possible. Do not keep the money at your house for long. I shall handle Tahasin matter," Aninda said.

"Ok, Sir, I shall do what you have told."

Next day, Aninda met Gumani Hussain at *Panchayat* Office. He knew that Gumani Saheb came to *Panchayat* Office at morning time before going to school. Aninda apprised everything about Tahasin matter to Gumani Saheb.

"Are you sure, your Manager didn't ask for money from Javed?" Gumani Saheb asked Aninda.

"I asked Manager before coming to your office. He was furious to know Tahasin's allegation. I am certain that nobody from bank asked any bribe through Tahasin. It is Tahasin's game play," Aninda replied.

"Ok, I shall enquire it. Do not worry. Please give loan today to Javed and tell him to buy horse and *Tanga* immediately without any delay," Gumani Saheb said.

"I have already advised Javed yesterday," Aninda said.

"Mr. Roy, I have no hesitation to say that it is not the first case. Tahasin asked money from other IRDP borrowers. I got information earlier too that Tahasin collected money from borrowers in the name of bank. Enough is enough. I shall take action against Tahasin," Gumani Saheb said.

Aninda left Panchayat Office saying good bye to Gumani Saheb. Although, Aninda knew well that Gumani Hussain could not be able to take any action against his most influential member of the board, Tahasin Sheikh who had connection up to the top level of the party.

When he reached Bank, he saw Javed waiting at the bank for him. Aninda asked his Assistant to complete filling up of the loan documents and prepared all other papers for Javed's loan. Loan documents were ready within a couple of hours and entire money was disbursed to Javed.

"Javed Bhai, buy the horse and *Tanga* within a day. Take one money receipt from the seller," Aninda said.

"I shall do, Sir."

"One more thing," Aninda lowered his voice.

"What?"

"Don't pay a single rupee to Tahasin or any *Panchayat* member."

Javed could not resist himself. His eyes were full of tears. Javed met Manager also. Manager told him the same thing what Aninda said. Manager also told Javed to repay monthly loan installment and interest in time.

Javed returned home. Salma was waiting for him. He gave the entire money to Salma and told her to keep in the box. Javed told every development to Salma.

"Abba, when will you go to Durgapur for buying the horse and *Tanga?*"

"I am thinking to go tomorrow."

"Why not today?"

Salma pressed him to go that day. Her sixth sense was giving bad signal that money should not be kept at house. Javed accepted Salma's advice.

It was afternoon time. Javed finished lunch within a minute and was ready to go to buy horse and *Tanga*. Salma wanted to go with him. Ruksana returned home from work that time. Ruksana also supported Salma. Javed agreed.

They reached Durgapur within an hour. Road was good. Javed met Noor Box Ali who was the owner of the horse and *Tanga*. Salma saw the horse. It was a white color horse. Health was good. Noor Box appreciated his horse like anything. Noor Box was using the *Tanga* for his own travel.

"Javed Bhai, please take care of my *Badsha*." Noor Box's eyes were full of tears. He had given the name of his horse, *Badsha*. Actually

Noor Box had arranged his daughter's marriage and that's the reason, he agreed to sell his horse and *Tanga*.

"Noor Bhai, your *Badsha* will stay at my house like my son."

"Badsha is very sentimental. If he does not get food on time, he will not eat at all."

Javed paid the full amount to Noor Box and requested him to give a money receipt for bank. Noor Box and his wife literally were crying when they bid good bye to their *Badsha*. *Badsha* was not ready to go with Javed but he liked Salma from beginning. Salma brought wet grams for *Badsha*. She gave him. *Badsha* followed Salma and Javed to his new home.

When reached, Ruksana, Danish, Nassir, Tashlima were waiting. That was their happiest day.

At the evening, Tahasin Sheikh came to Javed's house. His face was bleak.

"Javed Bhai, I want to know why did you complaint against me to Gumani Hussain?"

"Tahasin Bhai, believe me I did not complaint against you to Gumai Saheb."

"You do not know me. I shall see how will you run your *Tanga* in the village?"

Tahasin almost threatened Javed. Javed could not say anything to Tahasin. He knew that people like Tahasin could do harm to him if got any chance. Javed left everything to God's wishes.

Next day, Javed was ready early morning. It was his first day of new venture. Javed reached bus stand well on time before bus reached at Nayanpur. He got good number of passengers.

It is said that every after rainy days, sunny days are following. It is the cycle. It happens to nature as well as human life. Javed's rainy days were suddenly over. He saw lot of sunlight.

It is the human nature that every human wants comfort. When there was no alternative transport available at the Nayanpur bus stand, the travelers had to walk. They didn't have any choice. It happened that Javed's *Tanga* was ready there to receive and drop them at their door step. Travelers were happy and obviously Javed was more happy. Ruksana stopped working at others houses. Salma and Tashlima got new saris. Danish and Nassir got new dresses. Ruksana bought new utensils which she didn't have at kitchen. Javed repaired his house with new shed of asbestos. All members shared good food and laugh which they almost forgot. Months were going fast. Javed never forgot to pay installments to Bank. He was given 3 months moratorium. But Javed started paying installment from the first month. He met Aninda at bank and also at his residence and kept informed of his business. Aninda was happy.

One year was gone. Javed's business was going well. He paid almost half of his loan to bank. He was able to save money for Salma's marriage. Javed was searching a good groom for Salma. Salma was not ready to marry. She insisted Javed and Ruksana that she would marry when Javed would pay back the entire loan amount to bank. Javed didn't want to wait more. Salma already entered eighteen years.

It was one Sunday morning. Javed already went out with *Tanga.* Aninda came to Javed's house. It was his formal yearly inspection. Bank had the policy to inspect the assets which they disbursed to their borrowers once in a year. Aninda didn't come to Javed's house after loan disbursement. Javed either came to bank or to his residence for loan payment. Aninda was surprised to see Javed's house. It was remodeled totally. Aninda saw Salma after one year. That small shy girl had changed to a young lady. Salma welcomed Aninda to their house. Aninda saw the happy faces of all members of Javed's family. Aninda was happy that he had selected right person for the loan. Salma arranged cup of tea for Aninda. Aninda entered in their bed room and saw total changes there.

*Ajoy Ghosh*

Salma offered him a dish of vegetables fry which she made. Aninda saw Salma closely.

"Shall I say anything to Abba?" Salma asked.

"Tell your Abba that I came here to carry out annual inspection. It's a formal visit to know how is Javed Bhai after loan disbursement. I have got all information now."

Aninda thanked Salma for good tea and vegetable fries. He appreciated Salma's cooking too.

# Chapter-4

It was one regular day. Javed as usual started from home with his *Tanga* to Nayanpur bus stand. When he reached, one dark surprise was waiting for him. Javed was not at all ready for that. Javed saw at least 10 new *Tangas* waiting at the bus stand for travelers. He could not believe his eyes. He found unknown faces who didn't belong to his village. He knew one person only who was Yakub of Char Gopinathpur. Javed rushed to Yakub. Yakub greeted him with lot of smile.

"Javed Bhai, we got the *Tanga* from bank under IRDP loan scheme."

Yakub introduced Javed with all new *Tanga* riders.

They requested Javed to guide them as they just got loan and purchased *Tanga*.

"Javed Bhai, we are thankful to Tahasin Sheikh. Only due to his efforts, we got loan from Nayanpur bank. Tahasin persuaded our loan cases with Block Office and convinced them that there is tremendous scope for grant of more *Tangas* who will operate from Nayanpur bus stand." Yakub and others thanked to Tahasin Sheikh.

Javed remembered Tahasin's word on that day he got loan. Tahasin threatened him that he would see how Javed operated *Tanga* in the village. Javed sat on the ground. All his dreams were ended.

Number of *Tangas* were increased but number of buses and travelers not. Bad time had come, he had to face a cut throat competition for passengers. Suddenly, Javed's sunny days were ended. Javed shattered with lot of grief. He didn't ask how much Yakub and his friends offered to Tahasin for their loans. He was surprised that neither Aninda nor Manager told him anything that they were going to disburse more *Tanga* loans. He also realized at the same time why bank would say to him. It was their decision and pressure from Block Office. Tahasin was the man behind that project who did to ruin Javed. Javed realized everything clearly.

All the passengers were shared by all *Tangas* that day. Javed's income suddenly came down. Javed went home with lot of pain that day. He reared hope that he would arrange Salma's marriage one day and he was trying to save more and more money. Suddenly, one big question arose how would he repay bank's loan. He saw the writings of the wall.

Javed told everything to Salma and Ruksana. They were mum.

It happened what Javed thought. His regular income was reduced many times. As he was the oldest *Tanga* rider at the bus stand, the regular travelers initially preferred his *Tanga* to others. But after a few months, Javed saw that other *Tangas* were getting more passengers. Their rates were lesser than Javed's. It was also a game plan of Tahasin Sheikh.

Javed could not pay the monthly installment for the first time. He owed one half of the loan amount. One evening, Javed went to Aninda's residence at *Paschim* Nayanpur. Aninda just came from bank. Seeing Javed, Aninda asked, "what happened, Javed Bhai?"

Javed told everything of the developments. Aninda silently heard.

"Javed Bhai, it is Tahasin's plan. He managed IRDP Officer of the Block Office for sponsoring of more *Tanga* loans. Gumani Hussain didn't want to sponsor more *Tanga* loan applications until number of buses were increased. But Tahasin managed to get the new *Tanga* loans through Block Office."

Aninda was not sure how much Tahasin got from the new borrowers but it was rumor that he took hefty amount from all new borrowers. In fact, Tahasin took the revenge against Javed which happened one year before.

"Sir, what shall I do now? My income has gone down. How can I pay the monthly installments henceforth?"

Aninda could not reply.

"Sir, It's now difficult to manage family and food cost of my horse, *Badsha.*"

"Javed Bhai, I understand what you say. What advice shall I give you? Please wait and see what happens next."

Javed's days were more difficult. His daily earnings were lesser and lesser. It happened many days that he returned back empty hands. He could not decide what to do. He could not pay loan installments for last 3 months. Bank sent one notice to him demanding immediate repayment. He could not pay the school tuition fees of Danish and Nassir for several months. He had to buy foods for *Badsha* everyday even if he had no earning. He had already spent the money for house hold living expenses what he saved last one year for Salma's marriage. Ruksana took housemaid job again.

Javed discussed Salma what to do. Would he sell the horse and *Tanga* to repay the bank's dues? It was difficult to get a good price if it was sold in distress. Javed wanted to know Salma's decision. He depended Salma in all his critical matters more than Ruksana. Salma suggested him to meet Aninda one more time at his residence. Salma had trust that only Aninda could do something good for them.

When Javed reached Aninda's house, he was about to leave for dinner. Aninda took his lunch and dinner from the hotel everyday at *Paschim* Nayanpur Bazaar. Aninda did not know cooking.

Seeing Javed, Aninda told, "what happened? Are you ok, Javed Bhai?"

"Sir, are you busy? I want to talk."

"I am going for diner now. Please wait at my house. I shall talk after diner."

Aninda returned back within half an hour. Javed already nurtured one plan in his mind. He waited for Aninda's arrival.

Aninda as usual again asked, "what happened, Javed Bhai?"

Javed could not find words how to start. He told with broken words about his present condition. It was difficult for him to manage family, horse and bank loan together. Javed asked his advice. Aninda got all information. Javed wanted to sell the horse and *Tanga* for repayment of bank's dues. Javed asked his permission.

"Javed Bhai, don't be so frustrated," Aninda said. "Time will change. Please wait for a few months more. I hope situation will change. It is not wise decision to sell the business. Meantime, come one day to bank and tell your present position to our new Manager."

Javed knew that the earlier Bank Manager was transferred and in his place, a new Manager took charge.

"Sir, I have one request," Javed said.

"Tell me Javed Bhai, don't hesitate. I shall be happy if I can help you in any matter."

"Sir, everyday you are taking your lunch and dinner from the hotel. It is not good for health. Why are not cooking yourself? Homemade foods are always better than hotel's food," Javed said.

Aninda laughed and replied, "Javed Bhai, I am eating at the hotel from the first day I came to Nayanpur. What shall I do? I do not know cooking. Jangli Saha, my land lord, always gives me same suggestion. It is not possible for me to cook. I am happy with the food which is available at the hotel."

"Sir, I have one small suggestion. If you kindly permit, I can say," Javed said.

"Tell me, Javed Bhai, what is your suggestion?" Aninda asked.

"If you permit, I can send my daughter, Salma to help you in cooking and other house hold works. Salma knows cooking better and I am sure you will like," Javed said with lot of hesitation.

"No, no, Javed Bhai, I could not take all of these burdens. I have to make arrangements for kitchen utensils, cooking gas and other things. Every day I have to buy vegetables and grocery items for cooking. It's horrible. I can't do," Aninda said his inability.

"Sir, you need not do anything. My Salma will arrange everything. Just pay her and she will buy all kitchen utensils and make cooking arrangements. You can trust her."

Aninda became silent. It's fact that he didn't like hotel's food anymore. It was very difficult to digest. It's ok if you ate one or two days. He was eating for last 2 years from the same hotel. He wanted a change. Earlier, he thought to start cooking by hiring one maid. But he dropped that plan soon.

He thought a while of Javed's plan. Still he could not make up his mind.

"Javed Bhai, I shall inform you if I want to start cooking," Aninda replied lastly.

"Sir, if you hire my Salma, she can eat two square meals," Javed said. "I am a helpless father who cannot arrange foods for his daughters and sons now."

"What?" Aninda was shocked.

It was his beyond thinking what was the real financial position of Javed. One father begged to him for two square meals for his daughter. Aninda didn't think more. He told Javed to send Salma from the next day.

"Javed Bhai, I could not buy anything for kitchen," he said. "Please tell Salma to take money from me and buy everything what she wants."

"Sir, I am now relieved. I cannot repay your debt," Javed replied.

"Javed Bhai, one more matter. I shall pay to Salma for her service. If you agree, then send her, otherwise not," Aninda said.

"Sir, what shall I say? Please do whatever you like," Javed replied.

After returning home, Javed told everything to Salma and Ruksana. Ruksana didn't agree initially. She didn't send Salma for housemaid work so far. But Salma agreed instantly.

That night, Salma could not sleep properly. She was waiting whole night for the morning. She was feeling speed of her heartbeats. She would see Aninda closely every day. Suddenly, Salma was happy.

———— ∽∾⌀⌀⌀⌀∾∽ ————

"Madam, we have reached Krishnanagar," Pintu stops the car. Salma wakes up all of a sudden. She is, as if, dreaming.

"Madam, will you take a cup of tea," Nitish Babu asks. "Pintu will check the tire pressure here. There is a good Tea shop."

"Ok, let's have tea here. Pintu, you take tea first and then go for checking tire pressure," Salma tells.

Salma gets down from the car. The car already has travelled more than sixty miles and it needs rest for a few minutes. Salma follows Nitish Babu to the tea shop. Krishnanagar Bus stand is located on the highway. There are many sweet and other shops. Most of the cars, buses and lorries stop there and take rest. Krishnanagar is very famous for one type of sweets, *Sarbhaja*. Aninda bought *Sarbhaja* for her once. One sweet shop, "Nadia Sweets" is very famous for *Sarbhaja*. Aninda bought *Sarbhaja* from that shop. Salma could still remember the name of that shop. After tea, Salma asks Nitish Babu to find out if there is any sweet shop named "Nadia Sweets" there.

"Nadia Sweets" is a famous shop and the tea shop owner shows that shop when asked by Nitish Babu. It is at the middle of the Bus stand. Salma slowly goes to "Nadia Sweets" shop. Salma stands for a few minutes before the shop.

"Madam, will you buy sweets from here?" Nitish Babu asks.

"Yes, please buy one kilogram *Sarbhaja*," Salma says. Her eyes are suddenly full of tears.

The car is ready. Pintu requests Salma and Nitish Babu to board. Pintu starts engine and rolls the car. Salma asks Pintu, "how many hours more it will take to reach Kolkata?"

Pintu tells, "Madam, it will take not more than 4 hours."

Salma closes her eyes. Nitish Babu shuts down window curtain to avoid excess sun light inside the car. Salma is alone in the back seat. Nitish Babu is on the front passenger seat.

# Chapter-5

Salma could not sleep well that night. She was waiting for the morning. Javed told her to reach Aninda's house at early morning. Salma had to finish everything including Aninda's breakfast and lunch before he went to office. It was her first day. Salma was hurry to finish daily morning works at her house. Ruksana went to work early morning. Javed also left at the same time. She had to make breakfast for Danish, Nassir and Tashlima. She was elder sister. Salma finished everything hurriedly and started to Aninda's house. Sun just rises in the East. Color of the Sun was still reddish.

It took only 10 minutes to reach at *Paschim* Nayanpur. Salma knew the house of Jangli Saha where Aninda stayed. Salma wore her only good sari. The sari was given by Javed during last year *Eid*. Salma had no shoe. She combed her long black hair neatly. She was feeling the speed of her heartbeats.

Jangli Saha's house was two storied. There were several rooms in his house. Jangli Saha had been running one Grocery and vegetables shop at the ground floor. His family also resided at the same floor. All his tenants stayed at the first floor. There were 4 small apartments at the first floor. Aninda stayed at the corner apartment. Other 3 apartments were occupied by 3 local school teachers who stayed with their families. Aninda was not married and stayed alone.

Jangli Saha had big family. He had 4 sons and 4 daughters. His wife, Lolita, was from the same village, Nayanpur. Jangli Saha had a few acres of agricultural lands and fruit orchards. His sons helped him in business. Two sons were little aging below ten years who had been studying at the local school. His two daughters were grown up aged 16 plus. Jangli Saha was trying for their marriage. In rural areas, generally girls were married early, below 16 years. Jangli Saha at the time of construction of his 1st Floor last year, took loan from Aninda. The loan was being repaid by monthly rent of Aninda. All his tenants were good and all including Aninda came from outside. Aninda did not make arrangements for cooking. Jangli Saha once told him to arrange for cooking. He didn't agree. There was one Hotel adjacent to Jangli Saha's house. Aninda took lunch and dinner there.

Aninda was basically a careless boy. His bedroom was never cleaned for last 2 years he stayed at the house. Lolita requested several times for cleaning and arranging his apartments. Aninda every time smiled and told to come next week. However, next week never came. There was a washing laundry at *Paschim* Nayanpur. Aninda sent all his dirty cloths there for washing and ironing once in a month. Aninda was a smoker. Earlier when he was in college hostel, he used to smoke costly brand of cigarettes. At Nayanpur, he smoked *biddies*.

Aninda's father, Joydeb Roy, had been running one Kitchen Utensils business in Kolkata. Joydeb constructed one big house at Dover Lane area of Kolkata. Aninda had no brother and sister. His mother, Nirmala Devi, was a strong devotee of Goddess Kali. She spent most of her time in worship of her deities. Joydeb Babu would be above 50 years and Nirmala Devi was 5 years junior to her husband. Aninda was their only son.

Since childhood, Aninda was sincere in his study. Every year he secured good score in class examinations. After graduation, Aninda appeared for Credit Officer post in Public Sector Banks. He qualified in 4 banks together. Finally he had chosen People Bank and it was his first posting at Nayanpur.

Nirmala Devi was not ready to allow him to go to Nayanpur. She heard that the area was located at the remote corner of Murshidabad district. Murshidabad was considered one of the backward districts of West Bengal state the then time. Moreover, Nirmala heard that Murshidabad district was populated mostly by Muslims and Nayanpur had Muslim populations more than Hindus. Nirmala did not like his only son would stay at the area where majority of the population was Muslims. It was her superstition that if her son took food from any Muslim family, her son would be impure and lose the Hindu sanctity. Her attitude to Muslims was never changed. Joydeb was progressive minded. He didn't have any prejudice of Hindu Muslim factors. In his business, most of his suppliers and customers were Muslims. Aninda got his father's characters. He had many friends who were Muslims.

It was Aninda's first posting. As per People Bank's policy, all his newly hired officers would serve rural area for 4 to 5 years at their initial posting. Aninda served 2 years already at Nayanpur. He was happy with the branch and the people of Nayanpur areas. There was one Public Library at Nayanpur village. He hired books from the library and read those. He was a voracious reader and loved novels.

Aninda was having a number of typical attitude. He had no fixed time to get up from bed. Every night, he read books hours together. He forgot to see the time. Many nights, he went to bed at 2 o'clock. After getting up from bed in morning, he finished his daily works within half an hour and went to bank. He had no fixed time to go to office. Many days, he reached office so late that other staffs were ready to leave for lunch. It happened often, he reached early when bank did not open and the sweeping staff was cleaning the bank. Aninda often forgot to take breakfast even. There was a small canteen at his bank. He took only tea from the canteen and started to work. He had no fixed time to return from office. It happened almost all days in a week that he was the last who left from the office. Bank remained close only Sunday. But Aninda went to bank in all Sundays. He even forgot to go to Kolkata to meet his parents. His parents sent series of letters to him. Aninda had no time to read those letters. The bank had no telephone connection.

The Manager and all other staffs knew the attitude of Aninda. They protected him all the way in the office. During lunch time, they forcibly sent Aninda to hotel for lunch. The hotel owner by that time knew him well. Aninda often forgot to come to hotel for dinner at night time. Aninda forgot to shave and cut his hairs regularly. He had developed already long hairs and beard. He was tall about 6 feet and his complexion of body was fair. Above all, he was looked like a hero of any movie with long hair and beard.

Jangli Saha, his wife and all other tenants were familiar with the life style of Aninda. They always tried to take care of Aninda and asked Aninda if he needed any help from them. They always received the same answer, "Not now" and "Thank you for asking."

Aninda's attitude and behavior was like a child. Everyone would like him and love him if knew him and saw one time. His eyes were different, deep and mixed with lot of calmness. Nobody saw Aninda unhappy at any moment.

Aninda had two states of life. One was at his house and other one at his office. He was most serious and hard working officer of the bank. When at his office, Aninda was a different man. He was perfect in lending works. He didn't give any chance to his Manager and Higher Office to find faults in his works. He loved all his customers and extended help whenever they requested from him. Same thing happened to Javed's case. He personally took initiative to get Javed's loan approved. He strongly protested against the corruption of Tahasin Sheikh. It was a different Aninda at office.

When Salma reached, Aninda was sleeping. Aninda forgot totally that Salma would come early morning. Salma knocked his apartment's door. No response came from inside. Salma waited for a few minutes. No response still came out. Salma came down to ground floor at Jangli Saha's house. Salma saw Lolita and asked her help.

Lolita was surprised to see Salma. Lolita knew Salma. Salma came to her house earlier for buying grocery and vegetables from their shop.

Lolita asked the reason why Salma was there at the early morning. Salma told everything. Lolita immediately called Jangli Saha. They were surprised but at the same time happy to know that at last, Aninda agreed to hire one maid for cooking and other house hold works. Jangli Saha knew Salma well. Salma was soft spoken girl. By that time, other tenants came out from their apartments when Lolita and Jangli Saha were talking to Salma. Lolita introduced Salma with them. They were too happy to know the change of Aninda. They all loved Aninda.

Lolita said Salma, "it's God's mercy that Aninda agreed to hire you. We could not see Aninda's face. He is like a child. He will never say any of his difficulties. Is it possible to eat daily from the hotel? Aninda never cared of his health. Salma, it is your challenge to make Aninda in a shape. We all help you whatever you need. Come with me."

Lolita rushed to Aninda's apartment with Salma. She knocked the door repeatedly calling Aninda. At last, Aninda opened the door. He was surprised to see Lolita and Salma there.

Aninda asked, "what happened, Bhaviji? Why are you disturbing my sleep at the dead of the night?"

"Night? Aninda, please open your eyes. It is now morning 8 o'clock. When will you be ready to go to office?" Lolita asked.

"Office? yes, yes, I shall go now," Aninda replied. Again Aninda asked why Salma came.

"You told her to come at the morning for cooking. Did you forget?" Lolita said.

Aninda remembered yesterday's night talk with Javed. He became ashamed.

"I am really sorry, Lolita Bhavi. I forgot totally," Aninda replied.

"Bhai Sub, please allow Salma to enter into your apartment and tell her what she will do. I heard everything from Salma. I also told her that she will ask me whatever she needs. At last, God has given you good sense and you have agreed to hire Salma. I know Salma. She is a good girl and know how to cook good," Lolita said.

Aninda invited Salma in his apartment. It was one room apartment. Kitchen was small attached with the room. The toilets were common in Jangli Saha's house. There was one small corridor also. Aninda told Salma to start work and again went to bed. Aninda told Salma to get him up at nine o'clock and he would go to Office. Aninda didn't tell what Salma should do.

Salma was about to become senseless seeing the bed room and kitchen. She could not believe how one young man could leave so haphazardly. She, by that time, understood Aninda's life style. Salma was intelligent in all households matter. She didn't disturb Aninda anymore. Salma searched in the apartment if there was any broom stick or cleaning materials. There was none. The room was not cleaned for last 2 years. Salma borrowed cleaning materials from Lolita. Aninda was still sleeping. Aninda had one Time clock. Salma never went to school any day. But she learnt how to see the time in clock. Salma saw it was quarter past eight. Aninda would go to office at nine.

Aninda had a few furniture at the apartment. One Queen bed where Aninda was sleeping. Most dirty bed and the bed cover was never cleaned since it was purchased. There were one folding chair, small sofa, and one reading table. Aninda had one big suitcase. It was opened and Salma found full of shirts and pants kept haphazardly. There was one small almirah and it was full of books and news papers. There was old news papers heaped at the corner of the room. The floor was full of dust. Salma was shocked to see the kitchen. It looked like the dirtiest garbage store. There were lot of paper boxes, old cloths, buts of cigarettes and *biddies*. There were a few cooking utensils fallen on the floor. It was a total mess. Salma stood for minutes and could not decide where to start. She thought that it was not wise if she started cleaning before Aninda left. There were lot of dusts around and thousand of cockroaches, rats and flies were living happily. Salma waited when it would be nine o'clock. When clock showed exactly nine, Salma came in to the bed room and called Aninda, "Sir, it's now nine. Please get up."

There was no response from Aninda's side. Salma called loudly once again and that time Aninda opened his eyes. Aninda was not surprised to see Salma.

"Is everything done? You can leave now and come tomorrow," Aninda said.

"Sir, I have not started work yet. I am waiting when you leave. Then I shall do the work. It's not good if I start now as there are full of dusts and insects, rats in the house who are living with you, like master like your tenants," Salma replied.

Aninda smiled and perhaps enjoyed Salma's words. "Ok, no problem, finish your work and then go. Here is the key of the apartment on the table. Give it to Lolita Bhavi when you are done."

Aninda took his towel, soap and cloths and went to toilet which was common for all tenants and located at the corner of the building. Aninda was ready within half an hour. He was ready to leave to office.

"Where will you take breakfast?" Salma asked.

"Breakfast, no problem, Balaram will bring from hotel. Every day, he brings from hotel." Balaram was the peon of Aninda's bank.

"Sir, I have one request. Can you please give me money? I have to buy cleaning materials, soaps, broom, kitchen utensils and stove. I shall buy vegetables and other grocery items and from tomorrow, I shall make your breakfast and lunch. If I could finish early, I shall make your dinner ready today itself," Salma said.

"Breakfast, lunch, dinner at my apartment? I am not dreaming really. Is it?" Aninda said.

"No Sir, I shall do it today."

Aninda gave five hundred rupees from almirah.

"I am very angry," Aninda told Salma. "Why are you calling me "Sir"? I have a name. You can call me by name."

Salma's face became red. "I can't," Salma almost whispered.

"Then call me what you like. But don't say Sir."

Both were in a fix to decide which name Salma would call Aninda.

"If I say "Saheb", is it ok?"

Aninda smiled and agreed.

When Aninda left, Salma saw that the almirah was opened. Aninda took money but forgot to close the almirah. There was no lock in the almirah. Salma saw there was good amount of cash and coins inside the locker of the almirah. Salma could not think how to manage everything of this kid. Aninda's age was only increased but he was still like a kid. Salma was new and Aninda left everything to her. Salma was surprised how one man could leave everything including money to one lady whom he did not know fully. Man like Aninda was a surprise to her.

Salma didn't waste time for a single minute. She had only a few hours left to finish her works. Firstly, she had to buy lot of things and inform her mother that she could not go home till her works were done. Salma knew where her mother worked. She locked the apartment and went to market. On the way to market, she met Ruksana at her master's house. Salma told Ruksana about her position. Ruksana smiled. "Come home for a few minutes at noon and take lunch," Ruksana told Salma.

Salma moved one shop to another and bought lot of things. She took help of Kalu, elder son of Jangli Saha to carry all the materials. Salma bought all grocery and vegetable items from Jangli Saha's shop. He told Jangli Saha to deliver at Aninda's apartment after 2 hours. Meantime, she would clean the apartment. Lolita asked Salma again if she wanted any help from her. Salma didn't agree.

Salma managed her sari properly with tight knot and covered herself with a towel of Aninda. Salma started her cleaning works.

Salma was expert in all types of household works. She cleaned Kitchen first. Lot of dirts were there. She bought a few gunny bags. She put all garbage in the bags and threw in to the Panchayat's dustbin at the corner of the street. The bags were heavy and she took help of Kalu to carry from apartment to dustbin. Salma started cleaning of floor and walls after full removal of all garbage. Salma mercilessly thrown all old news papers. She didn't think to take permission from Aninda. She brought gallons of water from the well of Jangli Saha and applied with detergent powder for thorough cleaning of the bed room, kitchen and corridor. Total floor area of the apartment was small and it took only a few hours to clean perfectly. Salma thereafter washed all dirty cloths, bed sheet, blanket, trousers, towels, and other cloths of Aninda. The suitcase which was used by Aninda for keeping his clothes was thoroughly cleaned. Salma washed all the dirty clothes and after wash, kept those under Sun for dry. There was good sunlight and the day was hot. It was summer time. Lolita came to see Salma's work from time to time and gave necessary instructions to her.

After cleaning work, Salma went to take bath for cleaning herself. Her hairs were full of dust and sari was also dirty. She was sweating almost. Lolita offered her cup of tea with bread. Salma was indeed hungry.

It was 3 o'clock that time. She came to know from Lolita that Aninda usually returned back from office after 6 o'clock. So she would get another 3 hours time. By that time Jangli Saha delivered the grocery and other vegetables. Salma already bought a few kitchen utensils and one cooking stove from market. Today, she had bought only the necessary items which were needed for cooking. Slowly, other things she would buy with permission of Aninda. The condition of the apartment was totally changed. Both Lolita and Jangli Saha appreciated Salma's hard work and cleaning of the apartment. Salma checked the cloths she washed. Most of the cloths were dry by that time. She told Kalu to drop the shirts and pants to the laundry shop for ironing. She specifically told Kalu that all the garments should be ironed within an hour so that she could arrange everything before Aninda came.

Salma thereafter was busy in kitchen. She arranged all the utensils and grocery items properly. She managed a few glass containers from Lolita for keeping the oil and cooking spices. Salma also bought tea leaf, sugar, powder milk etc. for making tea. She also bought a few items of cookies and snacks for Aninda. She thought to serve those with a cup of tea to Aninda when he would come from office. Salma bought one pair good Tea cups and plates for Aninda. Five hundred was not enough to buy everything. Salma bought a few items on credit particularly from Jangli Saha's shop. That could be paid back later on from Aninda. Salma didn't find time to go home for lunch. She took lunch with Lolita that day.

Salma arranged the bed with the washed bed sheet. She arranged pillows and mosquito curtain perfectly. The almirah was thoroughly cleaned and door was closed. The apartment was given a new look.

Salma asked Lolita, "Bhavi, what type of food dishes Aninda like?"

Lolita did not have knowledge as Aninda never ate at her house despite several requests for last two years. But she heard from hotel that Aninda liked potato curry with onion and handmade chapatti. Aninda also liked *moong dal* fry.

Time was not sufficient. Salma became busy to make the items for Aninda. She made all arrangements but didn't cook as the food would be cold when Aninda took dinner at night. There was no fixed time for Aninda's dinner.

It was about 5 o'clock. Salma locked the apartment and gave the key to Lolita. "Bhavi, I shall come back again for dinner preparation within an hour. Please tell your brother," Salma told Lolita before leaving.

Aninda came before six. Lolita and Jangli Saha were there. Lolita gave key of his apartment and told that Salma would come for making dinner.

Aninda followed stair case to reach to his apartment. He opened the lock of the door. A big surprise was waiting for him. He was perplexed when entered. As if he entered into a different apartment. He was not sure if it was his apartment. Aninda stood like a statue for a few minutes. He could not believe his eyes even. He could not recognize his apartment where he lived for last 2 years. He went to kitchen and another surprise was waiting for him. Everything was so clean and arranged perfectly. Aninda remembered his mother's kitchen. He opened suitcase and almirah. All his dirty clothes were ironed and arranged neatly. He could not believe that it was his bed where he slept for last 2 years. He saw in the kitchen that Salma peeled the vegetables for cooking and also made arrangement for tea. Aninda was extremely happy and could not understand how it was possible for a girl of merely eighteen years old to make everything so perfect. Salma made his apartment from hell to heaven.

Aninda found Lolita coming to his apartment.

Seeing her, Aninda told, "Bhavi, Salma did it all? It is unbelievable. I could not believe my eyes. Is it my apartment where I lived for last 2 years?"

"I could not believe also how Salma made total change within a day. She worked whole day and did not go home to take lunch even. I forcibly offered lunch today. She did it after you left and didn't take rest for a single minute. Please give her a good tips. She is really good," Lolita said.

"Yes, of course, Bhavi. I must give tips," Aninda replied.

Lolita found that Salma entered silently. Seeing Salma, Lolita said, "Salma, you deserve good tips. Aninda promised me."

"I do not want. I shall give tips to your brother for allowing me to clean his apartment," Salma replied.

Lolita laughed. Aninda became shy.

"It's fact, Lolita Bhavi, I made everything mess in the apartment. I am sorry Salma. I have given you lot of pain," Aninda said.

"No sorry business, Saheb. You will follow my instructions whatever I say. If agree, then I shall come tomorrow. Otherwise, today is my first and last day."

Lolita again laughed. "Ok, Salma, I assure on behalf of my brother, Aninda that he will follow your instruction."

It was evening time. Lolita had lot of household works. She left taking permission from Aninda.

"When did you come?" Salma asked Aninda.

"Just a few minutes before," Aninda replied.

"Please wash your hands and change dress. I am making tea for you. By the by, Shall I cook rice or make chapatti for dinner? Which one do you like?" Salma asked.

"Whatever you like, do. But if you ask me, I like chapatti. In dinner, I do not eat rice. I eat rice only at lunch."

Aninda went to Bathroom for washing his hands. Salma closed the door of the kitchen There was one door between Bed room and kitchen. The entrance of the apartment is at the bedroom side. The apartment was small and that too unplanned. Aninda was alone and hence didn't face any difficulty so far. But now problem was that everything could be seen from the bedroom. Salma closed the door in between bedroom and Kitchen so that Aninda could change his dress.

Tea was ready within fifteen minutes. Salma knocked the door. Aninda opened. He had changed his dress and wore casual dress. Salma served tea and cookies on the table. There was no other place in the room. The reading table could be made for dining table temporarily.

Aninda asked, "Where is your tea?"

"I do not take tea at evening," Salma replied.

"Ok, I also do not take tea," Aninda said.

"Ok, Saheb, I am making tea for me now. Please do not get the tea cold."

Aninda smiled and made a long sip of the tea cup. He liked the leaf tea. After a long time, he had got proper taste of tea. His mother also made leaf tea and he last went to Kolkata about 6 months ago.

In Nayanpur, daily newspapers came at evening time when the last bus from Berhampore reached at Nayanpur. All daily newspapers were published from Kolkata. It reached morning at Berhampore. Kalu everyday went to bus stand to collect newspapers. The number of newspapers readers were a few in Nayanpur. Kalu came with newspapers and gave to Aninda. Aninda was busy in reading newspapers.

Salma came to him and asked, "what dishes do you like in dinner?"

Looking at Salma, Aninda said, "Salma, I forgot to tell you. I have one guest tonight. Please make dinner for two persons. You can make whatever you like. I have no choice. I have only satisfaction that I should not go to hotel tonight for dinner."

After tea, Aninda usually smoked. He could not find the box where he kept *bidi* and matches. Aninda asked, "Salma, where was the *bidi* box?"

Salma gave him the box. Aninda found that there was no *bidi*. One new cigarette packet was there. Aninda was happy to see the cigarette. He took one and fired the cigarette. Aninda thanked Salma again.

Salma was busy in kitchen. She worked whole day without any rest. She might be tired for continuous work. But Salma could not feel any tiredness that day. As if, Salma was getting thousand volts of energy.

Dinner was ready by nine. Salma asked Aninda, "when will your guest come? Dinner is ready now."

"My guest has already arrived," Aninda replied.

"Where? I could not see your guest."

"My guest is standing in front of me," Aninda said.

"You are really... a child," Salma replied.

"Salma, give two chapattis and small quantity of curry what you made. Take rest for you and your brothers and sister. I cannot eat more at night," Aninda said.

"You smoke a lot and takes many cup of teas in bank. Perhaps your appetite becomes less. Leave those and you can eat more," Salma said.

Aninda was happy that at least one girl in Nayanpur was present who was taking care of his heath. He remembered his mother's face. Nirmala always expressed unhappiness due to less eating of food. Aninda's health was medium. He was tall and slender. He never cared of his health. There were at least one or two days in a week, when he forgot either lunch or dinner. At least that thing would not happen. Salma served dinner on the reading table. There was no separate dining table. Chapatti and vegetable dishes were warm, just cooked. Aninda tasted the curry. It was delicious. He was happy to see the potato and onion curry along with *Moong dal* which were his favorite dishes. He was surprised how Salma could know his favorite dishes.

Aninda finished dinner. After a long time, he tasted homemade foods what he used to take in Kolkata. He got another letter from Nirmala yesterday. His mother literally appealed to him to come to Kolkata. Aninda didn't go to Kolkata for last 6 months.

After dinner, Salma packed the rest of the food with papers. She already washed the dishes and cleaned the kitchen.

She asked before leaving, "How was the taste of dinner?"

"Not bad, not good, so so," Aninda was kidding.

"Shall I come tomorrow?" Salma asked.

"If you don't come, I shall go to your house and sit there for a hunger strike," Aninda said.

Salma laughed. Within a few hours, Salma was free to Aninda. The barrier between master and servant was disappeared in the first day.

Salma returned home when it was 10 o'clock. Javed and Ruksana were waiting for her. Usually, in rural area, everybody finished dinner early. There was no recreation available. Moreover, everybody became tired due to hard work all the day. They preferred to sleep early and got up before Sun rises.

# Chapter-6

Another day began. Salma got ready before Sun rises and when reached at Aninda's house, he was still sleeping. Salma knocked the door. Door opened automatically. It was not locked from inside. Perhaps, Aninda forgot to lock yesterday night. It was not good at all. Although, in Nayanpur, the incidents of burglary was less, Aninda should take care of his belongings at least.

Salma entered inside. The room was dark totally. Salma put on the switch. No electricity power was there. In the dark, Salma crossed the bedroom and came to Kitchen. She lighted one lamp by matches. With that light, Salma found that Aninda was sleeping deeply. She saw lot of books and newspapers on his bed. Aninda forgot to unfold mosquito curtains. In rural areas, there was plenty of mosquitoes and the mosquito bite diseases were common. The pillows were fallen on the ground. Salma laughed seeing Aninda's condition. Really, he was a child like.

Salma closed the door of the bed room and started working at kitchen. Today, she would make breakfast and lunch right now. At the evening time, she would make dinner. Yesterday, Aninda specifically told her to make lunch and dinner for two persons.

Salma was thinking how to serve lunch to Aninda. He would take breakfast before going to office. But what about lunch? Salma searched if there was any lunch box in the kitchen. There was none. Salma got an idea. The lunch might be sent through Kalu at lunch time. It was good that Aninda would take lunch at the bank. Salma came to Lolita and asked if she had any spare lunch box. Lolita knew that one of her tenants, Mukul Gonai, had one spare lunch box. Lolita immediately went to his apartment. Mukul Babu gave the spare lunch box and told Salma to use it for Aninda. Salma thanked Mukul Babu.

Salma was busy in kitchen. She made flour *puri* and vegetable curry for breakfast. Salma bought a few vegetables yesterday. There was a problem of availability of fresh vegetables in Nayanpur. Jangli Saha kept vegetables in his shop but those were not fresh. The vegetable Market which the villagers called *"Hat"* operated only two days in a week. The villagers bought their requirements from the *Hat* and stored in house. *Hat* began at afternoon time. Salma thought to buy fresh vegetables from the next *Hat*. She made curry with the vegetables what she bought yesterday. It was about nine. Salma came to Aninda. He was still sleeping deeply.

"Saheb, please get up," Salma called. "When will you go to office? Breakfast is ready."

No response from Aninda's side. Salma again called. Aninda did not respond. Salma was impatient. Salma was hesitant to touch the body of Aninda. She was waiting when Aninda got up. It was half past nine. Salma could not sit idle. She put gentle push on his back.

"Saheb, please get up," Salma said.

Aninda opened his eyes. His face was full of morning smile seeing Salma.

"When did you come?" Aninda asked. "You didn't call me."

"I have come two hours before and made your breakfast ready which is getting cold," Salma replied.

"I am sorry, Salma. Please give me fifteen minutes time and I shall be ready," Aninda said.

Aninda got ready for office. Salma served breakfast.

"Delicious. I liked *puri* most. Again thank you Salma for delicious breakfast," Aninda said.

Salma made tea for Aninda.

"Why did you not lock the door yesterday night?" Salma asked. "You know somebody might enter and steal your goods."

"I kept it opened for you. Otherwise, I have to get up from sleep to open the door. It's good for me that my sleep will not be disturbed and you can enter at ease. Is it not a good idea?" Aninda asked.

"You are really a kid," Salma laughed.

"Lolita Bhavi also says so," Aninda added.

"What is your lunch time?" Salma asked.

"Lunch? What is that?" Aninda asked.

"I want to know what time you take lunch?" Salma was angry.

"Ok, I have no time. May be noon, afternoon, evening. Why are you asking?"

"I shall send your lunch box to bank. Kalu will go. I want to know the time you will take lunch."

"Why are you taking so pain? Keep the lunch here. I shall take when come from office."

Salma again laughed and could not think how she would handle this child.

"Ok, Kalu will go at 1 o'clock to bank with lunch box," Salma told. "Please finish your lunch, otherwise it will get cold."

"Ok, Madam. Thank you for taking pain for me." Aninda was about to leave with files and other papers for bank.

"I have one request. Yesterday, I bought some items from Jangli Uncle's shop on credit. Will you please give me money to pay back the dues?" Salma said.

"Take money whatever you need from the almirah," Aninda replied.

"I can't take. If you don't give, I shall not take."

"It is up to you. I can't help," Aninda left saying, "Please tell me when the stock of money will be over. I shall withdraw from bank."

Salma was surprised how one man could trust so on an unknown lady. Salma understood the typical nature of Aninda. Salma started her work again. She had to make lunch ready and send to bank before one o'clock.

Salma suddenly became unmindful. She was thinking the moment when she touched Aninda first time in morning. Aninda was sleeping deeply. He could not get up despite her several wake up calls. Salma had no other choice but to touch his body for getting him up. It was first time Salma touched the body of one young man. From that moment, she was getting an unknown pleasant feelings all over her body. She could not decide whether she did right or wrong. Aninda woke up. His face was full of morning smile. It was first time in her life, she touched one young and handsome man. Only touching could bring such sensation, it was beyond Salma's imagination.

Lunch was ready. Salma sent the lunch box through Kalu to the bank.

At the evening, when Salma came, Aninda already reached. Aninda had a casual dress and the radio was on. He was listening music. His eyes were closed. Hearing the footsteps, Aninda opened eyes. His face was full of smile. Salma went to market before coming and bought vegetables and other items. Salma told that she had repaid the dues of Jangli Saha and bought those items taking money from almirah. Salma opened the almirah to keep the balance money which was returned. Aninda didn't ask any thing of expenditure. As if it was Salma's own house and it was Salma's duty to manage the fund.

"Is the money enough? Shall I draw from bank?" Aninda simply asked.

"Don't you know how much you kept at the almirah? You didn't ask me the bills and price of items I bought. It is not good at all. You should not trust me fully. It is your money and I am your servant. If something happened, you will blame me for misappropriation," Salma said.

"Very good question. But answer is I do not know how much money I kept there. I never manage my own wealth in life. Please Salma, try to understand me. I shall never blame you. I am really happy the way you are managing everything. Please tell me when the stock of money is over."

Salma understood Aninda within two days. She didn't continue the arguments with Aninda.

"How was the lunch? Did you eat or forget?" She asked.

"It was delicious," Aninda replied. "You deserve another tips. Please write somewhere the tips amount I shall pay to you."

Salma was busy in kitchen for preparation of dinner. She made tea for Aninda and served with potato fries she made.

"Where is your tea, Salma?" Aninda asked.

"I do not take tea at evening," Salma replied.

"I also do not take tea at the evening," Aninda said.

"Ok, Saheb, I am now making my tea. Please take your tea. It will get cold either."

Dinner was ready at nine. Salma served dinner.

"Salma, bring your plate and join with me," Aninda said.

Salma was hesitant. She didn't want to eat on the same table with Aninda.

"Don't be shy, baby. Bring your plate here," Aninda again insisted.

"No, I can't. Please don't force me. I am taking dinner at the kitchen," Salma replied.

Aninda smiled. "Ok, no problem. As you wish."

Days were going. Salma followed the same routine every day. Aninda as if left everything of his household matters to Salma. Nowadays, he was very relaxed. Salma knew what type of foods Aninda liked most. She tried to cook those things. In that matter, Lolita Bhavi was her guide to teach the techniques of cooking. Aninda everyday appreciated her cooking. His appetite suddenly increased. Month was over by that time.

"Salma, now month is ended," Aninda told Salma one day. "You take your pay from the almirah."

Salma was surprised. It was her first job in life. She didn't know her pay amount.

"I can't take," Salma replied. "I have never heard that master himself does not pay to his servant. Instead, he is telling to take money how much servant wants. Are you mad? When will you manage your money yourself?"

"I told you at the first day that It is not possible for me to manage the money matters. Please tell me how much you want for your work?" Aninda asked.

"I do not know. If you want to pay, please give to my father."

"That's like a good girl. You are really a wise girl," Aninda replied with smile.

Aninda told Salma to send Javed to his bank at any time of the day.

Javed came at the evening time when Aninda was about to leave office.

Seeing Javed, Aninda asked, "Javed Bhai, please tell me how much money I shall pay to Salma. She didn't say anything."

"Sir, what shall I say? You have saved my family. I cannot take any amount from you," Javed said.

Aninda couldn't decide what to do. Both Javed and Salma were not ready to take any money for work. They left it totally to him. He further requested Javed who was not ready to take still.

"Javed, Bhai, I do not know why are you hesitating so? If you do not accept money, please tell Salma not to come from tomorrow."

Javed held Aninda's both hands. "Sir, please do not say so. My family is getting life from you. I have one request. If you want to pay, please deposit the amount to my loan account. You know that I could not pay the monthly installments of my loan for last couple of months."

Aninda appreciated his suggestion.

"It's very good idea, Javed Bhai," he said. "I thank you. I shall pay your monthly installment."

Aninda returned home. Salma by that time came and started her works. Seeing Salma, he ordered for a cup of tea immediately. He was looked happy. Other days, Aninda when came, sat on the sofa and took rest for some time. That day, he got extra energy from office as if. Aninda entered kitchen.

"Salma, hurry up. One tea right now."

Salma noticed Aninda's changed behavior.

"What happened? You are cheerful today," She asked.

"Yes, I am very happy. Today, I bought a girl from one person in Nayanpur," Aninda said.

"So, I shall not come to work from tomorrow. Who is that girl?" Salma asked.

"She is very sweet and pleasant. You will forget your name if you eat her dishes she cooks," Aninda replied.

Salma's face was changed suddenly. Aninda was enjoying to see the changed face of Salma. Tea was ready and Salma served with potato fry and egg omelets.

"Are you not interested to know her name?" Aninda asked.

Salma didn't reply.

"Ok, it's my duty to disclose her name. Her name is Salma."

Salma's face became red to hear those. She was happy to hear from Aninda.

"You bought me? How? Who sold to you?" Salma asked.

"Your father, Javed Bhai. You know Salma, I told your father that I shall repay his *Tanga* loan. Instead, I want to buy Salma and she will work at my house until loan is repaid," Aninda said.

Salma was happy to hear those. She knew that Aninda was kidding and adding some spices with his words.

"I shall not leave you even if you tell me not to come," Salma replied softly.

# Chapter-7

In rural area, all farmers wait for monsoon season. It is their season for sowing corps. Their hopes and desires depend on how much rain, God gives during monsoon. If monsoon is good, their corps will grow better and their harvest will be better. They sell part of their crops to market and store rest to their house for food. But in monsoon days, the roads become muddy and it is very difficult to walk.

Nayanpur was not exception. Only concrete road was up to bus stand. All other roads inside Nayanpur and other villages were muddy and it became non walk able during monsoon. Albeit, the monsoon is the most lovable season in rural Bengal. It brings their joy and happiness. It gives their food and sources for living. Most of the villagers have the busiest time during that period.

Aninda's work increased during monsoon time. The farmers came to bank for cultivation loans. Aninda had to process their applications and submit to Manager for approval. Hundreds of farmers turned up. They used the money for buying of seeds, manures, fertilizers and cultivation expenses. The loans were given for short period of 6 months. When the crop was harvested, the farmers repaid the loan to bank with interest. The good crop depends solely on the rainfall. If rainfall is good, crops are grown well.

Aninda left early during those days from house and even he had no time to take breakfast. He returned late. Salma was worried how to manage everything that time. When Aninda came back, he was tired literally for whole day work. Salma was coming early. She made breakfast quickly and served to Aninda. Salma forced Aninda to take breakfast before going to office. Aninda could not disobey. Since Aninda was busy with his works and came from office late, Salma was coming late in the evening time to make dinner for Aninda. Salma everyday returned home after 10 o'clock at night.

During rainy days, the supply of vegetables and other food items became less. But there were plenty supply of all types of fishes. Salma knew that fresh fishes were available at Char Gopinathpur village where fishermen caught fishes from river. Salma went there to buy fishes for Aninda. It was about two miles from Nayanpur and road was practically difficult to walk. Salma knew that Aninda liked fishes particularly the local fishes. She bought fishes for Aninda and cooked. Aninda left everything to Salma and never asked how she was managing.

Aninda's workloads became lesser when the monsoon time was over. He returned back to normal routine.

In Bengal, after rainy season, the sky becomes clear. Sun becomes bright. It is Autumn, a charming season.

The condition of roads improved. There was sporadic rains only and most of days got day long sunlight. The fields were full of grown crops. Main crop was rice and jute. Autumn is also the festive months in Bengal. The famous Durga Puja festival happens during that time. Unlike *Eid*, Durga Puja happens almost at the same time every year. *Eid* is celebrated 11 months interval every year. That year, *Eid* was fallen after Durga Puja festival. Both Hindus and Muslims were busy that time to celebrate their most important festivals. Muslims observe *Ramjan* for one month and *Eid* is observed after the month long fasting. It was the most auspicious time to all Muslims. They observed with full devotion. The rich Hindu families organized *If tar* before end of *Ramjan* month. Nayanpur was an exceptional village where both Hindus and Muslims lived together and celebrated their religious ceremonies most peacefully. Muslims gathered with Hindus at Durga Puja time. Durga Puja was celebrated at the ground between *Purba* and *Paschim* Nayanpur. At the same place, Muslims did their *Namaj* during *Eid*.

Aninda decided to go to Kolkata to see his parents during Durga Puja time. Bank would be closed for one week. Salma was not happy. She would not see Aninda for a week. Both Aninda and Salma could not remember when they came close to each other. Aninda noticed the change of Salma's behavior when he told Salma for his going to Kolkata.

"What item shall I bring for you from Kolkata?" Aninda asked.

Salma did not reply. Her eyes were full of tears. Salma had fear if Aninda didn't return from Kolkata.

Aninda noticed that. "Don't cry, baby. I shall certainly return after one week. It is only for one week. Smile please."

Salma smiled.

Aninda bought new dresses for Salma from Berhampore. He gave to Salma and told her to wear during *Eid*.

Aninda's parent was happy to see him. Aninda's health was improved a lot. His hairs were cut and beard was shaved. He was looked like a prince. His mother observed that. Aninda told everything to his mother for the secret of his improved health. He gave the entire credit to Salma. Aninda's mother, Nirmala Devi was not happy to hear that his son had hired one Muslim girl as maid at his house. Her son was eating food what that Muslim girl cooked. But his father, Joydeb Babu was happy to see Aninda's bright face and improved health.

"Aninda, hire one Hindu girl," Nirmala advised. "You know, it is not good for a Hindu boy to take food cooked by one Muslim girl. Our Hindu religion will not permit that. It is against the religion."

Aninda laughed loudly. He didn't make any comment.

"Nirmala, listen. We must forget this cheap sentiment of religions. There is no difference of all religions. It is nothing but the mind set up. It is wise to leave these superstitions." Joydeb reacted.

"I can't. I am surprised to hear your view. You should endorse my advice, rather you are giving lecture supporting Aninda. What type of man you are? My only son has hired one Muslim maid and he is taking food everyday from that girl. You tell me to support that. Never."

"Nirmala, world is changing and we should not give any cognizance of cheap religious sentiment." Joydeb's contention was clear. Moreover, he was happy to see Aninda. Aninda was a changed man and more beautiful than earlier. Joydeb thanked to that unknown Muslim girl, Salma who had taken so much care of his only son. Despite Nirmala's insistences, Aninda did not agree to fire Salma.

Durga Puja is the most important festival in Bengal. More than hundreds Pujas are organized every year in Kolkata. The festival continues for four days. Thousands of people gather to see the festival from outside districts and states. Foreigners also come to see.

Nirmala was busy during Puja days. There was one Puja organized at their own neighborhood. Joydeb Babu was the President of that Durga Puja committee. Aninda's distant relatives and uncles came to their house during that time.

Everybody in Bengal waits for those days. They forget their pains and sufferings during those days. The whole city was flooded with various lights. People were on the street moving to the famous Puja *Pandals*. Most of them came with their families from neighboring towns of Kolkata. Polices were vigil to control the traffics. Buses, Trams, Taxis were full of passengers. All offices and shops were closed during four days of Puja. In front of Puja Pandals, hawkers and fast food shoppers were busy with the customers. All over the place was full of noises from Loud Speakers, musical instruments and visitors.

Aninda was given voluntary works at the Puja *pandal*. He had many friends there. He was busy whole day and night. He didn't have time to come home for rest. It was the time, he met all his friends who stayed away from Kolkata.

Four days were ended quickly. Aninda's leave was over. It was the last day's night. Next day, Aninda would go back to Nayanpur.

At the dinner table, Nirmala told Aninda, "I have one proposal for you. After Diwali, I shall arrange your marriage. I have already selected a good girl for you. She is from our own caste. You apply leave for one month when you will join office."

"I am not ready to marry now. I shall tell you when I shall marry," Aninda replied.

"You are now 25 years. It is the high time to marry. I am not going to hear anything from you. I have seen a good girl for you and you will marry after Diwali this year. It is my final instruction."

"Mom, I told you already. I cannot marry now. Please try to understand me."

"What is your problem? Tell us freely. Do you like any girl? Tell us. We shall talk to that girl's parent if you have already chosen her."

Aninda didn't reply to her mother. He was eating silently.

"You are silent," Nirmala told Joydeb. "Tell something to Aninda. It is the most important issue I think. You are his father. You must convince Aninda to marry now. He is 25. When will he marry?"

Joydeb was smiling.

"Nirmala, it is Aninda's own matter," he said. "Why are you forcing him? It is a life time decision. He does not want to marry now. So we should not force him. Let's wait. He has just joined service. Let's wait for his transfer to city from Nayanpur. I know it is a remote village. It is not possible for our daughter-in-law to live there."

"You didn't answer my question," Nirmala again asked Aninda. "Did you see any girl already? Tell us freely."

"Mom, I cannot say anything in this issue. I shall tell you when time will come," Aninda replied.

"It means you have chosen one girl what I understand. Tell me who is she?" Nirmala insisted to know the name.

"I already told you that I shall tell everything when time will come," Aninda said.

Nirmala left a long breath. Joydeb didn't say anything more. All finished dinner silently.

After returning to Nayanpur, Aninda became busy at office. He had lot of pending works. Salma was busy with day to day cooking and other works. Days were going fast. Aninda after end of each month, deposited the monthly loan installment to Javed's loan account. He also gave extra money every month to Salma. He knew that Salma would not take any money of her own.

Salma nowadays looked more beautiful. Nobody could say that she was one of the most poor man's daughter in Nayanpur. Her height was higher than any average girl. Her complexion was exceptionally fair. Hairs were long and deep black. She looked like a princess with the dress bought by Aninda from Kolkata. She had completed 18 years.

After Durga Puja, the next most important Hindu festival is Diwali. It is the most important festival in Northern Indian states. In Bengal too, it is celebrated at every house. It falls at the time of Kali Puja. The festival is called *Festival of Lights*. The people celebrate it with lighting of the fire crackers and sweets.

Aninda's bank was closed for two days. Although it is Hindu festival, Muslims of Nayanpur also participated equally with Hindus. Jangli Saha and his sons bought many firecrackers. They had decorated the entire house with varieties of lights. Nayanpur was flooded with lights at the night on Diwali. Salma heard from Lolita that it was Hindu practice that every house would cook variety of dishes in dinner including sweets. Salma bought sweets and other things. Aninda didn't ask what she was doing for Diwali. He was busy with his books and papers.

Salma cleaned Aninda's apartment neatly and decorated with new lights. The apartment got a new look. She was busy in cooking of special dishes. Her face was full of joy. Aninda observed her activities. Outside, Jangli Saha, his sons and, other tenants started lighting of the firecrackers. Kalu called Aninda to join. Aninda at his request went there. All were celebrating with joys. The entire area was full of light and firecrackers' sounds. Aninda was asked to fire some crackers. The ladies also joined. Lolita Bhavi called Salma. That was the festival which made you to forget your caste, color and religion.

The fireworks continued for hours. Everybody wished each other and it was 10 at night, Aninda came to his apartment. Dinner was ready. Every lady would not sleep on Diwali night. It was a ritual in Nayanpur village. They would spend night by making sweets and snacks. Lolita Bhavi already told Salma to stay night at their house. Salma took permission from Javed and Ruksana. They gladly granted the permission.

Aninda was extremely happy to see varieties of dishes at dinner. He liked sweets too. Aninda appreciated Salma's cooking and took more food than usual in dinner. He told Salma to finish dinner and then joined with Lolita Bhavi.

After dinner, Aninda was looked satisfied. He took one cigarette and smoked after dinner. He laid on his bed. It was pre winter time. Only blanket was sufficient. No fan was needed. Temperature was comfortable. Salma finished her dinner and cleaned the kitchen. She would join with Lolita Bhavi.

Salma dressed specially for Diwali. She wore a new blue sari. She knew that Aninda liked blue color. She made little facial make up. She looked like a princess that night. Aninda called Salma. He saw her closely. Aninda became silent for a minute.

"What are you looking?" Salma asked.

"I am looking at you," Aninda replied.

"Didn't see me earlier?" Salma said.

"I am seeing a different lady whom I never saw before."

"Good, you have to give me tips now."

"I am ready to give tips. I am ready to give everything what I have," Aninda's voice was lower suddenly.

Salma came closer to Aninda. Aninda was feeling warm breath of Salma. That was an unknown moment to them. Aninda could not control himself. He stood up and extended his two hands to Salma. Salma closed her eyes and did not ignore Aninda's call. It was first time Aninda kissed Salma. Salma didn't try to be separated from Aninda. Aninda forgot everything; time, place, relation, all. He didn't know what he was doing. He put the light off and locked the door.

Two bodies became one. Two hearts were made in one. Two souls were united. Salma surrendered everything to Aninda.

Salma got up from bed and put the light on. She put one blanket on Aninda. Aninda's eyes were closed. His face was full of heavenly peace and satisfaction. Salma went to Kitchen and changed her dress. She had extra dress kept there. Salma saw her face on a mirror and made up her face again.

Salma was the happiest girl of the world that night. She opened the door and went to Lolita Bhavi.

# Chapter-8

Next day, Salma came as usual. The door was opened. Salma saw Aninda already got up. It didn't happen generally. Aninda didn't leave bed early. Aninda was on the sofa. His face was bleak. He was thinking something deeply. Aninda saw Salma but didn't say anything. Salma went to kitchen and started daily works. Bank was closed that day too. Salma asked Aninda if he would take morning breakfast and tea that time. Aninda didn't reply.

"Will you not give any answer?" Salma came to him and again asked.

Aninda raised his head and looked at Salma. His face was not normal. Aninda told Salma to lock the door so that nobody could hear their talk. Salma did that.

"Salma, I am sorry," Aninda said. "Please forgive me. I was not normal last night."

"Why do you apologize?" Salma asked.

"Please forgive me. It was an accident."

Salma didn't say anything. She went to kitchen and was busy in making tea and breakfast.

Breakfast was served with tea. Salma made egg omelets and bread toast.

"Take breakfast first and then forgive your all misdeeds," Salma said.

Her eyes were twinkling with smile. Aninda could not understand the behavior of Salma.

"Please Salma, please tell me that you have forgiven me. I promise it will never happen what I did last night," Aninda said.

"Ok, I have forgiven you. Now are you happy? I have lot of works to do."

Aninda got tremendous relief as if. He was happy that Salma didn't take the incident seriously. He was scared that Salma might tell to her mother or Lolita Bhavi. Nothing happened.

Salma got new energy that day and her activity was increased many times. Salma told Aninda that she would cook some special dishes of fish curry what she learnt from Lolita. It was holiday. Aninda again went to sleep. One big stone from his chest suddenly removed.

After Diwali festival, winter suddenly came out in Nayanpur. The fields were full of ripe crops. The farmers would start harvesting shortly. It was another busiest time. The buyers of the rice gains and other vegetables would come to Nayanpur and other villages. They came from Berhampore and other big towns. They bought directly from farmers house. The farmers got their price of hard labor during last six months. It was their celebration time. They repaid the loans at that time. Aninda was again busy with his work. The farmers were coming to repay their loans. They would take another loans for winter crops. In Nayanpur areas, the land was very fertile and there was good source of river water. The farmers grew two crops in a year from the same field.

The important Hindu festival, *Pause Parbon* is celebrated that time.

It was one Sunday morning. Aninda didn't leave bed as usual. Salma came late. She knew that Aninda didn't go to office and took lunch late. Aninda got up late. Salma served tea.

"Salma, I have one serious talk to you," Aninda said. "Please sit here close to me. Before that, please lock the door."

Salma was a bit hesitant. She locked the door and sat closer to Aninda on Bed.

"Salma, I am thinking one issue for months together," Aninda said. "Today, I must tell you. One request, please keep it within yourself and don't tell anybody even to your parents now."

Salma could not guess what Aninda would tell.

"Salma, I have thought a lot and decided finally," Aninda continued. "I want your consent. if you agree, I can proceed. I have no issue if you do not agree."

Salma still was in a dark and could not guess what Aninda would tell.

"Please tell me freely," she asked. "It will be within me and I shall not tell anybody,"

"Salma, I want to marry you."

Salma stood up instantly. As if someone gave her strong electric shock.

"Do you know what are you talking? Are you mad? How do you think I shall agree to marry you?" Salma reacted sharply.

Aninda was mum. He didn't expect that sharp answer from Salma.

"Sorry Salma, I apologize," Aninda said.

"You are really a child. You forgot that I am a Muslim girl. How will your parents allow this marriage? Did you ever take permission from your parents?"

"No, Salma, I didn't take permission. I first want to know your consent. Next week, I shall go to Kolkata and request my parents for permission. I am sure that my father will agree. I am not certain about my mother. I want words from you," Aninda said.

Salma didn't reply. She went to kitchen and sat on the floor. Aninda after a while went there.

Seeing Aninda, Salma said, "Saheb, you know I am an uneducated, uncultured village girl. My father is a *Tanga* rider. My mother is maid servant. I am also your maid servant. Please do not tell this again. You will get good girl from your own caste with good back ground. I cannot make you happy at all. Please do not make me weak by saying this."

"Salma, I have no hesitation to tell you today. I thought for last several months. I took the decision finally after deep thinking. Trust me, I seriously want to marry you. I cannot live without you now. Please try to understand," Aninda said.

Salma was silent and didn't give any reply. Aininda requested her again. Salma told him to give one day time to think. She also promised that it would not be told to anyone in this world.

Salma came early next day. It was total dark all around. She opened the door and was surprised to see that Aninda got up and sat on the sofa. He was waiting for Salma.

Salma didn't tell anything, went to kitchen straight. Aninda was still waiting. After 10 minutes, Salma came to him. Aninda looked at her eyes. Perhaps Salma didn't sleep whole night. Her eyes were swollen. Aninda didn't ask anything. He was waiting for Salma's reply.

Salma could not talk properly that day.

"If your parents permit,....." she told only a few broken words while leaving.

Aninda got reply. He jumped from the sofa. His face was changed suddenly. He was the happiest man in the world that moment.

Aninda took one week leave from office and went to Kolkata. His mother was surprised to see him. "Are you well?"Nirmala asked.

"I am fine, Mom."

Joydeb was happy to see Aninda. "Dad, I have something to discuss with you," Aninda told his father alone when Nirmala went to kitchen.

Joydeb guessed something. "Not now. It's not a good time. Tell me tomorrow morning when you Mom will go to temple."

Time was perfect next day morning. Nirmala was not in house and she would take several hours in temple that Joydeb Babu knew. Aninda came to him. Aninda was hesitant.

"Aninda, tell me freely without any hesitation."

Aninda told entire episode slowly. Joydeb Babu was silent and his face became dark totally. Perhaps, he guessed in the same lime. He got a slight hints during last Durga Puja time when Aninda came.

After half an hour, Joydeb said, "Aninda, I understand your position. You truly love that girl. I do not believe religion or caste in marriage. If a boy likes a girl, there should not be any issue of marriage. I thank you that you take a decision which will slap the face of our religion and society. I am proud. But..."

"What ?" Aninda wanted to know.

"Your mother will not permit. She will force you not to marry a Muslim girl at all. I do not know how you will manage your mother," Joydeb Babu said.

"Let me try, Dad. I know my mother. I have trust that my mother will permit me if I am happy with this marriage."

Nirmala came early that day. She gave *Prasad* from Temple to them. She prayed today before God for Aninda's success in life and good health. Aninda didn't find the time good to talk that issue. Nirmala was busy in kitchen. She instructed the cook to prepare special dishes what Aninda liked most.

Lunch was heavy. At the lunch table, Joydeb, Nirmala and Aninda joined together. Dishes were delicious.

On the way of casual talks, Nirmala told both Aninda and Joydeb to listen to her seriously in one matter.

"Aninda, during last Durga Puja, I told you that I shall arrange your marriage this year," Nirmala said with straight words. "I have chosen a good girl of our own caste. I saw the girl. She did Master's this year, very charming and gentle. I talked to her parent too. Your father also liked that girl. Now, tomorrow you will go to her house to meet. I am sure you will like. I know your choice," Nirmala told at a stretch.

"Mom, I have one thing to say," Aninda said.

"What will you say? I am ready to hear everything except your unwillingness to marry. It is our only wish and I want to show to all my relatives what sweet girl I have selected for you."

"Mom, please listen to me. I have selected one girl and I want to marry her," Aninda said with straight words.

The entire dining room suddenly became ice silent. Nirmala stopped taking lunch. She could not believe what she heard from Aninda. It was her beyond dream even. Since childhood, Aninda obeyed all her instructions. Aninda was her only son.

"Nirmala, please listen what Aninda says. Then you react whatever you like. Let him allow to say which is his own matter exclusively," Joydeb said.

"Who is that girl?" Nirmala asked.

"Mom, her name is Salma. I told last time that I have hired one girl for cooking. She is that girl."

"Aninda, do you know what you said?" Nirmala screamed. "You will marry one Muslim maid servant," Nirmala shouted to Aninda.

"Nirmala, listen and think before reacting on Aninda. He loves the girl. That is the final matter. Whether she is Hindu or Muslim or Christian, it is not a matter," Joydeb Babu said.

"Are you both mad? My only son will marry a Muslim girl that too she is a maid servant? You want me to permit. Not at all. I shall commit suicide if Aninda marries that girl against my wish. It is my final word." Nirmala raised her voice high.

She stopped eating lunch and started weeping.

"Aninda, you are my only son. I am living only for you. I have lot of hope and wishes around you. Please do not give pain to me. Please forget that girl. Please agree to marry the girl I selected for you." Nirmala's voice became heavy.

Aninda didn't say anything. He left dining table unfinished his lunch.

Nirmala was totally upset. She insisted Joydeb repeatedly to intervene and convince Aninda for not marrying Muslim girl. She was totally scared to think what would be the reaction of all her friends and relatives. In conservative Hindu family like her, no person could accept that marriage. But Joydeb refused to intervene.

He said, "Nirmala, it is Aninda's own matter and as a father, I don't like to intervene his personal choice."

"So, you will not tell Aninda to change his decision," Nirmala's voice became heavy.

"Listen, Aninda is matured enough to select his life partner. It's my suggestion to accept the marriage."

Nirmala sat like a stone piece. She tried to speak something but no voice came out from her mouth. She was terribly shocked.

"How will I say to all our relatives?" Nirmala's voice was not normal.

"Yes, you are correct. Our relatives will resist and not come to the marriage. They will not keep any relation with us. I believe," Joydeb said. "But as parent, we should sacrifice everything for happiness of our only son."

Aninda went to his room after lunch and locked the door. Nirmala went to her room and cried a lot. Joydeb was watching TV at the drawing room. There was no talk thereafter amongst them. Aninda didn't take dinner that night. Next morning, Nirmala found that Aninda left house already.

Aninda returned to Nayanpur. He joined office and was busy as usual in daily works. Kalu went to Salma's house and informed her of Aninda's come back. Next day, Salma came to work as usual. Aninda already got up that time and was reading one newspaper.

"Shall I make tea for you? Salma asked.

"Yes," Aninda said. Salma made tea quickly. Her heartbeats were high for one nameless fear. She didn't know why she was becoming unmindful often. She could not ask Aninda for a single time how he was during those past days in Kolkata.

Salma made tea and gave him.

"Can you please lock the door?" Aninda told. "Please sit here for a minute."

Salma followed without saying anything.

Salma looked at Aninda. His eyes were different which were exceptionally red in color. Perhaps, Aninda didn't sleep last night. His voice was also different.

"Salma, my mother didn't give permission of our marriage," Aninda said.

Salma got up from the sofa.

"You wanted to say this only," Salma said coolly. "I am now really relieved."

Aninda was surprised to hear the instant reaction of Salma. There was no symptom of unhappiness and disappointment in her face. Rather she was exceptionally normal.

"I want to marry you, Salma. I don't care what my mother says. I don't care of my society. Please tell me that you will marry me."

"Saheb, I told you earlier. I do not agree this marriage without your parent's permission. It is now final. Please forget me and try to concentrate your office work. Please marry a Hindu girl what your mother wants. You will be happy and your parent will be happy."

"No, I am determined now. I shall marry you."

"I do not want. Please stop it now. I have lot of works to do."

Salma was busy in kitchen works. There was no further talk then. Aninda left to office. Salma made lunch and sent to Aninda's office.

Aninda when came from office, saw Salma working in kitchen. There was no talk between them. Salma finished her work and left.

Aninda realized that Salma would not marry without blessings of his mother. Aninda didn't find any change in Salma thereafter. Every day, Salma came on time and did her works.

Aninda was struggling within himself. He tried to talk on the same issue with Salma. But Salma was silent and didn't answer to any of his questions. Aninda was sure that Salma would not agree to marry at his hundreds request.

Time was going on. Days were flying on. Months were passing one after another. Aninda stopped going to meet his parent for a single time.

One day, Aninda received his transfer letter and he was transferred to Kolkata. The Branch Manager and all other staffs congratulated for his coveted transfer to Kolkata.

Aninda next day told Salma of his transfer. There was no reaction in Salma's face. Aninda didn't understand why Salma was changed.

It happened a few days before Aninda's transfer. Salma came as usual.

"I have taken one day leave for packing of my belongings," Aninda said. "I shall vacate the apartment. Will you please help in packing?"

The entire day, Salma was in his apartment. She did all packing and cleaning works. She returned the utensils, lunch Box and other things which she borrowed from others. She worked like a machine.

At last, Aninda got courage and asked.

"Salma, I am leaving now. I know that you will never marry me without my mother's consent. Very good. I have decided not to marry you until my mother gives consent. I have one request. Please promise me that you will keep."

Salma raised her eyes to Aninda. She didn't tell anything.

"Please promise me that you will wait for me."

Salma didn't reply.

The final day came. Aninda said goodbye to everybody. Lolita Bhavi and Jangli Saha started crying. He was loved by them from heart. Other tenants also came to say good bye. Salma was busy in packing of Aninda's belongings. From next day, she would not come to work. It was her last day. Salma was working silently. Aninda didn't notice any change in her face.

"You have not given the answer," Aninda called Salma and said. "I shall not insist on answer. Please forget me and forgive me."

Salma was strong enough so far. But that moment, she could not control herself. Her eyes were full of tears. Aninda was emotional.

"Salma, you have not given the answer," he said. "But I have got answer from your tears. Please trust me and wait."

———

"Madam, we have reached Ranaghat," Nitish Babu says.

Salma opens her eyes. She was in a different world.

"Madam, will you take tea?" Nitish Babu asks. "Pintu will take ten minutes rest. The car engine has become hot."

"Nitish babu, it is 1 p.m. now. It is good time for lunch. Can you please find any hotel here?"

"Pintu, is there any hotel for lunch here?" Nitish Babu asks.

"There is one good hotel located at Ranaghat Station market. It is only one mile drive," Pintu replies.

"Ok, go there," Nitish Babu says.

The car reaches at the hotel within ten minutes and it is parked in front of the hotel. All enter to the hotel for lunch. Nitish Babu knows that Madam takes only vegetarian dishes. He orders at the counter for lunches for everybody and tells the Hotel Manager for special vegetables dishes for Madam.

Salma takes a little food. She is not feeling hungry today.

The day is typically warm as contrast to morning temperature. Temperature is rising gradually now. Nitish Babu tells Pintu to put AC of the car on.

Salma's thoughts are moving to those days. How could she forget?

Those days were extremely painful when Aninda left. She cried whole night. She was not knowing whether she could meet Aninda in her life. Ruksana smelled everything. She doubted already that her daughter developed a soft corner for the bank Officer, Aninda. She knew that it was not possible at all that Aninda would marry Salma. Her society would not allow their marriage. The Imam and other clerics would allow with only one condition that Aninda should give up his own religion and converted to Muslim. It was not possible. As a mother, she wanted happiness for her beloved daughter. But it was like a dream to her. Ruksana told Javed everything what was her guessing. Javed also got a few indications that Salma loved Aninda. Javed knew it was not be allowed by his society.

Javed's condition was worsening day by day. Aninda repaid his loan to bank fully. That was not an issue. Issue was his earning was not sufficient to manage his family. Salma didn't want to work at any house. Javed didn't force her. Nassir and Danish were grown up boys. Javed could not manage their school fees and they were dropped out from school. Javed could not decide how could he manage everything. He asked Salma for marriage. Salma refused totally and told she was determined not to marry. Javed and Ruksana could not force her. Salma told them to arrange marriage for Tashlima. Javed and Ruksana did not agree for Tashlima's marriage. How would the society say? Elder daughter remained unmarried and how they could arrange marriage for younger one.

Javed's income was going down day by day. Nowadays, there were many Tangas at the village. It happened that he couldn't earn a single rupee in a whole day. Javed didn't think how would he manage foods for his family members.

# Chapter-9

It happened after *Muharam* days. Javed was not well. He had developed fever. Salma told him to visit a doctor. There was one doctor at Char Gopinathpur. Javed didn't agree. He was lying on bed. It was morning time. Ruksana had gone to work. Salma and Tashlima were busy in household works.

Tahasin Sheikh came. Tahasin called Javed's name from outside house. There was another gentleman, Sher Ali Mondal with him. Sher Ali was a member of nearby Kurshi *panchayat*. Tahasin and Sher Ali were friends. Javed with sick body came out and invited both to his house.

Tahasin asked Javed, "how is your health, Javed Bhai?"

"I am not well," Javed replied with sick voice.

Tahasin and Sher Ali came to the room and sat on the bed. Javed was not feeling well. He was too weak to speak. Looking Javed's condition, Tahasin advised him to visit a doctor.

Javed could not guess the reason of Tahasin's coming.

Tahasin introduced Sher Ali with Javed. Javed saw Sher Ali earlier at bus stand and heard his name.

After some casual talk, Tahasin said, "Javed Bhai, what are you thinking about your elder daughter's marriage. I forgot her name. I think he is over 20 now."

"Her name is Salma. Tahasin Bhai, I didn't think anything of her marriage. I am now penniless. You know, my income is now meager. There is severe competition in *Tanga* business. I am old and not getting enough customers. I am now not good at all."

"Javed Bhai," Sher Ali Mondal first talked. "If you don't mind, I can say something about your daughter's marriage."

"What help will you do? I am penniless now," Javed said.

"Javed Bhai, please listen first what Sher Ali Saheb says. Then you decide what you will do. It's a good marriage proposal. Yesterday, I got the information from Sher Ali Saheb. It came immediately in my mind about your elder daughter's name. Please listen to Ali Saheb," Tahasin said.

Sher Ali said, "Javed Bhai, a few days before, two persons came to my house. One of them is finding a good girl for his own marriage. The groom has a business at one town in Bihar. In his town, there is dearth of good girls nowadays. He has one distant relative in our *Panchayat*. He came here about one week ago. His relative requested me to find a good girl for marriage. The groom, named, Moslem Sheikh is a perfect man. His age is not more than 40 years. He earlier married but his first wife died untimely. He had no son or daughter. When we were talking, Tahasin Bhai reached at my house. I requested Tahasin Bhai to find a girl for Moslem's marriage. Tahasin told your name and we came for that purpose. If you agree, please tell us and we can proceed further."

Javed was suddenly silent. He didn't say anything.

"Javed Bhai," Tahasin said. "Do not think a lot. Take a decision quickly. Moslem Bhai will wait only for one day here and he will leave if no girl is available for marriage."

"Let me talk to my wife and daughter," Javed said.

"Javed Bhai, you will take decision. In this type of issue, the head of the family takes decision. I am sure, your wife will agree," Tahasin said.

"I have no money to arrange the marriage now," Javed said.

"Don't worry of money matter," Sher Ali said. "Moslem Bhai told me that he will pay entire expenses of marriage. He is a businessman and earns good money every month. You are lucky that you are getting groom like Moslem."

"I am fully impressed with Moslem. He is a perfect match with Salma. He is a moneyed man," Tahasin said. "Javed Bhai, don't hesitate. It's a golden chance you are getting."

"Let me think," Javed replied in weak voice.

"Javed Bhai, tell us you decision by the evening today. I shall request Moslem to wait one more day. He will leave if you don't agree," Sher Ali said.

Tahasin told Javed that he would come at evening time to hear his decision.

Javed didn't say anything. Salma heard their talk from outside.

After Tahasin and Sher Ali left, Salma came to Javed. She didn't speak anything. Javed saw Salma.

"Did you hear what Tahasin said?" Javed asked.

"Yes," Salma replied.

Javed took a long breath and told, "I do not know what Allah has written in your fate. What shall I do now?"

Salma didn't speak anything. Left silently.

At the afternoon, Ruksana came from her works. Javed told everything to her.

"What shall I say?" Ruksana said. "Do whatever you feel better. It's fact that it will not be wise if we turn down the proposal."

Javed still was in a great dilemma. He was not sure of Salma's decision. He told Ruksana to ask Salma if she agreed.

Ruksana asked Salma. Salma was firm to her earlier decision. She didn't want to marry. All members of the family were in a fix. Javed called Salma and tried to convince her. He wanted to know the reason why Salma didn't agree to marry. Salma could not reply.

At the evening, both Tahasin and Sher Ali Mondal came. They asked Javed what he decided.

"My daughter didn't agree. What can I do?" Javed said.

Tahasin started, "Javed Bhai, you are her father. No girl will agree for marriage initially. You have to put pressure on her. I am telling, you will miss a lot if you do not agree. You have to think of your second daughter also. If your first daughter is not married, who will agree to marry your second daughter? We know your condition. How will you arrange marriage of your daughters? Moslem will bear entire expenses of the marriage. I think it is the best proposal. You will be fool if you turn down such a good proposal."

"What can I do? Salma didn't agree. I cannot force her," Javed said.

"Javed Bhai," Sher Ali started. "Please think once again. Moslem is waiting for you. If you say yes, we can arrange marriage within a day or so. Your daughter will live like a queen in Moslem Saheb's house. He is a rich man."

Ruksana entered at that time. Tahasin, seeing her said, "Bhavi, please try to convince Javed Bhai. He didn't agree to this marriage. I am again telling you, this is the best marriage proposal you are getting. Your groom has come to your door. Please do not turn down. You will never get such a good groom. He is a rich business man."

Ruksana tried to convince Javed to put pressure on Salma. All girls didn't agree first time at their marriage. Later on, under pressure, they agreed.

"Javed Bhai," Sher Ali started, "I forgot to tell you one thing."

"What's the matter?" Ruksana asked.

"Moslem Bhai has agreed to pay you cash of Rupees five thousand if you agree. He will pay all expenses of the marriage too. Look, five thousand is a good amount. Your business is not going well. You can start a new business with this amount. You can also arrange marriage of your second daughter. I am telling you that your family will be saved," Sher Ali said.

"Five thousand?" Ruksana could not believe her ears.

"Yes, he will pay five thousand and all other marriage expenses," Tahasin added.

"Tahasin Bhai, I am taking responsibility. I shall convince Salma," Ruksana was excited.

"Thank you, Bhavi, I am happy to hear these words from you. So we are going to request Moslem Bhai not to leave. The marriage is fixed," Sher Ali wanted to hear final decision.

"What is your opinion, Javed Bhai?" Tahasin asked.

"What shall I say? Ruksana is taking responsibility to convince Salma."

"Bhavi, please convince Salma. We want to hear the final words. Thereafter, we have lot of works to do. We have to arrange the *Nikkha* within a day. I do not know whether Qazi Saheb is available now. He is a busy man. We have to go to Berhampore for purchase of bride and groom's new dress and other things. At least 50 persons will attend the *Nikkha*. Time is short. Moslem Bhai will leave as soon as marriage is over," Tahasin said.

"Salma will also leave. She will not come back to Nayanpur. I shall not see her again," Javed started weeping.

"Javed Bhai, you are fool really. Every year, Moslem will bring your Salma one or two times. Bihar is not far. You can go and see your daughter there. Your daughter will live like a queen, I am saying," Sher Ali said.

"Ok, do whatever you think better. Ask Salma what she says," Javed told Ruksana.

"Ok, I am going to talk Salma now. Tahasin Bhai, please wait," Ruksana said.

Ruksana again tried to convince Salma. Salma didn't agree still.

Ruksana finally told, "I will commit suicide if you refuse to marry Moslem. It's a question of our life and death, Salma. Who will pay cash rupees five thousand to our family?"

Salma heard with tearful eyes. She didn't say anything.

"At least, our family will be saved from the real distress. You know, it is now difficult to arrange two square meals for all of you. Your Abba's health is deteriorating day by day. If something happens, we all be nowhere. Please Salma, please agree," Ruksana literally appealed.

Salma stood like a statue.

"Salma, I beg to you. Please say yes. Please save your parents, brothers and sister. It is the best proposal we have got," Ruksana's voice was soaked with tears.

Salma was crying. Her eyes were full of tears. She was remembering the face of Aninda. Aninda told her to wait. He would come back. Aninda left about 6 months before. She had got no information during that time. What Salma should do?

Salma didn't speak anything. Ruksana didn't give her much time. She told Tahasin and Sher Ali that Salma did agree to the proposal and they could safely go ahead for the arrangement.

Tahasin and Sher Ali were extremely happy to hear. "Bhavi, thank you. We shall arrange everything within a day. You should not think even," Tahasin said.

Next day, Tahasin and Sher Ali came early morning. They made a list of items for purchase. Tahasin hired a few persons for working. They were over busy. Sher Ali called Javed in the mean time. He gave five thousand cash to him. Javed's hands were trembling. He was hesitant to receive the money. Sher Ali told him to keep the cash safely. In the marriage day, many invitees would come. Javed gave the money to Ruksana. Her eyes were suddenly brightened seeing five thousand in her hands.

*Nikaah* was scheduled on day after next day. They got only one day for arrangements. Sher Ali sent one guy to Berhampore for shopping. The vegetables, grocery items and sweets were available in Nayanpur. He sent another guy for local purchases. Tahasin went to Qazi Saheb's house to invite him. He was the most important person who would administer the total marriage process. Salma sat like a stone piece that day. Nobody had any time to talk to her.

By the evening all arrangements were completed. Nassir and Danish were involved fully and Tashlima also was helping them. Ruksana was supervising everything. Already, all his local relatives came to their house. Only Javed sat idly at one corner. Nobody bothered to ask him or discuss with him in any issue.

Salma got up early. She would be colored by *Mehndi*. The ladies would give turmeric paste on her face. Her hands would be beautifully decorated by *Mehndi*. Next day, her *Nikaah* would be sermonized. She was remembering Aninda's face again and again. She didn't know where he was. She wanted to see him for last time. Her eyes were full of tears. She could not eat for last two days when her marriage was announced.

Salma sat like a stone piece. Ruksana was busy to complete *Mehndi* ceremony early. Ladies already came. All were busy to decorate Salma.

The day came. It was Salma's *Nikaah* day. Qazi Saheb came early morning. He was the chief person who would officiate the *Nikaah*. The *Barat* would come any time. Everybody was busy to finish the works. The ladies were busy in cooking. Gentlemen were busy in making arrangements for marriage. Guests already started to come. *Barat* should be given special treatments.

Tahasin came early. He hired a few guys for work. He was managing entire works. Sher Ali would come with *Barat*. The house was full of people and guests.

*Barat* reached at forenoon. All were busy to welcome them. Danish and Nassir were asked to welcome and serve *Sherbat* to groom. Moslem reached by one *Tanga*. Danish and Nassir could not speak seeing Moslem. They were seeing first time. They were not ready to see such an old groom who might be older than their father. Nobody saw Moslem early. They believed what Tahasin and Sher Ali told. Tahasin and Sher Ali were busy to complete the marriage formalities. There were only a few *Baratis*. Moslem Saheb entered with *Baratis* in the marriage room.

Qazi Saheb went to Salma. Qazi started the ceremony.

"Salma Beti, do you accept this marriage?" Qazi asked.

Salma had to say, *"Qubul"* meaning she accepted the marriage.

Salma sat like a stone piece. Her eyes were full of tears. Qazi was impatient. Until Salma said *"Qubul"*, he could not proceed further. Salma didn't say any words. Ruksana observed. She came to Salma.

"Salma, say *Qubul*,"

Salma didn't respond.

Ruksana again requested Salma, "Beti, please say *Qubul* for the sake of our family." Salma didn't say.

Ruksana held Salma's both hands, "Salma, do not waste time, say Qubul."

"Ruksana, I am going to pronounce that Salma does not accept the marriage. I have one more marriage today to attend." Qazi didn't allow more time to Salma.

"Salma, if you do not say Qubul, your Abba and me have no other alternative but to commit suicide. We cannot show our faces to this village. It's better to finish our life if you do not say Qubul," Ruksana's voice was torn. Her eyes were full of tears.

Salma saw her mother. She uttered five letters, *"Qubul"*.

Ruksana embraced her and blessed for her happiness.

Qazi was busy to complete the process of *Nikaah*. *Baratis* and guests were invited at lunch.

Salma saw Moslem. She accepted her fate.

Moslem asked permission to leave from Javed next day. He had to return back to Bihar with Salma as early as possible. All his relatives were waiting there. It would take one full day to reach to his home town. Javed requested him to stay one more day. Moslem didn't agree. He promised Javed and Ruksana that they would certainly visit in the next year. He had a big business there and it was not possible for him to come often.

Salma left Nayanpur with Moslem. Tahasin hired one *Tanga* for their going up to bus stand.

Javed, Ruksana, Tashlima, Danish, Nassir and all their relatives came to say good bye to Salma. Salma was going to her groom's house. Javed could not control himself. He was crying. Ruksana and Tashlima also were crying. There was no change in Salma's face. She was moving like a stone body. She was doing what was asked her to do. Salma was going to her groom's house for ever. She didn't know if she could come back to Nayanpur in her life.

Tahasin and Sher Ali were busy to start the journey. They were literally impatient. They would also go with them up to bus stand. From there, Moslem and Salma would go to Berhampore by bus.

When they reached at Bus stand, Moslem told Salma, "Wait for a few minutes here. I have something to talk Tahasin and Sher Ali Saheb. Next bus's time is after half an hour."

Moselem went to talk to Tahasin and Sher Ali to one tea stall at bus stand.

Bus came on time. Tahasin and Sher Ali said good bye to them. They were happy. Their faces were full of smiles. "Ok, Moslem Bhai, take care of Salma. Wish you happy journey," Tahasin said.

Bus was almost empty. Moslem and Salma got two window seats. Bus reached at Berhampore within two hours.

"Salma, we shall go to Kolkata by train now. We shall catch tonight's train from Howrah station," Moslem said. Salma didn't know where she was going. What was the name of the place she was going? She didn't ask her husband.

"Will you want to take lunch here?" Moslem asked.

Salma didn't want to eat. She didn't feel hungry.

They reached Kolkata at the evening of the day. They went to Howrah station straight to catch the train which would go to Moslem's native town.

Moslem bought two tickets. The train started at night. The compartment was full of passengers. They had no reservations. Moslem managed the Ticket Collector with money and got two berths for sleeping.

Moslem again asked Salma, "will you eat something?" Salma still didn't feel hungry. Moslem bought fruits and water. He ate those. Salma drank water only.

The compartment was full of passengers. Train started at dead of night. Salma didn't ask what's the time. She didn't know where she was going. She didn't ask Moslem. Salma laid on the berth. She got a lower berth. Salma was terribly tired. She couldn't eat literally for last couple of days. Initially she cried a lot. Her tears were dried up. She made up her mind that she would never cry.

Salma was remembering Aninda's face. It was that city, Kolkata where Aninda lived. Aninda could not know that she was married and left forever. She would never meet Aninda in her life. Salma didn't know when she slept.

# Chapter-10

Salma opened her eyes. The train reached one station. A few passengers were getting down and new passengers were boarding. Someone called porters for help. Tea hawkers were selling teas. There was lot of noises around. Outside was becoming clear. It was morning time.

"Salma, will you take tea or any breakfast?" Moslem asked.

"What is the name of the station?"

"It is Barauni. We shall get down at Samastipur and it would take another 2 hours."

Salma came to know that her final destination was Samastipur. She didn't hear the name of the places ever. She went to Berhampore one or two times only. She didn't have any idea of the places beyond Berhampore. She never went to Kolkata even. It was the first time she came to Kolkata and beyond.

"Will you take tea?" Moslem again asked.

"Yes, one cup please."

She was absolutely normal in behavior. Salma surrendered everything to her fate. She didn't think what would happen to her. Moslem bought one cup tea for her. Train would stop here for more than half an hour.

Barauni was a big junction. It was a busy station. Several important trains were scheduled to pass through Barauni.

"Salma, I have one friend who will meet us here," Moslem said. "I am waiting for him. If he does not come, we shall get down and wait for my friend."

Salma didn't ask anything of his friend.

"Let me have a look on the platform if he has come already," Moslem said. "You wait for a few minutes. Train will stop here for half an hour."

Moslem got down from the train and went to find out his friend. When returned, train was about to start. He found his friend at the station.

Moslem introduced his friend with Salma. "Salma, this is my friend, Ashadul."

"Salam, Bhavi," Ashadul greeted Salma.

"Salma, I have an urgent work at Barauni. Ashadul will go with you up to Samastipur. I have told everything to Ashadul. He is kind enough to help," Moslem said.

"Bhavi, don't worry. I shall go with you," Ashadul added.

"Ashadul Bhai, please stay at any hotel nearer to Samastipur station. I shall go as soon as my works are done."

"Moslem Bhai, you know me. I shall take all care of Bhavi. Do your work peacefully," Ashadul assured Moslem.

"I have got enough relief from your words, Ashadul Bhai. You know, Salma is new to our area. Please take all care. Please stay at a good hotel. Do not think about money. I shall pay to you," Moslem was emotional.

"Moslem Bhai, go and finish your works. I shall be always with Bhavi."

"Ok, then good bye, Salma. Take rest at the hotel today. I shall reach as soon as my works are done here."

The train was about to start. Moslem got down from the train and the train started.

Ashadul was a middle aged man with well built body. He asked, "Bhavi, will you take tea or any breakfast?"

The hawkers were selling tea and breakfast within the compartment. Salma wanted to have one more cup of tea. Ashadul bought one for himself and other for Salma.

"Bhavi, who are in your family in village? What is the name of your village?" Ashadul asked.

Salma was exceptionally normal in behavior. She replied to Asahdul.

"Bhavi, please do not take it otherwise. Is it your first marriage with Moslem Bhai?" Asahdul was hesitant when asked.

Salma smiled. "Yes, it's my first marriage."

The train reached at Samastipur station. It was also a big station. Samastipur was the district head quarter. The town was also big. Ashadul and Salma got down from train and came out of the station. He hired one rickshaw and told the rickshaw puller to drop them at Modern Hotel.

Modern Hotel was not far from the station. It was located just outside the Samastipur Station market. The area was not crowded like station area. Ashadul paid money to the rickshaw puller. Salma had only one small suitcase. She had a few saris and cloths only. It was not heavy in weight. Ashadul entered to the hotel.

The Manager of the hotel welcomed Ashadul. Ashadul greeted him and other workers of the hotel. Everybody knew Ashadul. Manager gave him the key of one room. As if, they were waiting for Ashadul. It was a small hotel having a few rooms only.

Ashadul opened the room. It was a small room with double bed. Salma didn't ask why Ashadul took only one room. Where would he stay?

"Bhavi, take rest now. You can sleep, if you like," Ashadul said. "I have told waiter to serve lunch in the room."

Salma saw there was an attached bath with the room. She was hesitant as Ashadul was in the room. Ashadul noticed that.

"Bhavi, feel free. You can change dress and take rest in my presence. I shall not mind at all. Actually, there is no other room available now in this hotel. It is only a matter of one night. Tomorrow, we shall leave the hotel. We can manage one night," Ashadul said.

"When will my husband come?" Salma asked.

Ashadul didn't reply. He said, "Bhavi, I have an urgent work and I have to leave now. I shall come within an hour. Do not leave the room. If you want anything, push the calling bell. Manager or any waiter will come. Lunch will be served within an hour."

It was afternoon time. Salma was feeling hungry.

Asahdul left. He didn't tell when Moslem would come. Salma left everything to her fate. She could not think any more.

She found that Ashadul locked the room from outside. She could not go out of the room. She didn't understand why Ashadul locked the room from outside.

Salma took bath and wore a new sari. She was terribly tired. One waiter came with lunch plate. The waiter kept the lunch on the table. He brought one bottle of water. He told Salma to push the calling bell if she wanted more food. The waiter locked the room from outside.

Salma was hungry. She finished the lunch quickly. She pushed the calling bell. The waiter came. She told him to take the empty lunch plate out of room. Waiter did and locked the room again.

Salma suddenly felt drowsy. She laid on the bed and soon went to sleep.

Salma didn't know how long she slept. She heard that someone was opening the lock. There was dark all over. She found from the window that evening already came. Salma slept a lot. She felt some pain on her head. She heard the voice of Ashadul outside. He was talking with someone. Ashadul opened the door and came inside. The Manager of the hotel was with him. Both entered and again locked the door. They closed the window of the room. It was pre-winter time. The temperature was charming. It was neither hot nor cold. Manager put on the switch and the room was full of light. Salma already got up from bed and sat one corner of the bed. Ashadul and Manager sat other side of the bed. Salma didn't see Moslem still.

"Will you want to eat something now? Ashdul asked. Salma was not hungry. She didn't want to eat.

"When will my husband come?"Salma asked Ashadul again.

"Your husband? Your husband will never come. You will get a new husband tonight," Ashadul said coolly.

Salma could not understand what Ashadul said. She was scared all of a sudden. Her voice became chocked. She could not speak. She was sweating literally.

She again asked with weak voice," What are you talking? My husband told me to come soon. He told you to take care of me and wait till he comes. Who are you?"

"You will get a new husband better than Moslem." Ashadul and the Manager laughed loudly. "You will enjoy whole night with your new husband. Are you not happy, baby?" Asahdul said.

Salma realized that she had been trapped. Still the entire picture was not clear to her. Ashadul made everything clear soon.

"Salma Bibi, your so called husband who married you and brought from your village, sold you to me for twenty five thousand rupees.

His name is Abu. He told his name to your family as Moslem. It is his business to buy fresh girls from villages of Bengal and sell to his clients. Every year, he marries hundreds of fresh girls and sell. He managed some persons in the villages who helped him to find good looking girl. I bought you from Abu. You are now my property and tonight I am your husband," Ashadul chewed the words and told with rude voice. "If you try to move, I will kill you and cut your body into pieces. Manager sub and all other waiters are guarding you. Don't try to move from this hotel. Do whatever I shall say."

Salma's senses were not working. Nothing was entering inside her ears. Still she didn't cry. Salma understood why Tahasin and Sher Ali Mondal were so interested for her marriage. Moslem bribed them with good amount for a girl. Tahasin knew her father's financial condition and she was the softest target. She knew that Tahasin and Sher Ali gave money to her mother. She understood why the unknown man was ready to marry her. She was bought from her parents and sold to Ashadul. She knew that she couldn't do anything. She could not return back to her village. She cried a lot before marriage. Nobody bothered. Tahasin and Sher Ali showed extra interest for her marriage. Everything was clear to her. She had been trapped and nothing could be done. Salma realized everything. But she couldn't cry.

Manager didn't speak anything when Ashadul was talking. Salma understood that the Manager was also a part of the racket. Girls were bought and sold in that hotel. Manager called one waiter for a bottle of whisky and chicken fries. Drinks and fries were served. Manager opened the bottle and both cheered the drinks. Asahdul asked Salma if she would like to have one glass of whisky. Salma didn't reply. She sat like a stone piece on the bed. Her body was full of sweat. She knew that she could do nothing.

Manager and Ashadul drank pegs after pegs. They smoked cigarettes one after one. The room was full of smoke. Salma's eyes were burnt. She faced difficulty to breath. They didn't bother what Salma was feeling. They finished drinks and food. The whole bottle was empty. Ashadul got up from the chair. His body was hanging.

"Manager Sub, I am going out," Ashadul said.

Salma was now Manager's property. Ashadul went out and locked the door. Manager's eyes were completely red. His movement was not normal. He put off the lights and came close to Salma. For more than an hour, Manager raped Salma repeatedly. When he was completely exhausted, he got up from the bed. Salma laid on bed. Salma didn't resist at all when Manager was eating her flesh.

Manager knocked the door. Ashadul opened. Manager left and Ashadul entered. Salma became half conscious. Her senses were not working. Asahdul was hurry to act. He started eating her body. Asahdul raped her. It was about dead of night. Ashadul was exhausted. He got up from bed. He covered the body of Salma with a blanket. He put on the light and entered into the toilet.

Salma lost her senses completely. Two wild animals ate her body for last several hours. Asahdul went out. Salma didn't know how long she laid on bed in such condition. When her senses returned back, she saw another stranger on her bed. The man had no dress. The stranger was smoking. Salma had felt lot of pain all over her body. She had no strength to get up. She didn't realize if she was dead or alive. The stranger dressed up and left. Salma could not remember how many persons had eaten her whole night. She again became senseless.

When Salma got up, she saw Asahdul was sleeping on the bed beside her. Salma had no strength to get up. Her body was burning. She could not open her eyes properly. She felt lot of pain in her entire body. Salma stayed hours at the same condition. Asahdul got up when it was late morning. Ashadul called touching her body. Salma had no sense to reply. Asahdul got a wrong signal. He called Manager who rushed to the room. Manager touched forehead of Salma and felt the high temperature. Ashadul's face was changed.

"What shall I do now?" he asked Manager. "She has lot of fever. She might have other complications."

"I can't call any doctor here. He will ask lot of questions which will not be answered properly. It's better to buy some medicines from Pharmacy shop. The owner of Pharmacy shop knows me. I am sending one person for medicines. Don't worry, she will be ok within a day," Manager said.

"How many persons you sent last night?" Ashadul asked.

"I sent only one person. I think he did something wrong. The girl's condition has been worsened."

"What shall I do now?" Ashadul murmured. "I have already informed Badi Aunty to come today. She is coming from Chaturbhuj Sthan, Muzaffarpur and will arrive at any time. If she sees this condition, she will not agree to buy. Then entire liability will come to me. I want to sell the girl as early as possible," Ashadul said.

"Don't worry, tell Badi Aunty that girl had fever and not well. Tell her that due to lot of travel, she fell sick. I think your Aunty will understand," Manager said.

"I am not sure. She is also lady. She may doubt something wrong seeing her condition. She will not believe that girl had only fever. She will guess the actual reason which cannot be hidden. She told repeatedly that we should not touch her body. She wants fresh girl. Now, even if she agrees to buy, she will not give me desired price. I already paid twenty five thousand," Ashadul said.

"Ok, what can we do now? I am bringing medicines and apply to her. Let's see what happens," Manager left.

After one hour, one waiter came with a few medicines. He told Asahdul to feed it to the girl. Asahdul tried to feed. He asked Salma to open her mouth. Salma still was not in conscious condition. Could not open her mouth properly. Asahdul forced her to open and fed the medicines with water.

Salma laid on bed like a corpse. There was no sign of any improvement. Her fever was rising. Asahdul was tensed.

Badi Aunty came at noon. She was a middle aged lady of mid forties. She came from Muzaffarpur. She lived at Chaturbhuj Sthan at Muzaffarpur, the famous red light area. Manager informed Ashadul that Badi Aunty came and waiting at the counter. Asahdul was scared suddenly. He knew that Badi Aunty would not agree to buy the girl seeing that condition. If agreed, she would not be ready to pay good price. Anyway, Ashadul went to meet Badi Aunty.

Badi Aunty came after a few minutes. Salma was still in same condition. Her body was like a hot oven. Aunty entered the room and saw Salma. She touched her forehead and realized what happened.

"Baby, get up. I am here," she called gently to Salma. "You have no fear to me. I shall take all of your care. Get up baby."

There was no movement at all. Salma laid like a dead body. She could not open her eyes.

"How many persons worked on her?" Badi Aunty asked. "It is not a normal case. I told you repeatedly, I want fresh girl. Who will take all of this burden? I am not going to buy."

"Please Badi Aunty, please listen to me. She had fever due to long journey for last couple of days. She has come from Bengal. She will be ok within a day. You know my condition. Where shall I keep this girl? I have bought only for you," Asahdul requested with soft voice.

"I told you should not touch her. I am sure you sent some illiterate persons to her. They damaged her body brutally. This is not a simple fever. I have doubt whether she had other damages. She is not ok now. I cannot buy," Badi Aunty said clearly.

"Please Badi Aunty, please take her. It's my request. I shall give you a beautiful girl next time afresh. I swear," Ashadul promised.

"Ok, you are my old friend and supplied many girls. It's ok, I shall buy. But I shall pay ten thousand for this girl. Please tell me if you agree," Aunty wanted to know.

"Ten thousand only? I bought her for twenty five thousand. How can I sell for only ten thousand? Please give me twenty five thousand. I do not want any profit."

"Are you mad? How do you expect I shall pay twenty five thousand for this sick girl? She is over aged and sick. Nowadays, customers want young girls not more than 16. I think she is more than 20. It's my last price that I can pay fifteen thousand. If you agree, tell me. Otherwise, I am leaving. I have to see another girl at other hotel," Badi Aunty said.

Asahdul was in dilemma. He was not ready to hear that type of answers from Badi Aunty. It was not possible for him to bear loss of huge ten thousand from that girl. He could not decide what to do.

Badi Aunty told him to deliver the girl at Paradise Hotel where she was going to see one more girl, if Asahdul agreed for fifteen thousand.

Badi Aunty left. Ashadul didn't agree to sell. He talked to Manager. It's better to wait for a few days. By that time the girl would be better and he would get a good price from other customers.

Manager endorsed his views. There was another risk what Manager told. It was risky to keep the girl long at the hotel. Nowadays, polices were very vigil. They could raid the hotel if they got any information of the girl. It's wise not to call any doctor. Medicines could be bought from pharmacy. The girl would be ok if she was given medicines and rest.

"Do you know any person who buys girl?" Asahdul asked Manager.

"There is one Chowdhary at Ranitola village who owns hundred acres of agricultural field. His name is Chowdhary Lal Shyam Singh," Manager said. "Singh sub buys girls for his agricultural and household works. He has 15 to 20 girls what he has bought and they are in his house."

"Can we not request Chowdhary for this girl?" Ashadul asked.

"We can talk. I know he pays good amount if he likes the girl. Your girl is no doubt good, young, and fresh. Her body is attractive. What is your experience?"

Ashadul's eyes were twinkling.

"I have got this type of girl after a long time. That is the reason, I agreed to pay twenty five thousand to Abu," Ashadul said.

"But, there is one problem," Manager said.

"What?"

"Chowdhary Sub buys only Hindu girls. If he knows the girl is Muslim, he will not agree to buy," Manager said.

"What shall we do then? How to deal with that issue?" Ashadul asked.

"Ok, I am going to Ranitola," Manager said. "I shall tell that the girl is Hindu. He knows me. He will not disbelieve me. You can go with me if you like. But don't say that you are Muslim."

Asahdul didn't want to go. If he was caught by any means, Chowdhary would not believe that the girl was Hindu. It was then difficult to sell the girl. Asahdul knew that he could not know the deal how much price Chowdhary would offer.

"Manager Sub, please try to convince Chowdhary for at least fifty thousands, Ashadul said. "I am ready to pay you five thousand rupees as commission." Manager was Hindu and Chowdhary would not destruct him.

Ranitola was located only 10 miles from Samastipur town. Next day, Manager reached at forenoon. Chowdhary was present in his house that time. Manager sent information to Chowdhary that he wanted to meet him.

Chowdhary was literally land lord of the village. He had hundred acres of lands. His house was also big. He had security guards at the main gate. The guards searched the body of Manager and then allowed to enter. Manager was asked to wait at one big room which was made for visitors. Manager saw many people working at his house. He heard that Chowdhary had five sons who were looking after the business and agricultural operations.

Chowdhary's age would be around 60. He lost his wife a few years ago. He had total command on his family. All his sons were married and they had children. Chowdhary had number of businesses at Samastipur and Patna which were managed by his sons. He was a big gun in the area.

Manager waited for half an hour. Chowdhary was busy in lunch. Manager was asked by one servant if he would prefer to take lunch. Manager said no.

Chowdhary came to see him at the visitor's room. Manager bowed and touched his feet. Chowdhary asked his well being. He knew Manager.

"How can I help you, Manager?" Chowdhary asked.

"Chowdhary Sub, I have a small request. One bird has come to my hotel. I want to present the bird to you. I am sure you will like," Manager said.

"How much do you want?"

"Sub, what shall I say? I got an offer of sixty thousand," Manager lowered his voice.

"Bring your bird. Let me see first. I cannot deal without seeing the item."

"Sub, the girl is fresh and young. Just come from Bengal. She belongs to a higher caste," Manager said.

"Ok, go and bring here. When shall I see?"

"Sub, give me a few days. She has just come. She is tired due to long journey."

"No problem, bring next week," Chowdhary said.

Manager again bowed his feet and asked permission to leave.

Manager was happy to know that Chowdhary was ready to buy. Only big question was how much he would offer for the girl.

Manager on return informed everything to Ashadul. He wanted to know the condition of the girl. There was certain improvement after applying medicines. Her fever was less. But she was too weak to get up from bed.

Manager told that the girl should be presented before Chowdhary when she was completely alright. If Chowdhary did not agree to buy, it was difficult to sell the girl. Polices were active in Samastipur and if they got any clue, they would send them behind the bar and the license of the hotel would be seized.

Salma was recovering slowly. She was given medicines from time to time. After a week, there was sharp improvement in her condition. Ashadul himself was looking after her. Salma could go to toilet and bath herself. Manager was enquiring from time to time about her health. Salma became well.

Manger discussed with Ashadul what would they do next.

"Ashadul Bhai, make sure that the girl should not say that she is Muslim," Manager said.

"How can we do?" Ashadul asked.

"Her name is Durga and she is a Hindu girl. No problem with her surname "Sarkar", it is used both Hindus and Muslims. Chowdhary will not doubt," Manager said.

"Great idea. Come with me and teach her now,"

Ashadul and Manager taught Salma what she should say to Chowdhary. They told her that she would be happy at Chowdhary's house. Chowdhary's family was well known and respected in the village. She would be lucky if Chowdhary would agree to hire her. They didn't tell that they were going to resell her to Chowdhary.

Salma lost everything. She was taking food against her wishes. She wanted to end her life. She had no interest at all in her life. She thought that at least she would be freed from the clutch of Ashadul. If she stayed further with Ashadul, she would be brutally tortured any time. It's better to take the shelter of Chowdhary and for that she was ready to tell any lie.

Salma was dressed like a bride with new sari. Ashadul bought facial make up for her and instructed to make up her face and body neatly so that Chowdhary would agree to hire her. Salma did what Ashadul told. She looked like a newlywed bride. Salma was going to her new groom's house.

Manager hired one rickshaw to go to Ranitola. They reached before noon. The day was not hot. Manager and Salma took the permission of the security guards outside the house. They were asked to wait at the visitor's room. Chowdhary came to see the visitors.

Chowdhary was tall about 6 feet height with fair complexion. He was old but strong in his movement. Chowdhary sat on his chair. Manager bowed his feet and asked his blessings. Manager told Salma to touch the feet of Chowdhary. Chowdhary was extremely happy to see Salma. His eyes were twinkling with lust and happy face was giving signal that he liked Salma. Chowdhary asked, "what's your name?"

"I am... I am... I am..."

"Tell your name," Chowdhary again asked.

Manager asked Salma to tell her name. "I am Durga. Durga Sarkar," Salma replied.

"Very good name. I do not want to know anything of your past. Go to the next room and wait there," Chowdhary said.

He instantly called one maid servant and told the maid to take Durga to another room. He had some discussion with Manager of the hotel.

"Now Manager Saheb, tell me how much do you want for the girl. I want to make sure one thing that if any police complaint arises,

I shall shoot you. Make sure before me that there will not be any police case with this girl. Then I shall buy."

"Chowdhary Sub, you know me for several years. You know I never lied you before. I am assuring you there will not be any issue with this girl. She came from Bengal and she is a Hindu high caste girl. Her father sold her to one of my friends. I guarantee you there will not be any issue with this girl."

"Do you know the girl is married or not?" Chowdhary asked.

"I heard she was married earlier but her husband left her. She had no kid."

"Good, I like married girl. Now tell me how much do you want?" Chowdhary asked.

"Chowdhary Sub, I want sixty thousand. See the face and body of the girl. I can get much higher price if I sell her to Muzaffarpur or Patna. I have come to your house as you like young Hindu girls," Manager said.

"Are you mad? You want sixty thousand. No, I can't pay sixty thousand for one girl. If you supply another girl of this type, I can pay sixty thousand for both girls. It's not possible for me to pay sixty thousand for one girl," Chowdhary said.

"Chowdhary Sub, I have come with lot of hope. Please don't say so. Please consider my case. Nowadays, the prices of all items are gone up. It's true that one year before girls were available for twenty or twenty five thousand. Now, even one cow is not available less than ten thousand. Please favor me. I am not asking high price. It's the present rate," Manager requested.

"No, I can't pay such huge amount. Of course, I liked the girl. But I can't pay your amount," Chowdhary said.

"How much will you pay ?" Manager asked.

"I can pay maximum thirty five thousand. Tell me if you agree. You will get cash now," Chowdhary told his final words.

"Chowdhary Sub, please make it forty. It's my request."

Chowdhary thought a little and said, "Ok, take forty. But keep in mind, if any police case arises, I shall shoot you like a dog. You know me and my sons."

"Chowdhary Sub, I guarantee you, it is a fresh girl and there is no issue with this girl."

Chowdhary told him to wait for ten minutes. He called his Munimji and asked him to pay cash of forty thousand to the Manager.

Salma heard everything what was discussed with Manager and Chowdhary. She was sold for forty thousand.

Her name was Durga, a Hindu girl. She was Durga Sarkar. Salma Sarkar just died.

# Chapter-11

Salma was escorted by one maid to another house. The main house where Chowdhary and his sons lived, was a three storied building with several rooms, guest house, visitors room, kitchenette. There were other two houses located at the same compound. One was made for female servants and other was for male servants. There were about 30 servants working at Chowdhary's house and his farm. The whole compound was protected by concrete boundary wall. The height of the boundary wall was high so that no outsider could see anything from outside. There was one gate at main entrance of the compound. Chowdhary posted security guards at the gate. They were armed with guns and rifles.

Chowdhary had several cars for use of his family members. By caste, he was *Bhumihar*, a higher caste in Bihar. He was the chief of the Village *Panchayat*. The villagers dared him a lot. His three sons were looking after all his businesses at Samastipur and Patna and other two sons were busy in farm operations. Chowdhary was 60 years old and left all his business and farms to his sons. He had three daughters, all were married. All sons were married and having two to three kids on an average. The elder son's age would be late thirties and the youngest one would be mid twenties. He lost his wife about five years before. The family was completely vegetarian.

Chowdhary preferred ladies in his household as well as farm works. Altogether there were 15 ladies working at his house and farm. Chowdhary liked young ladies. Once the lady became old and slow to work, he drove them away from his house. The gents were mostly working in the farm and managing the cattle yards. The house of the female servants was located adjacent to main house. It was a store house like with several rooms. Each room was double bedded and two girls stayed in one room. There was a separate kitchen for female servants.

The male servants house was located at the last corner of the compound which was again surrounded by one boundary wall. No male worker was allowed to enter inside the ladies house area. There were 2 guards posted. Chowdhary had strict rule. If any male worker was seen nearer to the ladies area, Chowdhary and his sons, if came to know, would give severe punishment. He would not be given any food and water for several days and he would be beaten mercilessly. All servants were sacred and dared to Chowdhary and his sons.

Chowdhary had several houses at Samastipur and Patna also. His three sons with their families stayed there. They came on Sunday and holidays at Ranitola with families. Their children were studying at Samastipur and Patna school. In Ranitola house, his two sons and their families stayed. Their kids also admitted at Samastipur and Patna school. There was no good school at Ranitola.

The maid showed Salma which room she would stay. The maid was older than Salma. Her name was Savitri. Salma would be her room partner. Savitri told her to change the dress and take bath if she liked. There was common bath for all female servants. It was about evening time, Salma didn't like to bath. She was not feeling well. She had no fever but had developed one name less fear. Savitri brought a cup of tea and puffed rice for Salma.

"What is your name?" Savitri asked her name.

Salma told her name, "Durga Sarkar."

Savitri didn't speak more. She had works at Chowdhary's house. Savitri was the kitchen assistant of Chowdhary's main house. Salma was so dared that she could not speak freely with Savitri. Savitri left hurriedly and told that she would come within an hour after her work and tell everything to her.

Salma took the tea and puffed rice. She was hungry. Salma was not sure what Chowdhary would do with her. Savitri could throw some light about her future she thought. Salma was waiting for Savitri.

Salma saw most of the rooms empty. The girls were possibly working at Chowdhary's house. Salma came out of the room. She saw ray of light coming from one big room at the last end of the house. She went there. It was kitchen for female servants. Two ladies were busy in cooking. Salma didn't meet with them. She returned back to her room. She locked the room and sat on bed. There was no other furniture. Two big size wall almirah made inside the wall. She opened one. It was Savitri's almirah. Savitri kept her saris and clothes there in. Other was empty. It could be used by her, Salma thought. Salma opened her suitcase. She had a few saris and petticoats. Salma arranged those in her almirah.

Savitri came after her work.

Savitri knocked the door. Salma opened. Savitri entered. She looked tired. Savitri laid on her bed.

After a while, Savitri asked, "Durga, how did you come to this hell?"

"I didn't come. I was sold and Chowdhary bought me."

"Ok, I shall hear all your stories one day. You are new here. I shall not ask now."

Salma didn't want to ask Savitri how did she come there?

"Do you know why Chowdhary has bought me? What will he do with me?" Salma asked.

"You will know tonight what he will do with you," Savitri replied.

Salma understood why Chowdhary bought her.

"Chowdhary will call you at his bed room tonight. You are new and he will taste you," Savitri said.

Salma was scared and literally was trembling with fear. She could not speak anything.

"Don't worry, Durga, Chowdhary is old, has lost his vitality. He will only play with your body. He will be finished within five minutes. He will taste you till he will lose interest on you. Then his sons will taste," Savitri said.

Salma became a statue.

"Don't worry, you will be given light works at Chowdhary's house. No work at farm now. At least 6 months to one year, you will get light household works. Once their interest on your body will be lost, they will send you to farm works in the fields," Savitri said.

Salma was speechless. Again, she left everything to her fate. What could she do? It was better to accept the fate.

Salma didn't ask anything to Savitri. Savitri was telling one by one.

"One thing, always keep in mind. You cannot fly from this hell. If you try once, the security persons will shoot you. Another thing always keep in mind. Don't forget to take birth control pills every night. Open my almirah, you will see a lot of birth control pills there. If you are pregnant, that will be your last day. Your body will be vanished. Chowdhary will not allow any pregnant girl in his house. It happened two years before. One girl was pregnant. When it came to the notice of Chowdhary, the girl was vanished overnight. Nobody could see her any time here."

There was silence in the room. Salma was feeling speed of her heartbeats. She lost her senses as if.

"Were you pregnant anytime?" Savitri asked.

"No," Salma replied.

"Did you take birth control pills earlier?"

"No."

"So you never used the pills before. Do not forget to take pill every night. I also take it daily. Although I am not called every night. On Sunday, when his sons come from Samastipur and Patna, his eldest son called me. He liked me. He brought sari, perfumes, facial make up for me from Patna," Savitri continued.

It was about nine o'clock. Dinner would be given at nine. "Durga, be ready. We go for dinner now," Savitri told.

Salma was ready and both went to the dining hall for dinner. Salma found there were five /six girls taking dinners. Most of them were elder than her. They were talking, laughing, and enjoying the lunch. Savitri introduced "Durga" with them. They saw Salma critically and commented words of praise seeing her body.

One girl said, "Old Chowdhary will get a fresh item tonight."

"How long will he sustain with this item?" Another girl said.

"You know, Old Chowdhary nowadays is taking medicines for becoming young."

Hearing that, all ladies laughed. Salma had no appetite. She took one chapatti and vegetable curry only. Savitri insisted her to eat more for good health.

Salma and Savitri finished dinner and came to their room. Salma was terribly tired. She laid on bed. Savitri was changing her dress. Suddenly the door was knocked. Savitri opened and saw one security guard. The guard whispered something to her ears and left.

Salma was trying to sleep. Savitri came close to her and said, "Durga, please get up and be ready. Chowdhary wants to see you now."

"What?" Salma was scared to hear those words from Savitri.

Savitri didn't say more. She repeated, "Please don't delay. Chowdhary will be angry. Please be ready."

"I shall never go. Whatever he wants to do, let him do. I shall never go to his bed room," Salma shouted.

"Please keep patience. Try to understand. If you don't go, Chowdhary will send security guards to take you to his room. It's wise to go silently."

Salma knew that she had no other alternative but to follow the instructions. She wanted to see what was written to her fate. She was changed totally. She was a different woman. The innocent and simple Salma of Nayanpur died already.

"Durga, please change the dress and take bright make up on face."

Salma followed the instructions and was ready to meet her groom that night. Savitri was instructed to accompany Salma up to Chowdhary's bed room. Salma followed Savitri and came to Chowdhary's house. Savitri knocked the door. Chowdhary opened and asked Salma to come inside. Salma followed and the door was closed.

Salma didn't know what time she was freed and asked to leave Chowdhary's bed room. Salma returned to her room. Savitri already slept. Salma changed her dress and laid on bed. She felt that thousands of poisonous insects were crawling on her body as if. She couldn't sleep. She was remembering her days in Nayanpur. The faces of Javed, Tashlima, Ruksana, Danish and Nassir were appearing before her eyes one by one. She was seeing Aninda, his smiling face. Really, Aninda was like a child. Everybody would love him if saw at a glance. Salma felt as if Aninda came to her room and sat closer to her. Salma was getting fragrance of Aninda's body. Her eyes were full of tears. Salma cried whole night.

Savitri got up early. Salma was sleeping that time. Savitri went to her work. She came after a few minutes. Salma opened her eyes.

"Be ready, Durga, Chowdhary has given you work in the kitchen. Don't delay. He will be angry," Savitri said. Salma was ready and went to work.

Chowdhary bought all female and male servants. The servants were bought from remote villages of Bihar and Bengal. They were given only food, clothes and shelter. No wages were paid to them. They worked as bonded labors till their death. When they would be very old and unable to work, they were thrown out of the house. There were many servants who worked at Chowdhary's house, nowadays were seen at the Railway station or market areas of Samastipur. They were street beggars.

Chowdhary was a big gun at Ranitola. He purchased the local police and even district administrators by money. The Officer-in-Charge and other officers of local Police station visited his house once in a month. They stayed night at Chowdhary's house. Chowdhary sent the beautiful girls to their room.

Salma came to know everything gradually. Salma accepted her life. She nowadays never cried. She could laugh and enjoy like other maid servants. She never told anybody even Savitri that she was a Muslim girl. She was sacred if Chowdhary knew that she was not Hindu, he could do anything to her. She knew that Chowdhary hated lower caste Hindus and Muslims. Chowdhary when purchased any girl, made sure that the girl belonged to Hindu higher caste. It was his prejudice.

Once Savitri secretly wanted to know about her religion and caste. Salma didn't lie to Savitri. Savitri was her only friend and guide. Savitri loved her like younger sister and always helped in all matters. They were close to each other. Salma confessed her religion and real name to Savitri. Savitri swore that she would not tell her religion to anybody. Savitri told her real name and religion. She also confessed that she belonged to a lower Hindu caste which was called *Dalit* in society. When she was bought, the middleman told Chowdhary that Savitri belonged to a Hindu caste, *Brahmin* which was considered higher caste in Hindus. Chowdhary belonged to *Bhumihar* which was also a higher caste in Bihar.

Salma could not understand the reason of that prejudice. Chowdhary only liked higher caste ladies. It's fact God has not differentiated the body of one higher caste Hindu girl with one Muslim or Hindu lower caste girl. All girls irrespective of religion and castes are same. There is no difference in body structure. But if Chowdhary came to know that he slept with a Muslim girl or any *dalit* girl, he perhaps would shoot the girl. Chowdhary was happy to know that he slept with only those girls who were Hindus and belonged to higher castes. It was the funniest thing. Oh God, you made all women in this world with same body structure. The higher caste girls had no extra in their body which Salma or Savitri had not.

Days were flying, months were running, year was passing. Salma was confined at Chowdhary's house, during day time at kitchen and night time at Chowdhary's bed room. Nowadays, she was given attention by Chowdhary's youngest son. Salma was called to his room also when Chowdhary went to Cities. Salma accepted her life. She never forgot to take birth control pills.

Salma was given the post of head cook. She knew cooking better. She knew many delicious dishes. She learnt from Lolita Bhavi at Nayanpur and cooked for Aninda. Those days were really like a dream to her. Aninda, how could Salma forget him?

Years were flying and Salma was aging. Seven years were gone. Salma's age also grew. She would be late twenties. She forgot her past totally. Nowadays, she couldn't remember the faces of her father, mother, sister and brothers. But only face she would never forget was Aninda. Salma still dreamt that Aninda came to her room. Aninda's face was full of heavenly smile.

He asked her, "How are you, Salma?"

Salma didn't reply to him. Aninda again asked, "If you do not reply, I shall never talk. I shall fly now. You will never see me."

"Please Aninda, don't go. Please." Salma got up from her dreams. She felt the fragrances of Aninda. As if Aninda was in her room and just left. Again, Aninda would come. Salma was waiting for him. Salma would wait for whole life.

—————

"Madam, we have reached Jagulia. Pintu wants to load fuel in the car. The petrol pump is nearer. It's better if we take a cup of tea here. Pintu will take about ten minutes. If you like..." Nitish Babu asks.

Salma opens her eyes. "It's ok. Let us have a cup of tea. I want to walk a while. My legs are stretched. I am old now, Nitish Babu."

Nitish Babu opens the door and Salma comes out of the car. Pintu takes the car to the petrol pump for fuel. Nitish Babu has gone to one Restaurant for tea. Salma follows him. Salma asks the time.

"It is now 4 o'clock. The road is not good. It is taking more time," Nitish Babu says.

"How many hours to reach in Kolkata?" Salma asks.

"Madam, the distance is not long but the road is not good. Moreover, the road from Jagulia to Kolkata remains busy with traffics all the time. It's very difficult to say the actual hours. But, by evening we shall reach," Nitish Babu says.

"Ok, no problem, we have no work today. The main function will be tomorrow," Salma says.

Tea is served. Nitish Babu asks if she will take a cookie or anything. Salma says no. Car has been fuelled and Pintu comes. Salma boards in the car. Pintu starts the engine. Nitish Babu tells him to drive carefully as the road from Jagulia to Kolkata is busy with lot of traffics. Salma is looking outside through windows. Lot of shops and buildings are newly constructed. The road is full of traffics. Pintu drives the car carefully and the speed is slow.

Salma closes her eyes. She is travelling down memory lane. She does not know why her past is knocking the door of her memory.

## Chapter-12

Chowdhary had three daughters who were married long ago. The eldest daughter, Meena had settled in Delhi. Her husband, Arvind Sahi had one golden jewelry business at Noida. He had set up one factory there where more than 50 goldsmiths worked on hourly wage basis. His business was big. Arvind exported gold jewelry to Middle East countries. He was regarded one of the leading businessmen in gold jewelry in Delhi. Meena and Arvind had two sons and one daughter.

They could not find time to visit Ranitola due to their hectic business works. Meena also helped Arvind in business. They came to Ranitola after several years. Chowdhary was not well nowadays. He wished to see Meena and Arvind and their sons and daughters. Just to fulfill the wish of her father, Meena came to Ranitola with full family. Salma never saw Meena and her family. Salma was busy in kitchen. The family hailed from Delhi and the kids first time came to Ranitola. Salma was instructed to cook some special dishes for them. Chowdhary's sons and their families who stayed at Samastipur and Patna came to meet their sister. The house was full of members. Chowdhary was recovering slowly. One doctor was hired for full time for his treatment. Salma was happy nowadays that she was not called at Chowdhary's room at night.

Salma made special dishes for Delhi guests. Arvind Babu appreciated her cooking. Arvind asked Meena to enquire about the cook. In fact, Meena and Arvind were finding one cook for their factory. 50 full time workers were hired at their factory for making jewelry. Arvind Babu bought on big house at Noida for their staying. He also hired one cook for their lunch and dinner. Recently, the cook left job. Meena and Arvind tried to find one good cook but they didn't get any one good. Meena came to know the lady who made those dishes was Durga and she was from Bengal. Meena wanted to take her to Delhi. Arvind endorsed her proposal instantly.

Meena one day told her father, "I have one small request. Please don't say no."

"What is that Meena?" Chowdhary asked.

"I want Durga at my Delhi house."

Chowdhary was silent.

Meena guessed his unwillingness to allow Durga to go with her. "Dad, my sons and daughters like dishes made by Durga very much. You know, nowadays, I have no time to cook due to busy work schedules in business. I am helping your Son-in-law in business."

Chowdhary was still silent.

"Please Dad, please give me Durga."

Chowdhary didn't reply. Meena was his eldest daughter and Chowdhary loved her. All knew that Chowdhary had a soft corner for Meena whose face had total resemblance with Meena's mother, Chowdhary's late wife. Though Chowdhary didn't say yes, Meena repeatedly requested him whenever getting a chance.

Meena lastly told Chowdhary, "Dad, I shall take Durga for a few months and as soon as we find one good cook, Durga will come back to Samastipur. Please don't say no to me," Meena's voice became soft. Chowdhary agreed to her proposal.

Meena called Salma(Durga) and told, "Durga, you will go to Delhi with us. My father has given permission."

Salma listened silently.

"You will stay there. We have one factory where 50 persons work. You will be the cook of the kitchen," Meena briefly told her job in Delhi.

Meena didn't ask Salma if she agreed or not. Meena knew that her father bought the lady and hence, there was no question to ask if she agreed or not. The lady would follow what her master told. She had no choice. Still Salma was really happy to know that she would go to Delhi. More so, She would go out of that jail.

Savitri was not happy to hear. She had developed a real friendship with Salma. Savitri literally cried when heard that Salma would be leaving her. It was master's instruction. They had no choice but to accept. The day came when Salma left Chowdhary's house and boarded train with Meena's family at Samastipur station for Delhi.

The train started on time. It would take about a day to reach Delhi. Salma got one window seat. Meena, Arvind and her kids were in the same compartment. Train was running fast. Window was open. Salma closed her eyes.

A new life was waiting for Salma alias Durga in Delhi. Arvind Babu was a rich business man. He had one palatial house at Noida. His factory was located nearer to his house. His main business was importing gold and making jewelry as per orders. He exported majority of ornaments to Middle East countries where there was steady demand of Indian made gold jewelry. In his factory, about 50 persons worked. They were not local. Most of them came from rural areas of West Bengal state. Arvind bought one two storied house for those workers. One big kitchen was made for them in the house. Arvind hired maids and cooks for their lunch and dinner. All workers stayed at the house. Recently the head cook left job about six months before. Arvind hired one local cook but the workers didn't like the food. Being Bengali, they preferred to take Bengali type foods. Arvind and Meena searched a lot for one Bengali cook. But they could not find any one suitable. When they saw Salma and came to know that she was Bengali, they decided to bring Salma as cook. They were told that she belonged to a higher Hindu caste. So the Bengali workers would raise no issue at all, rather they would be happy to know that their food would be blended with Bengali recipe.

Meena instructed Salma what she would do. There were 3 other maid servants in the house who helped in cooking and cleaning of the rooms. The cooks and maids were given one separate room. Meena instructed everything to Salma. Meena didn't know that Salma was Muslim and Durga was not her real name.

Salma joined the work. It was her new job. The maids in the house welcomed her heartily. Salma was sincere in cooking and tried to make the foods for workers delicious. Soon everybody started appreciating her cooking. Workers were happy, Meena and Arvind too.

Salma started her work before sun rise. Firstly, she made breakfast and tea for the workers. There was a big dining hall. The workers assembled there. The maids served them. Lunch was given at 1 o'clock and workers gathered in the dining hall that time. They were given one hour lunch break. That was busy time. The workers tried to finish lunch early and wanted to serve food as early as possible. During lunch time, Salma helped the maids in serving food. There was no fixed time for dinner. It started from 9 o'clock night and generally ended by 11 o'clock. There were a few workers who came late. Salma went to bed after that.

The factory remained closed on Sunday. The workers mostly went outside to watch movies or sightseeing. There was no rush for lunch and dinner. Salma felt relaxed on that day. The food was given free to all workers. Entire food costs were born by Arvind Babu. Arvind Babu hired one person who bought vegetables and grocery items from local market. Meena came at least one time a day. She trained Salma and other maids to manage everything properly. Meena didn't like any wastage. Meena fixed the menu of lunch and dinner every day.

The business of Arvind Babu was growing fast. Many times, workers were asked to work on Sunday and holiday. They were paid overtime.

Days were flying and by that time two years were gone. Salma fully adjusted there. She forgot everything about her past. She forgot all. She forgot Nayanpur. She forgot her father, mother, sister and brothers. Salma was there as a Hindu lady who was fondly called by all workers "Durga Didi." Didi meaning elder sister. Salma forgot to cry at night.

Salma didn't forget Aninda still. She remembered him in dream. She loved to dream him again and again. Salma had no faith on God. But still every day, she prayed to Allah for Aninda.

Arvind Babu got one huge order from Saudi Arab. He had to supply within one month. The order was huge which involved several cores of money. The capital invested by Arvind in business was not sufficient enough to execute the order.

"Why don't you apply for a temporary loan from our bank to meet the working capital requirements?" Meena suggested.

Arvind appreciated Meena's advice. He had bank accounts with People Bank, Noida but all accounts were Savings and Current in nature. He never took any loan from his bank. Actually, he didn't need any loan. He was able to manage with his own capital. But it was a different case. He needed huge fund to execute the order.

One day, Arvind and Meena went to People Bank for short term loan. Arvind already phoned the Chief Manager of the Bank for an appointment. Meena and Arvind reached at scheduled time. Chief Manager was busy with other customers. He told Arvind to wait for a few minutes. Chief Manager called both Arvind and Meena at his chamber. He offered teas to them. Arvind briefly told what was his requirement. He wanted a short term loan for six months only.

"Mr.Sahi, I suggest you to apply for one year. After the first order, if you get any more order, again you have to apply afresh. It's wise to apply loan for one year and you can execute all orders which will come within one year," The Chief Manager suggested.

"Thank you, Sir, for your advice. I appreciate," Meena thanked the Chief Manager for his advice.

The Chief Manager asked Arvind, "Mr. Sahi, can you please tell me what is your requirement of loan?"

"Sir, I need one crore rupees. I have invested almost same amount in my business. I am sure that I shall be able to execute the order with this amount of loan."

"Ok, no problem. It is within my power. Your application will not go to our higher office. It will be decided at branch level," the Chief Manager said.

"Sir, I have one request. I have to execute the order within one month time. Time is not enough. If you please approve as early as possible, it will be immensely helpful to me," Arvind requested.

"Mr. Sahi, I cannot commit anything before inspecting your factory and processing your loan application. I want to visit your factory. In fact, before start of processing your case, I want to study your business carefully. It's a new type of loan case to my branch. This branch never processed this type of proposal."

"Sir, please visit any day when you will find time. It is not far from your branch. You are most welcome to our factory," Meena opened her mouth.

"No, problem, I shall go tomorrow. Is it ok?" the Chief Manager asked.

"Very much ok, I shall send my car tomorrow. Please tell me what is your good time?" Arvind asked.

"Don't send any car. I shall go before close of branch, say by 5 p.m. Is it ok?" The chief Manager again asked.

"Ok, Sir," Meena replied.

"How many days you will take to approve the loan after inspection?" Arvind asked.

"Mr. Sahi, after inspection, we shall start processing of your application. There are a few steps of processing of your case. It will be done internally. My Credit Officer will do the detail financial analysis of your business data. By the by, what type of collateral you want to offer to secure your loan? the Chief Manager asked.

"What is that, Sir,?" Arvind asked.

"It means, what type of property will you offer for mortgage to the bank as security against your loan?"

"Sir, I have the factory building and one Staff house. You can take these two properties for mortgage," Arvind said.

"What is the property of staff house?" Chief Manager asked.

"I bought one two storied house with several rooms adjacent to the factory. All our staffs reside there. They are from outside state, mostly from West Bengal. The house has about 10 to 12 rooms and one big dining hall with kitchen. We have hired cook and maids for cooking and maintenance of the house. All the workers are provided meals free. It is the part of their employment. We bear all cooking and other expenses."

"It's a novel idea," the Chief Manager said.

"Sir, any other thing which you want to discuss relating to the loan proposal," Arvind asked.

"Mr. Sahi, I want to tell you in brief what are the steps of approval. Tomorrow, I shall go to your factory for inspection. My Credit Officer will go with me. Please make the property papers ready. If the inspection is ok, we shall send your property papers to bank's advocate for searching and legal opinion of your property. If legal opinion is ok, we shall send your property papers to bank's approved Valuer for valuation of the properties. By the by, we shall visit both your factory and staff house. Also please make ready of last 3 year audit reports and income tax returns for verification. My Credit Officer will give you one loan application. Please fill it and sign. I am thinking to allow you one Over Draft limit for one year initially. The facility can be renewed every year if you want to continue. Otherwise, you can close it after one year. Interest of Over Draft will be decided after completing one pricing exercise which is primarily based on your business financial strengths and value of primary and collateral securities. It will take about 15 days to complete everything, I believe," the Chief Manager said.

"Sir, time is very short. Can you please make it within a week?" Arvind asked.

"The legal opinion and searching of your properties are not in our hand. You know, Advocate will take minimum one week time for legal opinion. I suggest you to talk to your client and request him to extend the order execution period for minimum one more week. If you get extension of one week or so, there will be everything proper in time."

"Ok, Sir, I shall talk. I believe my client will agree for extension."

"Another thing Mr. Sahi," the Chief Manager said. "Please commit me that you will talk to me without hesitation. If anybody asks for any bribe for the loan in my name or in my Credit Officer's name, please do not entertain if such request is received by you from any corner. Before start of your proposal, I want to make this thing clear. You know, in banking loans application, it is very common to bribe to Manager and Credit Officer. I hate those."

"Ok Sir, I shall tell you secretly if anyone asks for bribe," Arvind said.

"Sir, I have not seen you earlier in this branch. I think you have joined recently," Arvind asked.

"Yes, I have joined just one month ago. I am new in Delhi."

"Sir, I have last request. Please approve my case. It's the first time I am applying for loan. You can see my Accounts records in your branch. I have been maintaining business accounts for many years and I have good deposits at your branch," Arvind said.

"Mr. Sahi, I have already seen your Accounts. You are a valued customer to this branch. You have Current and Savings accounts. This is the first time you are requesting for loan. I am assuring you that I must look into your matters personally and try my level best to approve the limit. But I cannot say yes at this juncture before completing the process," the Chief Manager said.

The Chief Manager called his Credit Officer, Mr. Priya Ranjan and introduced with Arvind and Meena. Priya Ranjan knew them well. The Chief Manager also told him about the new loan proposal of Mr. Sahi and next day's inspection.

Arvind and Meena left with happy mood. Meena was charmed with the attitude and attention the Chief Manager paid to them. She told many good words about him to Arvind.

Next day, the Chief Manager and the Credit Officer, Mr.Priya Ranjan came late. They sought apology for late coming. In fact, one Officer from their Regional Office came to the branch and they were busy with that Officer.

Arvind and Meena welcomed them heartily. The Chief Manager and Priya Ranjan met the workers of the factory and wanted to know how the gold ornaments were made from gold bar. It was a new experience to them. They studied every manufacturing step one after one.

They asked for the audit and income tax returns of the factory and studied carefully. Arvind made prior arrangements. The Chief Manager asked for the property papers.

"Mr.Sahi, I appreciate your endeavor in running this business. I am happy to see your factory," the Chief Manager said.

"Thank you, Sir, for your kind appreciation," Arvind softly thanked to the Chief Manager.

"Ranjan, tomorrow, send the property papers to our Lawyer for legal opinion. Tell him to submit the report within a week time."

"Ok, Sir, I shall send," Priya Ranjan replied.

"Ranjan, give the loan application to Mr.Sahi and list of documents which he will submit with the application."

Priya Ranjan opened his file and gave one loan application form and list of documents to Arvind.

"Mr.Sahi, it's our formal loan application form. Fill it up and signed. If you need any help, ask Ranjan. See the list of documents. Please attach all papers and documents with your application when ready," the Chief Manager told to Arvind.

"Ok, Sir, I shall make everything ready by tomorrow. I have all documents and papers ready," Arvind said.

"Ranjan, if you have any question, ask Mr.Sahi."

"Sir, I have no question now. I shall ask Mr.Sahi if I want anything during process of the proposal. Let me check the audit reports first."

"Mr.Sahi, you told me that you have one staff house where the staffs stay."

"Sir, we are going there now. I have one small request. I have arranged coffee for you there, Sir," Meena requested the Chief Manger with her soft and polite voice.

"Madam, why are you busy with such formalities? I shall take coffee when your loan will be approved."

"Sir, Meena personally arranged coffee for you and Mr.Priya Ranjan. Please do not say no. It's our request," Arvind requested the Chief Manger.

The Chief Manager smiled."Ok, as you wish."

The staff house was located behind the factory. The Chief Manager and Priya Ranjan made one round of the house. Meena after visit requested them to go to the dining hall where coffee would be served. The dining hall was big and maintained neatly.

Meena went to kitchen hurriedly. Salma was busy in kitchen. She was making fries of potato.

"Durga, is everything ready?"

"Yes, Madam, fries are ready. I am making coffee right now."

"Bring fries and coffee to the hall. Guests are there. Check the plates and cups before serve. These should be perfectly cleaned."

"Ok, Madam."

Meena earlier told her to wear a good sari and dressed properly.

Salma brought Coffee and fries for the guests at the dining hall where the guests were sitting.

Salma slowly entered into the dining hall and served the plates to the guests. Salma didn't look at the Chief Manager. The Chief Manager raised his eyes and looked at her. Salma looked at him.

Salma couldn't believe her eyes. What was she seeing? How was it possible? The Chief Manager looked at her again but didn't tell anything. His face color was changed suddenly. His hands were trembling. He couldn't hold the cup properly.

Aninda's brain was not working at all.

"Are you ok, Sir?" Arvind asked him.

"Yes, I am ok," Aninda, the Chief Manager replied.

Salma didn't wait for a single minute. She left the hall. Salma's heartbeats were speeding like a superfast jet plane. She still was in a semiconscious condition and didn't believe her eyes. He was Aninda. She didn't make any mistake. He was Aninda. Oh, Allah, how was it possible? Salma left all hopes that she could ever meet Aninda in her life. There was no talk between them.

Aninda thanked a lot to Arvind and Meena and assured them to process the loan case at the earliest possible time. He also thanked for nice coffee and fries.

Salma could not sleep that night. She was weeping whole night after seeing Aninda.

"Aninda, I have a lot to speak you," she said herself.

Aninda was changed totally. His health had been deteriorated like anything. His hairs became thin. Color became changed. He had exceptionally fair complexion. Only eyes were not changed. Salma couldn't remember how many years after she saw Aninda. It might be more than one decade. Salma didn't know.

Two weeks were over. One morning, Arvind received phone call from the branch. Priya Ranjan was at the other side.

"Mr.Sahi, congratulation. Your loan is approved."

"Thank you, Sir, for this good news."

"If you are not busy now, please pay a visit to our branch and collect the approval letter. Our Chief Manager wants to see you."

"We are coming right now, Sir."

On the same day, Arvind and Meena went to the branch. The Chief Manager, Aninda was in the branch. He was waiting for them.

"Congratulations Mr. and Mrs. Sahi."

"Thank you, Sir," Arvind's voice was perfectly soft.

"Sir, we are really grateful to you for your help. Only due to your efforts, our loan is granted so early," Meena added spices to her words.

"Mrs. Sahi, it's not my credit at all. You deserve the loan. Our bank has done right thing for right customer."

Aninda offered cup of tea to them and handed over the Approval letter. Next, they had to execute the loan documents and could avail the loan for their requirements.

The tea was finished and Arvind asked permission to leave. Aninda requested them to sit for a few minutes. He wanted to say something personal.

"Mr. Sahi and Madam, I have one request. It is up to you whether you keep or not."

"Sir, please tell us without hesitation. You have done a lot for us and it is now our turn to keep your request," Meena said.

"Thanks for your words. You know that I have just joined the branch one month before. I took one apartment at Dwarka area. I am yet to arrange everything in my apartment. What major problem I am facing here that is food. I have hired one maid. But the lunch and dinner she makes are not at all good to me. I am from West Bengal and prefer to Bengali foods. I have problem in digestion also. The maid being North Indian makes dishes like North Indian style. It is not her fault. But I do not like her cooking at all."

"Sir, why are you alone? Where is your wife?" Meena asked.

"I am bachelor," Aninda smiled.

"We understand your problem. What help you need from us, Sir?" Arvind asked.

"I am hesitating to say. Again I tell if it is not possible, please ignore my request," Aninda said.

"Sir, please tell us what you want? We shall try our level best to keep your request," Meena wanted to know.

"That day, I saw your cook. I think she is Bengali and the dish given to me was made in Bengali style. Is it possible if I hire your maid for cooking at my apartment?"

Arvind and Meena could not answer. They were silent.

"I am sorry. I think I should not request," Aninda said.

"Sir, actually, that lady earlier worked at my father's house at Samastipur," Meena replied after a while. "We have requested my father for working at our house temporarily. I have to take permission from my father. Please give me one day time. I shall talk to my father and tell you."

"You are right Sir, the lady is Bengali and her name is Durga. I forgot her surname. I do not know much about her," Arvind added.

"Durga!" Aninda said. "Ok. no problem. Please try if possible."

Arvind and Meena left. Aninda lost in himself suddenly for a while. He repeated the name "Durga". He was sure that he didn't make any mistake. She was Salma. Aninda didn't understand how Salma was changed to Durga.

Arvind and Meena discussed long about Durga.

"Meena, it's my feeling that we should honor the request of the Chief Manager," Arvind said." "He is alone and just come to Delhi. As a neighbor at least, we should help him. He is from our neighbor home state also."

"How ? Tell me? Will you think my father will agree? I heard that she bought Durga. I heard other things also that I can't say to you. It's my shame."

"I know, Meena. I know everything. That's the reason I didn't want to keep any relation with your father and brothers. It is sin. Your father did all these sinful deeds. How one person can buy a woman? God will not pardon your father and brothers, I am telling you," Arvind murmured.

"I also didn't want to see their faces. I didn't go to Ranitola for last several years." Meena said. "I know my father and brothers. Not only Durga, my father bought at least 20 women and made them sex slaves. It's my bad luck that I am daughter of such person. I know you have pardoned me in all way knowing my family."

"Meena, don't say so. Just think how we can help the Chief Manager. You know, most of the Bank Managers ask bribe for loan. I heard from many of my friends who got the loan approved from banks. This Chief Manager is exceptional. On the first day what he told? Remember, he didn't ask anything for approval of loan. This is the small matter he has requested," Arvind said.

"One thing, I have not asked to the Chief Manager. He told that he took one apartment on rent. He is living there alone and is bachelor. Where will Durga stay? It's not possible for Durga to commute everyday from Noida to Dwarka."

"I think, the Chief Manager has thought this issue also before requesting us. He will certainly arrange for her staying. It is his matter. Now think about how you will convince your father," Arvind said.

"I have one plan. I shall not talk to my father at all. Already two years are over and he didn't ask me to send Durga so far. Let's see. If my father asks, I shall lie to him with any story. I am sure I can manage the case."

"Then can we tell the Chief Manager yes?" Arvind asked.

"You are really fool. Should we not ask Durga if she agrees or not?" Meena said.

"Oh, I forgot. It's good suggestion. Tomorrow you talk to Durga."

Meena told Salma next day.

"Durga, the Chief Manager of our bank wants to hire you for cooking at his apartment. You saw that Manager who came last time here. What shall I say to him?" Meena asked.

Salma was mum. She couldn't speak.

"Durga, tell me if you want to go. I shall not put any pressure on you. It is up to you," Meena asked her again.

Salma wanted to say something. Her lips were trembling. What would she say? She was waiting for that moment.

After a while, she said, "Ok, whatever you say, I shall do."

Meena was happy to know her consent. Meena knew that her father bought Durga and didn't pay a single rupee to her as wage. In Noida, Meena every month paid her hundred rupees.

"One more thing, Durga, don't ask any salary for your work there. Do accept whatever the Chief Manager pays," Meena said. "He has indigestion problem, I heard. I suggest you to use less spices and oil in cooking."

"When shall I go?"

"Let me talk to Chief Manager."

"Where shall I stay?"

"I think, he will arrange for your staying. Don't worry, he will take care. He is a perfect gentleman and has come to Delhi recently. I forgot to tell you, he is a Bengali."

Arvind telephoned Aninda that they had no issue to send Durga to him. Arvind wanted to know when Durga would go. Aninda told him that he would come on next Sunday and picked Durga from the factory.

Meena told Salma to be ready on Sunday. The Chief Manager would come.

Only 3 days were left. Salma could not sleep at all during those days. The factory workers heard. The maids also heard that "Durga Didi" was leaving them. Their "Durga Didi" was a silent worker. She spoke less. Yet, she had already created a soft corner in everybody's heart. They would miss her. Everybody expressed that.

Sunday came. Salma today wore a blue sari. Aninda liked blue color. That sari was given to her by Meena. Salma knot her hairs and made light make up in her face. Salma found a few hairs white. She couldn't guess her age. She thought she was aged enough so the hairs became white.

Aninda came late. Salma was ready. She took bath early. She had a small suitcase only. She had a few saris and other cloths. She took all. Aninda came with a car. Meena and Arvind were present there. They welcomed Aninda. Salma touched the feet of Arvind and Meena. The maids and workers said good bye to their "Durga Didi". Salma put her suitcase inside the dickey and boarded the car. Aninda sat beside the driver on the front seat. Car engine started.

# Chapter-13

The car reached at Dwarka Sector 13. It was a residential house complex. Several multi storied apartments were built up there. The area was calm and quiet. Roads were good and newly constructed. Dwarka, a few years before was like desert lands. State Government undertook developmental works there and made the land converted for house constructions. Several house societies were constructed during the past years. In Delhi, it's very difficult to get accommodation in main city area. People were preferring to the new township for comforts and peace. Dwarka township had been connected with metro line.

Aninda took one apartment in the house society named "Prerana House Society". The owner of the apartment was a banker who currently lived in Dubai with family. Aninda was lucky to get the apartment without any deposit money. The land lord was good and provided all furniture, washing machine, TV, fridge, etc.

The car reached at the House complex. Aninda paid the fares to the driver and asked Salma to get down. Salma took her small suitcase and followed Aninda.

The apartment was located at third floor of the building. It was 3 bed room apartment. Aninda and Salma entered into the apartment.

Till time they didn't talk. Aninda locked the door. Salma stood like a statue and could not decide what next she would do.

"Salma, it is your apartment," Aninda said.

"Why did you bring me?" Salma asked.

"I do not know. You can go If you like," Aninda said.

"Please tell me where shall I stay? I am sure, I shall not stay here at the same apartment with you."

"You are wrong. You will stay at this apartment with me. There are 3 bedrooms. I have arranged one corner room for you. Go and keep your belongings. Don't delay. I am hungry. Go to kitchen and make lunch. Before, give me a cup of tea," Aninda ordered.

Salma smiled. Aninda didn't change his attitude. He remained same. Only exception, he had aged. Hairs were thin. A few hairs looked white. He had taken a spectacle. He lost his fair color. Salma knew the nature of Aninda.

"How was it possible to stay at the same apartment? How the other neighbors would say? Salma asked.

"Don't worry. I have told everybody that my cousin's daughter will come from Kolkata. She is coming for her treatment. Here nobody has shown any curiosity about personal matters of any resident. Don't worry about that matter," Aninda said.

"I have already fired my maid," Aninda continued. "So, nobody will disturb you here. All neighbors in other apartments generally do not show any interest what is happening to other apartments. It is Delhi and everybody maintains safe distance with any one's personal matters. Don't worry. Stay safe. I guess lot of cyclones and storms you faced during last several years. Take rest, try to forget everything what happened in your life. Today is holiday and tomorrow, I have taken one day casual leave. I have made an appointment with one doctor for your check up. Please don't say no to any matter what I shall tell you. When you will be ok, you will order me and I shall obey. Please go to your room and if possible, prepare lunch. Everything is in kitchen."

Salma couldn't believe if it was a dream to her. She went to her room. It was nicely arranged. Aninda bought one new bed for her. In wardrobe, she saw new saris and petticoats. She saw soaps, hair oil etc on the dressing table. Salma locked the door and changed her dress. Every room in the apartment had attached bath. Salma went to bath and washed her face with water. After fifteen minutes, she went to kitchen. She found that the door of Aninda's bedroom was closed. Salma saw that Aninda bought everything for cooking in that kitchen. Salma became busy in making lunch. Lunch was ready within an hour. Aninda finished the lunch. He didn't talk more and went to his room for rest.

Aninda was tired and slept. When he got up, it was almost evening time. It was autumn time and the day was becoming shorter. Evening comes early. Durga Puja festival was only after one month that year. Aninda saw that the door of Salma's room was closed. He heard sounds that Salma was crying. Aninda didn't disturb her. Let her cry. All her pains would be washed out. It was the best medicine for her.

Aninda remembered, it might be 10 years after he met Salma. 10 years was a long time. He didn't know what happened to Salma during the last 10 years.

Aninda was transferred to Kolkata from Nayanpur and worked only for a few days there. He was again transferred to South India. He was posted at a small town in Kerala. He was surprised how bank transferred from one remote village of West Bengal to the extreme Southern state, Kerala. Later on, he came to know that his mother met the Zonal Head of the Bank in Kolkata and requested him to transfer Aninda to the farthest point so that he could not visit Nayanpur easily. It was his mother's plan to save Aninda from the clutch of Salma. Nirmala went to Kerala and stayed with him. Nirmala wanted to keep Aninda out of shadow of that Muslim girl whom Aninda wanted to marry. Aninda was posted there for 3 years. During that time Nirmala tried to arrange his marriage but Aninda didn't agree. It was his bad luck that he didn't get any chance to go to Nayanpur ever from Kerala. Nirmala never left him. Joydeb tried to convince Nirmala to accept the marriage with that Muslim girl. Nirmala was firm that she would not make the marriage happen in her life.

Aninda concentrated to his works. He got promotion due to his performances to Senior Manager when worked at Kerala branch. Thereafter, he was transferred to Gujarat. There too, Nirmala came with him. He was posted at Bhavnagar town for 3 years and then transferred to Surat. He was there for another 3 years.

Aninda was totally cut up with Nayanpur and could not find what happened to Salma. He tried to talk at the Nayanpur branch on telephone but the branch staff couldn't say anything about Javed and his family. When he was transferred from Kerala to Gujarat, he got an opportunity. He managed Nirmala that he wanted to go to Bhavnagar before joining there to find one residence. Nirmala agreed first time and allowed Aninda to go to Bhavnagar. That was the opportune time. Aninda bought one air ticket to Kolkata next day. He didn't tell anything of his going to Nayanpur to anybody. Aninda secretly went to Nayanpur.

The village was changed. The mud road became concrete and number of buses were increased. Aninda didn't see Javed at the Bus stand. He asked one *Tanga* rider about Javed. That person could not say clearly about Javed.

Aninda reached to Javed's house. He saw the house was empty. He waited there. After about 2 hours, Aninda saw Ruksana coming. Ruksana didn't recognize Aninda. Ruksana was looked sick and her health was broken totally. Aninda told his name. Ruksana could remember. She invited Aninda to her house. Aninda came to know everything from Ruksana.

Salma was married long back. Ruksana couldn't remember the year. She told that groom came from Bihar and married Salma. The groom assured them that Salma would visit Nayanpur every year. But Salma never returned back any time. Javed developed one serious disease. They had no money to go to Berhampore for treatment. Javed died. At the time of his death, Javed wanted to see Salma. Nobody could know which town or village in Bihar, Salma lived.

It happened after death of Javed, that groom, Moslem Sheikh again returned back to Nayanpur. He told that Salma was not well and seriously ill. Salma wanted to see Tashlima. Moslem told that Salma lived like a queen. But her health was not ok. He also added that due to his engagement in business, he could not give time to Salma. If Tashlima could go for one month, it would be helpful to him. Salma could be treated properly. Tashlima agreed immediately with a hope that she would meet her sister. Tahasin and Sher Ali also came to their house and told that same thing. It was only a matter of one month they told. Danish and Nassir agreed. Tashlima went and till that time, never returned back.

"I moved from Tahasin's house to Sher Ali's house. They could not tell anything," Ruksana left a long breath.

"Did you not receive any letter from Salma?" Aninda asked.

"No, we didn't get any letter neither from Salma nor Tashlima," Ruksana continued. "Tahasin sent one letter as he told but didn't get any information. Year after year passed, neither Salma nor Tashlima returned back. I didn't know the name of the town or village where my two daughters lived. Oh Allah, I lost everything. I lost my two daughters. It's my fault. Why did I agree to Salma's marriage? Salma didn't want to marry. She cried a lot. I forced her to say yes. It's my fault. Allah has given me punishment. What should I do now?" Ruksana cried.

Aninda couldn't say anything. By that time, both Danish and Nassir returned. They recognized Aninda. They were grown up and working at the agricultural fields as daily labors. They stopped going to school long ago.

Aninda returned from Nayanpur with broken hearts. He was totally disturbed to know that he could never meet Salma. Aninda gave a few thousand rupees to Ruksana and told her to start a new business for Danish and Nassir.

Aninda joined at the new branch. He was totally frustrated. He couldn't find the reason to live even. The entire world was dark to him. He was a victim of metal depression. Nirmala noticed everything. She tried to convince Aninda for marriage. Aninda even stopped talking to her mother. Joydeb rushed to Bhavnagar from Kolkata. Both husband and wife tried their level best so that

Aninda could come out from his depressive state. They apprehended if Aninda committed suicide. Joydeb tried to find out the cause of Aninda's serious depression. Aninda didn't tell anybody what actually happened. Joydeb and Nirmala consulted one renowned Psychiatrist there. There was no improvement. They brought Aninda to Kolkata for treatment. The doctors in Kolkata also tried to find out the cause. His condition was deteriorating day by day. Nirmala guessed something. She was Aninda's mother. Nirmala finally surrendered. Nirmala told Aninda that she would accept that Muslim girl as her daughter in law. Nirmala wanted to save his son's life. That was too late.

Aninda came out from his depressive stage after long treatment.

Gradually, Aninda came to normalcy one day. He joined at the branch. He was there for 3 long years and transferred to Surat. He worked in Surat for 3 years. By that time he got promotion to Chief Manager cadre and transferred to Delhi.

When he was posted at Surat, Nirmala suddenly fell sick. Nirmala was taken back to Kolkata. Nirmala was not well. Nirmala got success in her mission that she would not allow his only son's marriage with a Muslim girl. It happened Aninda didn't marry Salma. At the same time, he didn't marry at all. At later years, Nirmala perhaps understood that she had voided the life of Aninda. Ultimately, due to her firmness attitude, Aninda remained bachelor throughout his life. Nirmala felt guilty conscious at the later years. Nirmala passed away despite all efforts of doctors.

Aninda never dreamt that he would meet Salma again. It was the biggest surprise to his life when he saw Salma at Arvind Sahi's factory. He couldn't believe his eyes. He didn't talk on that day. He was not sure what would happen if he talked to Salma in front of Arvind and his wife. He took immediate decision not to talk that moment. He would get enough time. He planned to bring Salma and finally it worked. Salma agreed to come to his apartment. Aninda didn't know what exactly happened to Salma after her marriage. Why did she change her name to Durga? He could not guess at all. It's wise to wait and he would get enough time to know. It was not the right time to ask. Salma was crying alone. "Let her cry. Let all her pains wash out," Aninda thought.

Aninda didn't call Salma. Didn't knock the door. It was about dinner time. Aninda ordered one Pizza packet for delivery at his apartment. The delivery man came on time with pizza. Aninda took that and paid. Salma still was confined in her room. Door was locked. No sound was coming out from her room.

It was about 10 o'clock at night. Aninda knocked the door. After a few minutes, Salma opened. Her eyes were dark red. Face was swollen. Salma cried throughout the time.

"Salma, I have bought pizza for dinner. Don't prepare dinner tonight." Aninda behaved normally.

Salma brought the pizza on the dining table and served to Aninda.

"Take one please," Aninda said.

"I have no appetite. I cannot eat."

Aninda finished dinner and went to his room. He didn't talk any more to Salma that night.

Aninda took one day casual leave. He made an appointment with one doctor for Salma. Aninda was late riser. When he got up, it was late morning. He saw Salma working at Kitchen. Salma took bath early morning. It was her old habit. Today, Salma wore one white sari. Her hairs were long and fallen on her back. Aninda saw her for a minute.

Salma noticed that Aninda got up. She didn't talk. Salma put one cup tea on dining table with cookies. Aninda sipped the cup.

"Salma, we shall go to doctor's chamber at 10 o'clock. I have taken leave for a day."

Salma didn't reply. She was cutting vegetables for lunch. The newspaper vendor already delivered the daily newspaper. Aninda was watching the headline news.

Salma's health had been fallen like anything. It was hard to believe that she was the same lady whom Aninda saw her in Nayanpur 10 years before. At Nayanpur, Salma was vibrant, full of energy, and caring. She used to talk all the time with Aninda. She had good sense of humor. She had been changed totally. She was a different lady.

Salma was ready before time. They reached at the doctor's chamber. It was located at the next block. Many patients were waiting there. Aninda made an appointment already. Doctor checked up Salma thoroughly. He advised for all medical tests and asked to visit when the tests reports would be available. Aninda did all tests on the same day. The Laboratory was located at the same block. When they returned, the time was 3 p.m. It was too late for lunch. Salma quickly made one dish of *Puri* and *vagi* for Aninda.

Reports were available within a week and Aninda met the doctor with reports. There was no major issues in Salma's health. Aninda was happy. She had severe anemia. She had been suffering from certain trauma which caused serious mental disturbances. Doctor advised Aninda to consult with one Psychiatrist. Aninda was victim of mental depression a few years before. He had enough knowledge of the issues. Aninda perceived earlier that Salma had also been victim of deep mental depressions and disturbances. Thanks God, she didn't have any major diseases excepting anemia. Doctors prescribed medicines for her and advised Aninda to keep her in full rest.

Salma didn't speak at home. She followed what Aninda asked. She behaved like a stone piece. Aninda knew that it would take time to recover fully. Her past life had been haunting her all the time. Aninda didn't tell her that Javed died and her sister, Tashlima had been the victim of human trafficking like her. It was not good time to say. Aninda took every care of Salma.

The Psychiatrist checked Salma. He was an experienced doctor. He handled hundred of metal patients. He wanted to know the past life of Salma which would help him to diagnosis. Salma didn't open her mouth despite the doctor's best efforts. Treatment was continuing and the doctor didn't lose hope. He had experience that such type of patients took longer time to open up herself. The trauma had been haunting her always. She would not be normal unless her past life was revealed. Aninda didn't know anything about her past ten years. Only he knew that Salma was married about 10 years before with one guy who came from Bihar. When he last met, her name was Durga. How Salma was changed to Durga, Aninda didn't know.

When there was no good improvement in Salma's mental condition, Aninda thought that he would meet Arvind Sahi who knew everything of Salma. Earlier, he didn't want to talk anything about her past life with Arvind. He was not sure what Arvind Babu and his wife took if asked about past life of one maid servant.

Aninda didn't wait further. One day he phoned Arvind and requested him to meet as early as possible. Arvind Babu came at the evening time. Aninda was waiting for him. Arvind couldn't guess the reason of the Chief Manager's urgent call. Aninda offered him a cup of tea. Aninda was hesitating where from he would start.

"Mr. Sahi, I have one request," Aninda lastly told with hesitation. "It is about Durga. It's not a serious matter."

Arvind still couldn't guess what happened to Durga.

"Did she do anything wrong?" he asked. "Sir, what happened? You look a bit disturbed today. What the lady did? Please tell me freely."

"No, she didn't do anything wrong. That is not the issue. She is fine and working nicely. In fact, I have one curiosity. I want to know about her past life. How did you get the lady?" Aninda asked.

"Sir, we brought the lady from my father-in-law's house at Samastipur. She was there as maid servant. About two years before, we went there. My father-in-law was not well. We saw Durga there. We requested father-in-law for Durga as our cook at the factory staff quarters. I do not have any idea about her past life. Only thing

I know that she is Bengali and lived in my father-in-law's house for several years," Arvind said.

"Ok, got it. Anything more you know about her? Please tell me if you know," Aninda asked.

"Sir, it's our shame to say. I could not say," Arvind said.

"What's matter? Please tell me. It's my request," Aninda asked.

"I heard from my wife that my father-in-law bought Durga. There are at least 15 to 20 women working at his house which I heard, he bought. This much I know. I don't know anything more," Arvind said.

"Can you ask your father-in-law where from he bought Durga? I mean who sold Durga to him?" Aninda asked.

"Sir, I can't. I have request please don't probe in to the matter further. I know it is illegal and unlawful. If the matter comes to light, we will be in deep trouble. Please Sir, don't go further. I request you to please return the lady to us. We shall send her to my father-in-law's house again. We don't want any disturbances because of the lady. The question you are asking indicates that you have started probing of her past life," Arvind said.

"Mr. Sahi, I am not going to probe," Aninda replied. "I have no intention to lodge any police complaint. I simply want to know her past. She has some mental problem. I want her to be treated properly. That's the reason I should know her past."

"Why are you bothering unnecessary for her treatment? It is useless," Arvind said. "If you think she is a mental patient, hand over to us and we shall send to Samastipur. You will get good working Bengali lady in Delhi. Don't waste time for treatment of one maid servant."

Aninda laughed and couldn't speak anything more to Arvind. He came to know that it was not possible to collect full story of Salma. He had to wait till Salma told herself of her past.

It was sure that marriage of Salma was a drama and the guy who married her sold in Bihar. Finally Salma was bought by Arvind's father-in-law.

Anyway, Aninda knew something about Salma's past. It's wise to wait. Time is the best medicine, Aninda knew. Salma would be well one day Aninda hoped. Aninda made everything easy. He talked normally with Salma. Salma spoke less. There were many days in a week when Salma did not speak at all. Salma did her work like a machine. Aninda saw that his breakfast was ready before he got up. Aninda's lunch box was ready before leaving office. Dinner was served on time. Salma was like a machine without any feelings.

Days were flying, weeks were passing, month was going. There was no good improvement in Salma's behavior. Treatments were continuing.

One Sunday, Aninda proposed to see the local sightseeing in Delhi. Salma didn't show any interest to go outside. She wanted to confine herself in the apartment. It was good thing that Salma was taking food normally.

"That is a great improvement," the doctor said. "In most of the mental patients' cases, they don't take food normally. It indicates that the treatments are on the right track."

Aninda remembered that Salma spoke a little when first came there. After that, she stopped speaking. It means that she had several states of mind. Sometimes, her senses became active and she could behave normally. There was a good hope. Salma worked as cook at Arvind Babu's factory. Nobody told about her mental issues. Aninda got enough light and hopes.

It was Durga Puja days. In Delhi, Durga Puja was celebrated at many places. There was one Puja at Dwarka sector. Bank remained closed for one day. That was the last day of Puja. Aninda was in house. It was morning time.

Aninda was reading newspaper lying on bed. Salma brought tea to him. She took bath as usual. Salma put the tea cup on tea table.

Aninda suddenly touched her hand. Salma was shocked and her body was trembled all of a sudden. As if she had been given high voltage electricity.

"Don't touch," Salma shouted suddenly. "Please don't touch me. Please."

Salma cried and her eyes were full of tears. Aninda could not understand the reason.

"I am sorry Salma," he said. "I am really sorry. I swear I shall not do it."

Salma was crying. She sat on the bed.

Aninda was happy. Tears were the best medicine to her. Her pains were melting.

"Please Salma, please forgive me. I should not do that," Aninda said.

"Please promise me that you will never touch me," Salma said. "I am a dirty woman. My body is dirty."

Aninda was mum. He didn't ask any question further.

# Chapter-14

Salma's behavior was changing day by day. Aninda was happy to notice. Salma answered when Aninda asked her anything. Salma didn't talk of her own. It was a good improvement, the doctor told. Salma was coming to the right track. Doctor hoped that she would be completely alright soon.

Salma cooked those dishes nowadays which Aninda loved to eat at Nayanpur. Salma didn't forget. Still Salma was reluctant to go outside despite requests of Aninda. Aninda didn't force her.

Aninda saw smiling face of Salma quite often. It was one evening. Aninda returned early. He was not feeling well. He had fever. Aninda laid on bed without changing dress. Salma noticed that. Aninda was shivering with high fever. Salma came to his bed. Aninda seeing her requested to bring the medicine box and one glass of water. Aninda took one medicine. He kept all regular medicines for normal fever, stomach problems etc. Salma made one cup coffee. Aninda relished the coffee. After one hour, Aninda felt better. It was the effect of medicine. Salma came to his room and sat on a chair nearer to his bed. Aninda's face was full of smile like a child. Salma suddenly went to those Nayanpur days. Those days.

"Salma, tonight I shall not take dinner," Aninda said. "You make something for you."

"Don't speak now. You have fever. You have to eat something. Otherwise you will be weak. I shall make something light for you

tonight. Please tell me when shall I give you the next medicine?
"Salma asked.

"Salma, I have no appetite," Aninda said. "I cannot eat. Yes, give me one more medicine at nine o'clock."

"Ok, you have to eat something," Salma said.

"If I do not eat, what will you do?" Aninda's face was naughty.

"I shall feed you like mother feeds her kid," Salma replied.

"Then I must eat. Make my dinner. But you have to keep your words," Aninda again became naughty.

"Salma, please come here, sit on my bed. I swear I shall not touch you."

Salma sat on the bed at one corner maintaining distance with Aninda.

"Salma, I shall wait for you," Aninda said. "I shall wait for whole life. It is up to you when you will come. I shall wait only."

Salma was silent. Her face was changing. She tried to speak something but could not speak.

"Salma, my door will remain open for you," Aninda continued.

Aninda was better on next day. Salma told him to take rest one more day. Aninda didn't agree. He had lot of pending works at office and it was pre Diwali time. All his customers were busy in renewing of their loan facilities. As a Chief Manager, he had to take decision on those accounts. Every day he returned late from office.

Bank was closed for two days during Diwali. Many of his customers offered sweets and gifts to him. It was the main festival in Northern India particularly in Delhi. The city became full of lights. The houses were colored. The shops were crowded with customers. It was the busiest business time too.

Since evening, the boys and girls with their parents fired up the crackers. All streets were decorated with beautiful lights. All houses were decorated with lamps and lights. The residents of Prerana House complex organized a Diwali get together. The neighbors came to Aninda's apartment with sweets. Aninda also offered gifts to them. The sky was full of various color firecrackers. All over, there were lot of sounds coming out from firing of crackers. It was a beautiful festival. Salma decorated the apartment with new lamps and lights. She knew how to celebrate Diwali festival. Salma wore a new sari and made facial after long years. She looked like a queen that night.

Salma made special dishes for Diwali. It was 10 o'clock. Salma served dinner. Aninda told her to join with him in dinner. That night Salma could not disobey. Dinner was beautiful. Aninda expressed words of appreciation again and again. He liked those and ate all. Salma laughed.

Aninda went to his room. Salma cleaned the kitchen and washed the plates. Then she went to her room. Salma couldn't sleep. She could not close her eyes. Fire crackers were still lighting on the streets. The sound was breaking the silence all over.

It was another Diwali night at Nayanpur, Salma remembered. It was one night many years before. Salma offered herself to Aninda that Diwali night first time. That was the night, Salma could remember every seconds what happened that night. Another Diwali had come after many years. Aninda was sleeping in the next room. Aninda told that he would wait for her whole life.

"Aninda, how could I live without you?" Salma talked herself.

Salma came out from her room. She was roaming to a different world. Salma pushed the door of Aninda's room. It was not locked from inside. The door was opened. The room was dark. But the lights from fire crackers were making the room full of lights momentarily. Salma saw Aninda lying on bed. She could not guess whether Aninda slept already. Salma walked to his bed with slow steps. Her heartbeats were going fast. Salma came closer to Aninda. Salma stood a while. She saw Aninda raised his two hands towards her. Salma forgot all for the moment. She could not restrict herself. Salma took shelter on Aninda. Aninda didn't sleep at all. He told he would wait for her whole life. He told he would never ask her to come. He waited for the day when Salma would come of her own. That day finally came. Salma was crying. Her tears were falling on Aninda's chest. It was another Diwali night after long years.

That day came when Aninda asked Salma about her father and others at Nayanpur if she knew any information. Aninda didn't tell that he went to Nayanpur. Salma had no information. She was cut off from the world literally for last 10 years. She asked Aninda if he knew anything. Aninda told what happened to her father and how her sister was trafficked by the same guy who made drama of marriage with her. Salma became faint hearing her father was no more. She was crying to know the same fate of Tashlima and the same person, Moslem Sheikh destroyed the life of her sister. Salma could not believe at all. But it was the truth. She had to accept.

Aninda told everything about his visit to Nayanpur. Aninda asked Salma if she wanted to go to Nayanpur. Salma didn't agree.

Aninda lost his mother one year before. His father Joydeb Babu was alone. Aninda told Salma of his mother's last words before her death. Nirmala wanted to see Aninda's marriage with Salma before her death. It was her last wish. It was not fulfilled. Aninda confessed to Nirmala that he didn't know where was Salma and how was she? After death, Joydeb requested Aninda several times to make a search for Salma through police administration. Aninda didn't agree.

That was the story of Aninda. He told to Salma. Aninda didn't show any interest to know what exactly happened to Salma after marriage and why her name was changed to Durga. Aninda knew that day would come when Salma would tell her past hidden chapter of life.

Yes, that day came. Salma told her pains and sufferings to Aninda. It was heart breaking and Aninda could not control himself. Were they were humans or animals? It was difficult to believe. How the innocent poor village girls were trafficked by the culprits. It was a real case. Who would save all those innocent girls? Aninda didn't have the answers.

He wanted to shoot those beasts who did business with Salma's body and soul. Aninda could not believe that one human could be sold and purchased at the end of twentieth century. The world was progressing fast. Still, there were people who were doing flesh business of women. The local people like Tahasin and Sher Ali Mondal who were the faces of village administration were promoting that business for money.

In Delhi, winter was severe that year. The month was December. There was no Sun continuously many days. Dense fog was seen every day morning. Trains and buses were running late. Aninda took Metro from Drwarka Station to go to office every day. He started from home that day and when reached at station, there was announcement that train service had been stopped due to dense fog. The Station Officer could not tell when the train service would be resumed. Hundreds of passengers waited at the station. There was no alternative transport available to go to office. Aninda thought to take leave for the day. He had no such urgent works at office. Aninda took one rickshaw and returned to residence.

Salma was surprised to see him. But, her face was looked happy. She would get Aninda for the whole day.

Aninda phoned to the branch that he could not come that day. He told his Senior Manager to inform the Regional Office of his absence.

Aninda changed his dress and asked for one cup tea. Salma made it quickly. Aninda was watching TV news in his bed room. Salma came with the tea cup. Aninda'a face was naughty. His eyes were twinkling seeing Salma.

"Don't be naughty now. I have lot of works to do," Salma said.

"I have no control on myself. I am sorry,"

"Watch an old mythological movie and take long breath in and out for ten minutes. Your body will be calm,"

Aninda laughed. "I shall not do any wrong thing if you sit here. Forget your works. Today, no work, only talk. Come on, Salma,"

Salma knew that it was wise to give company to Aninda for sometime otherwise he would not allow to finish her works.

"Salma, I have one thing to say. I want to make our relationship official," Aninda said.

"What is that official? I do not understand,"

"Ok, it means, we will marry now,"

Salma was silent.

"What happened? You are silent, not saying anything," Aninda said.

Salma didn't say anything. Aninda was adamant and started forcing Salma for her consent.

"No, it is not possible," Salma broke her silence. "Please forgive me."

"Why? What's the problem? Tell me today."

"Please don't ask me again. I am not good. My body is dirty. I told you everything."

"It is not your fault. You are the victim. Forget everything what happened. Think about the life ahead. I didn't marry only for you. Think about me."

"Please don't ask me to marry. I cannot."

"I tell you, my father will happily accept our marriage. Your marriage with Moslem was nothing but a drama. It was not marriage. He did the drama just to eye wash to your parents and villagers. Man like Moslem Sheikh did that drama with hundreds of poor village girls."

"I told you, I am not good for you. Please marry another girl, if you like. I shall leave you if you want."

"Salma, it's all nonsense talk. You know, I shall never marry any other girl. If you do not want, I shall not force you. But, I want you to think it again. I am not convinced what you said. You were a victim only. I assure you that we will marry at the Marriage Register office and there will not be any celebration. Only a few friends and my father will join. It will be kept secret if you want."

Salma didn't agree. She was firm. She was a dirty woman, she believed. Her body and soul were dirty. She was not pure. How could she offer the dirty flower to her god? It was not possible for Salma to marry.

Aninda didn't request further when came to know that Salma would not agree at all to marry him.

Aninda's branch performance was considered best at the end of the year. The branch did unexpected business under his leadership. His works had been appreciated by his Regional Manager and Zonal Manager. He was rewarded as the Best Chief Manager of the bank.

Aninda got a reward. He was selected for overseas posting for 5 years period in New York. People Bank had one office in Manhattan, New York. Regional Manager and Zonal Manager congratulated him for his overseas assignment. He was asked to apply for passport and visa for self and family members.

Aninda was happy. At the same time he was sad. It was for Salma.

Aninda told Salma of his New York posting. There was no reaction in Salma. Aninda already decided to take Salma with him to New York. He would not live without Salma. Salma had become an integral part of his life.

"Salma, be ready. You will go to New York with me," Aninda said.

"How can I go? What do you say if anybody asks our relation?"

"You will go with me as a relative," Aninda thought and replied. "Bank will not raise any issue. Please tell me yes. I have lot of works to do. Time is very short."

Salma agreed at last.

Aninda took leaves from office for completing the necessary paper works. He applied passport for self and Salma. He took Salma when ever visited the offices for making the papers and documents ready. They moved from one office to other.

In one office, Aninda asked Salma to sign in one register. Aninda signed first in that register and Salma signed after Aninda. The Officer gave a bunch of forms and asked Aninda to fill up. Aninda filled in and signed. He asked Salma to sign after his signature. Salma could sign her name. Aninda taught her at Nayanpur. Aninda also bought Bengali books for her at Nayanpur. Aninda taught her every evening. Salma could read and write only Bengali.

Aninda got passports and other papers ready within a month and then applied for Visa at US Consulate Office, Delhi. Aninda and Salma went to US Consulate for Visa interview. The Visa Officer asked many questions to Aninda. The Officer didn't ask any question to Salma. Salma didn't know how Aninda managed all. Salma didn't know English. She couldn't understand what were the questions and what answers Aninda given to Visa Officer. They got Visa one fine morning.

The day came. All staff members of Aninda's branch organized a hearty farewell for him. Aninda thanked all for their help and support. Without their support, it was not possible for him to achieve the finest performances and as a reward, bank had given him posting in New York.

The journey day was fixed. Prior to flying to USA, Aninda went to Kolkata to meet his father, Joydeb Babu. Aninda stayed with his father for one whole week.

Aninda and Salma reached at JFK Air Port, New York one fine morning. One Officer from New York office received them at Air port. The country was America. Salma couldn't believe that she landed in America.

"Welcome, Sir and Madam, to USA. I am Vijay Tyagi." Aninda got the information earlier from New York office that one Vijay Tyagi would receive them at JFK Airport.

"How do you recognize me?" Aninda asked.

"I saw your and Madam's photographs in work permit processing forms."

"Great! Thank you Mr.Tyagi for coming."

It's a dream land, they came. Salma became speechless to see the city. The cars were running on the road as if those were flying. They reached at one place.

"Sir, this is Flushing. One apartment has been taken on monthly rent for you here," Tyagi said. "Please come with me."

Vijay unloaded the suitcases and baggage from the car. They moved to the apartment. The apartment was located at 20th Floor of the building. It was a huge building. Each floor was having 10 apartments. The bridling had 36 floors. Vijay helped Aninda in carrying the luggage. They reached at 20th Floor. The apartment number was 20 J. Vijay opened the lock and entered into the apartment.

"Sir, I am staying at the opposite building. Most of the officers of our Bank stayed here at different buildings," Vijay said.

The apartment was really good. Flushing area could be clearly seen from the windows. There were two bed rooms in the apartment with latest newly purchased furniture.

"Sir, I have bought a few vegetables, milk, tea, coffees and biscuits," Vijay said.

"Why did you take so pain for us, Mr.Tyagi?"

"It's not taking any pain, Sir. It's our bank's practice to arrange for the officers who come from India."

"Thank you very much, Mr.Tyagi."

"Sir, I have one request. Tonight, please take dinner at my apartment. I shall come at 9 o'clock to bring you and Madam."

"Mr. Tyagi, you are taking really lot of pains for us. We shall take something tonight. We have brought ready foods from India."

"No sir, It's my request. Otherwise, my wife will get hurt. She has arranged for your dinner."

Aninda smiled. "Ok, no problem. we shall go."

"One more thing, Sir, I want to say. You will feel sleepy after a few hours due to jet lag. It is due to differences in time period of India and USA. It's very common and it lasts maximum two to three days."

"I am feeling sleepy right now," Aninda yawned.

Salma laughed at seeing Aninda's posture.

Vijay left and told that he would come to bring them at 9 o'clock night for dinner.

Salma thought all the happenings like a dream.

Aninda came closer to Salma. Salma walked backward to maintain a safe distance. She knew the nature of Aninda. Aninda could do anything at any time. She was afraid of Aninda nowadays.

Everybody spoke in English in that country. Salma couldn't understand what Vijay told to Aninda.

"What did he say to you?"

Aninda translated in Bengali. "He has invited both of us to dinner at his apartment."

"I do not want to go."

"I shall think and decide on this critical issue later on. I want one cup of coffee right now."

"No Sir, I am now busy. Please make 2 cups yourself. One for me."

"It's easy to jump from the 20th floor of this building than making coffee."

Salma laughed. "Please wait for a few minutes."

Salma was busy in unpacking of the suitcases and baggage. They brought lot of things from India. Aninda bought lot of new dresses for her. They bought utensils for cooking also. Salma found that Vijay arranged everything for them. She made two cup of coffee. Aninda sat on a sofa and cheered the coffee with long sip.

Aninda went to sleep. Salma changed her dress and was busy in works.

It was summer time. But weather was not hot at all. Aninda heard that New York's temperature never goes high even during peak summer days. But winter is severe and there is continuous snowfall during winter days. Temperature goes below freezing point.

When Aninda got up, it was evening. He felt tired and could not open his eyes. Perhaps he had jetlags. Aninda called Salma. Salma was busy in her work. She didn't sleep. Aninda asked her to give a gentle massage on his body. Salma scolded his shoulders two times and refused to massage him. Aninda requested for one cup of coffee. Salma made and served.

"I shall not go to dinner at Vijay's house," Salma again told.

"Ok, Madam. Take rest." Aninda agreed.

Vijay came on time.

Aninda lied that Salma was not feeling well and she wanted to take rest. Vijay didn't request further to Salma. Aninda went with Vijay for dinner.

Next day, Vijay came at early morning. He already told Aninda that he would accompany him to go to office. It was Aninda's first day. They would catch 7 Metro train from Main Street, Flushing. Their bank was located at Manhattan and it took one hour journey to reach. Aninda reached before time. He met Chief Executive and other Officers and Staff members. Everybody welcomed him heartily.

Aninda returned from office early that day. Salma was waiting for him. Salma changed the look of the apartment. Every item she placed properly. Her kitchen was fully ready. Two bed rooms were nicely arranged. Aninda was happy to see. Salma had no jet lag possibly, Aninda thought. He left office early as he was sleepy in office. His colleagues told him to leave early.

Aninda changed his dress. Salma made Potato *Pakora* for him. Aninda liked Potato *Pakora* most.

—————vm·o·o\e+o·o+e/o·o·vvv—————

"What happened, Pintu? Why did you stop the car?" Nitish Babu asks Pintu.

"Sir, one tire has been flat. I have to change the tire. Road is not good. There are many holes in the road."

"How much time you will take?" Nitish Babu asks.

"Sir, only fifteen minutes. I have one spare tire," Pintu says.

"Madam," Nitish Babu calls Salma.

Salma has been roaming into a different world. She opens her eyes.

"Yes, I am hearing. No problem," Salma says. "Can you find any tea stall here?" Salma asks.

"Ok, Madam, I am going to find. Please get down from the car. Pintu will take time to change the tire," Nitish Babu says.

Salma gets down from the car. Nitish Babu goes to find tea shop. Sun is spreading his last rays for the day. After a few minutes, Sun will disappear into the horizon. Another evening will come. Another night is following the evening. The cycle is going on.

The place is beautiful, calm all around. The birds are returning to their nests. Sun is saying good bye for the day. Tall trees are receiving the last rays of the Sun. Vehicles are moving fast on the road. Salma walks around. She sits on the grass bed. Pintu is busy in changing the flat tire. Salma looks at the Sun's disappearance into the horizon. Aninda loved evening. Every day evening time, certainly he would come out from his room to see the last rays of the Sun. He told both sun rise and sun set are the symbol of new life, new hope. It's the most important time.

Aninda had no faith on any God. Salma didn't see any picture of any God in his house. He never went to any temple. Salma never asked him why he did not believe in God. But he was strict during the *Ramjan* days. He took every care of her so that Salma could observe *Ramjan* with full devotion. Salma forgot whether she was Muslim or Hindu during those darkest days in Bihar. Aninda arranged everything at his apartment in New York so that she could do *Namaj* every day.

Nitish Babu returns with two cups of hot tea. He gave one to Salma and second cup to Pintu. He told that he has taken tea at the tea stall.

The car is ready. Pintu starts the engine.

# Chapter-15

A new life was started In New York. New York, the world's finest city, the world's business capital.

Salma arranged the apartment beautifully what she wanted. Aninda helped her a lot and fulfilled her wish. Aninda left office everyday at eight morning and returned back at about 8 o'clock night. The bank remained close on Saturday and Sunday. They had two days full leave. Aninda didn't move any time from apartment in those two days. Salma went to shopping for buying vegetables and grocery items. There were many Indian and Pakistani shops in Flushing. There was no problem in speaking. The owners of those shops could speak Hindi as well. Salma could speak Hindi well.

Aninda liked new dishes and Salma had to cook. Aninda always preferred to eat fresh. He didn't like to eat frozen foods. Nowadays, he had become more naughty, more childish. It was difficult to understand whether his age was going up or down.

Time was going fast. They were settled fully at the new place. One day, Aninda brought a packet when returned from office. Salma asked what was there in the packet.

"I bought books from Jackson Heights Market," Aninda said.

Salma heard there were many Indian, Bangladeshi, and Pakistani shops at Jackson Heights area. It was called Mini India, Pakistan, and Bangladesh. Salma didn't go there. Aninda went quite often to buy fishes.

"These books are for you," Aninda said. "You will now read and I shall teach you."

"Do you know how old I am now? I am an old lady and have no interest in reading," Salma replied.

"No, It's my order. You will start reading from today. I bought basic Bengali and English books for beginners. You will start reading and writing both Bengali and English," Aninda said. "Salma, you don't know what's the benefit of Knowledge. You started at Nayanpur. At least, you can sign now. Then what's the problem?"

"No, there is no problem. But can I learn at this age?"

"Yes, I shall teach you. There is no age of learning," Aninda said. "Nonetheless, we have lot of free time. My office is closed on Saturday and Sunday. I can give you two days full time. Every day, after office I can give you time. I shall give you home task and you will do whenever you will get time."

Salma took the advice of Aninda. In fact, she had much free time. It was difficult to pass time. In New York, everything was so mechanized and systemic, she didn't spend much time in cooking and other works. Even, she did not spend time for washing cloths. Laundry machine was at the basement of the building. Salma had a lot of free time.

A new chapter was started. Aninda started teaching to Salma from the basic level. He gave tasks everyday and asked Salma to finish before he came back from office. Salma was an obedient student. Gradually, she got lot of interests in study. Aninda started from basic. He bought all books of Primary education level. He stressed in English language most. Salma started from Alphabets of English language. Aninda knew that Salma would take longer time to learn. There was no time issue and School tests. He was giving time so that Salma could learn everything with full confidence. On Saturday and Sunday, he didn't waste time in watching Television or reading newspapers. He devoted full time to Salma.

Salma sometime became angry when Aninda put hard pressure to her. Mathematics was a difficult subject to her. She could not do well in Mathematics. She was good in Bengali and English language learning. She loved to read other subjects like History, Science, Geography etc. Progress was slow but Aninda was happy with her progress.

Aninda cheeked her home task and fined her for every mistake. Nature of fine was peculiar. For every mistake, Salma had to give one kiss to Aninda. Salma was eagerly waiting to know how many mistakes she did in her home tasks. Her heartbeats were increasing and she was anxiously waiting to hear the numbers. Aninda enjoyed that moment and looked at her face from his half spectacle. Salma's face became red. Aninda lied the number for more kisses from Salma. Salma didn't want to agree. And it happened that Aninda forced her.

Salma was serious in study. She got lot of interests and did minimum mistakes in those tasks. Aninda was not happy as number of kisses were getting lesser.

Six months were over and Salma finished all primary level books. She could read and write basic English. She had no fear in Mathematics. Aninda wanted to continue few more months in Primary level. The books were repeated one more time.

Aninda one day told, "Salma, I shall take examination next weekends."

'No, Sir, I shall not sit in examination." Salma didn't agree.

"Examination is scheduled. You will appear and it is final." Aninda's tone was authoritative.

"If I cannot pass, I am not confident," Salma had fear if she failed.

"You will get a secret punishment if you fail," Aninda declared.

Salma didn't talk to Aninda for the whole day hearing the idea of secret punishment.

"Ok, don't cry, baby. I shall lower the punishment if you get at least nearer to pass marks," Aninda encouraged.

Aninda set up question papers for each subject. Salma would appear examination for 5 subjects namely Bengali, English, Mathematics, History, Geography and Science. Examination would be held on both Saturday and Sunday. 1st day, 3 subjects and 2nd day, 2 subjects had been scheduled. Each subject, there was 100 marks and Salma had to score minimum 50 for each subject to pass and avoid Aninda's secret punishment.

Salma wanted to have one more week for study. Aninda was kind enough to grant her request. Salma forgot everything. She studied whole day and even she studied up to late night. Time was short and she had to study a lot. Among all subjects, she had fear on English and Mathematics. Salma studied seriously all the time.

The examination day came. Examination started at morning 9 o'clock. Aninda was strict invigilator. He collected all books and charts from Salma and kept in almirah under lock. There was no chance to consult books. Salma requested Aninda to set up the questions easy for her. Aninda only gave a cruel smile. He didn't comment anything. It was not wise to tell whether questions would be essay or difficult to the student. Aninda followed the rule.

Salma prayed to Allah for easy questions. Aninda gave question paper. 1st examination was for English test. Salma was anxiously waiting for the questions. It was neatly typed by Aninda. He did all at his office. Salma was happy to see the questions. She could answer at least 60 percent. Time was allotted for two hours. Salma started writing the answers. Aninda already ordered lunch from one Indian Restaurant. There was one hour lunch break after 1st paper. Salma had one request. Aninda should not look at what she was writing. When her examination would be over, he could see only that time. Aninda agreed.

Salma was tired when examination was over for the day. She wrote continuously for whole day. She was more or less happy with the questions. She tried her level best to write correct answers. Sunday was another difficult day for her. Sunday morning, she had to appear Mathematics subject. She had still lot of fear in Mathematics. Salma was tired. Still she studied up to late night and practiced Mathematics.

Salma was happy to see the questions. She could answer more than 50 percent correctly she guessed. Lunch came from restaurant that day too. Aninda made tea for the examinee from time to time. Salma thanked him when tea was served. Tea was made by Aninda. It was difficult to recognize if it was tea or other unknown liquid item. Salma laughed. Aninda could not make a cup of tea of his own. Salma still thanked Aninda for his efforts in making tea.

Examination was over. Aninda would check the answer papers. Result would be announced in Sunday night. Salma was terribly tired. She went to bed after examination. Her brain was not working at all. In the last paper, she could not remember what she wrote. She requested Aninda for allowing her half an hour extra time. Aninda was kind to allow her fifteen minutes. The last paper was History.

After an hour, Salma went to kitchen. Last 2 days, food came from restaurant. Salma didn't like restaurant foods. They used more spices and oil which were not good for Aninda. Aninda had indigestion problem. Salma took maximum care while cooking for Aninda.

Aninda locked the door of his room. He was checking the answer papers and making score sheets. The results would be declared after dinner. Salma was unmindful. She was worried to know the results. She couldn't concentrate in cooking.

Aninda finished checking and scoring the papers. The result was kept secret.

"What is my results?" Salma asked.

Aninda was a strict teacher. He didn't disclose before dinner. But his face became changed. Salma got wrong signal. She didn't know what would be the secret punishment if she didn't get the pass marks.

Dinner was finished. Salma could not eat properly.

Result was announced. Salma passed in all subjects and scored more than pass marks. Salma was so happy that she started laughing and jumping like a kid. Aninda was not happy. He missed to punish Salma what he declared as a secret punishment for not getting pass marks.

Salma was so happy, she accepted the secret punishment Aninda gave her that night. Night was long and cheerful.

Salma could read English at ease. Aninda told her to read daily newspapers and if any word seemed to be difficult, she should ask the meaning from him.

Next day, Aninda bought another set of books from Jackson Heights. The books were for middle class level. Those were not easy like primary level books. Salma found difficulty in understanding initially. Aninda was a good teacher. He devoted more time to make the subjects easy and understandable to Salma. The progress was slow. Aninda made it slow knowingly so that Salma could receive correctly.

One year was passed by that time. Salma devoted her time in study. Salma became a member of Queens Library and borrowed Bengali novels and poem books from the library. She loved to read books of Rabindranath Tagore, Sarat Chandra and other writers. She was equally serious in study too. Aninda encouraged her all the time to read more and more not only study books but also novel, story, and poems. Plenty of various books were available in Queens Library. The library was located nearer to their residence.

"Salma, now try to speak in English when you will go to Library or shop," Aninda said.

"I am really hesitant to speak in English."

"Try to speak. Even if you could not speak correctly, you should try. You should not be ashamed at all."

Aninda started speaking in English with her. He used small sentences and taught Salma how to speak in English.

Aninda followed the routine and gave home task every day to Salma. Initially, Salma faced difficulty to understand the higher subjects, slowly she understood the subjects and higher Mathematics too.

Aninda was happy with her progress. When Aninda found that Salma received well the subjects of Middle class level, he took examination. Like first time, Salma didn't fear the examination. She did well in all subjects, English particularly. Aninda was extremely happy with her score. Salma was not a student of ordinary merit. She was quite intelligent, Aninda perceived. She had appetite to learn. Salma could speak in English at ease. She got lot of confidence outside. She became smart. That Salma whom Aninda saw at Nayanpur was lost. It was a new Salma. Education and environment could make a person different.

Aninda one day bought one computer. Salma saw such type of machine in library and other officer's apartment. Aninda had no computer earlier in house. Aninda told Salma to learn computer operation. It was totally a new thing to Salma. She was initially scared to handle it. Aninda broke her fear slowly and taught how to operate computer and internet. Within a few months, Salma got lot of interest in internet. She spent hours before computer.

Aninda already started teaching of High school level subjects. The subjects seemed to be more difficult to Salma. Aninda knew that. He gave proper time to each subject for better understanding. He made every subject clear and understandable to Salma. He repeated time and again if he found that Salma could not follow properly. Salma was sincere and put hard labor in study. In one side, she was learning computer and other side, she devoted to her study.

It is told that everything could be achieved if one person sincerely and honestly tries. Salma's improvement was good. She learnt well in computer operations and internet. She could write letter in English in computer using Microsoft Word. She learnt excel and other operations too. She read newspapers, books etc. in internet.

Three years were gone. Salma was transformed to a new Salma. That shy village girl was disappeared within new Salma. Aninda was happy.

Aninda was more naughty. After returning from office, when Aninda taught her, he asked Salma to sit closer to him. Aninda inserted his fingers in her long and thick hairs. He played with her hairs, fingers, kissed her repeatedly. Salma left the reading table showing her displeasure. Aninda again took her to the reading table.

"Are you growing old or your age is going down?" Salma asked him one day.

"I am ever green, my fair lady," Aninda replied.

Salma wanted Aninda to play with her hairs, ears, fingers more and more. She loved to see happy Aninda all the time, all the life.

Salma got good marks in High school level subjects also. Aninda told her to borrow different books of under Graduate college level from library. He told that Salma would not study for any degree from any school or college. She would study for knowledge only. Hence, there was no fear of pass or fail.

Queens Library had huge collection of books. It kept newspapers from most of the important countries in world. Salma everyday at afternoon time went to library and read books and newspapers. She got a few friends there who came from India, Bangladesh and Pakistan. Their husbands either working at different companies and banks or had business in New York.

Salma found a new world. Salma's appetite in reading books was growing. She already read Shakespeare, Milton, Mark Twain, and world class novels of many renowned writers. She read Tagore's books of all volumes which were available in library. She was equally serious in studying Under Graduate college level books. She had interest in History and Psychology subjects. Aninda told her to concentrate her study in those two areas more. Those subjects were easy to her and she got real interest. Salma borrowed Hollywood and Indian movies DVD from library. There was no fees for borrowing those movies. It was a thrilling experiences to her. Aninda encouraged to watch those classics Hollywood movies of great directors.

Still Salma could not forget her mother, Tashlima, Danish and Nassir. How were they? She became unmindful when remembered them. She didn't know where was Tashlima? Moslem sold her already to another Ashadul or another Chowdhary. Hundreds of Salma and Tashlima were lost forever by those human traffickers. Who would save those poor village girls? Salma was lucky. She had got Aninda. How many girls would be lucky to get man like Aninda? She didn't know.

Salma wanted to go to Nayanpyur. But she was afraid of what she should say to her mother, brothers and neighbors, what happened to her after that so called marriage? She wanted to unmask Tahasin and Sher Ali Mondal. Salma wanted to take revenge. She had strong belief that she would get an opportunity.

One day Aninda told Salma to borrow books from library on works of Muhammad Yunus. Salma first time heard the name.

She asked, "who was that man?"

"He lived in Bangladesh," Aninda said. "He founded one bank in Bangladesh which provided Micro finance to women in rural areas for their self employment. It was an unique idea, Yunus Saheb introduced in Bangladesh. Most of the underdeveloped countries and India now are following his model. In India, Government is now encouraging formation of Self-Help groups in villages."

"Self-Help group?" Salma never heard the name.

Aninda was a banker. When he was posted in Kerala and Gujarat, he formed many Self- Help groups.

"Search in internet. You will know the life and works of Muhammad Yunus from internet. There were books available in Queens Library also," Aninda told Salma.

Aninda said in a few words, "Self-Help group is formed with women members in villages. It may be formed with 10 women or more. Any women can be a member. Only minor below 18 years cannot be member. They form a group and do one gainful activity."

"Activity? What is that?"

"It may be anything, they will select for extra earnings. Say, the group thinks that they will make bungles for ladies or make shirts and trousers for kids or dry food items. That is their activity."

"How will they do that? I think they don't have any experiences in making those."

"There are training centers run by Government at each district who will train them in their activity."

"Who will give fund? God?"

Aninda smiled. "Good question. Every member will contribute some amount as per their capacity and one bank account will be opened. It is the starting point. The women will make the products during their free time. The products will be sold either locally or in towns. The profit will be shared by the members. It is really an innovative idea. It gives a scope to poor and helpless village ladies to stand on their feet."

"It's really a new idea," Salma commented.

"I forgot to tell you. The group can open a Account with any local bank and they can save their contribution and earnings in their account. Bank will allow loan depending on their savings. The loan will be given for their capital in making items," Aninda said.

"Muhammad Yunus introduced this model first and he is called the father of Self-Help groups."

"Do you know name of any book where I can get more information?" Salma asked.

"Salma, you can search in internet and Library. You will learn more about this. I think it is the way, the poor and helpless village women can be saved. I do not know how far it will be successful, but the process has been started in many states in India." Aninda said.

Salma collected books on works of Muhammad Yunus and Self-Help groups. One lady in the library helped her to find those books. Salma searched the articles on Self-Help groups in internet. She got true interest in those articles. She as if got a new avenue. Salma asked Aninda when she could not understand any matter. Aninda had deep knowledge and experience as he himself formed many groups. Salma studied a lot. She got a new vision as if.

Aninda completed four years in New York. Time was flying as if. Those 4 years were important in his career also. He got recognition and promotion to Assistant General Manager cadre due to his performances. He was given posting for 5 years. It meant that he could stay in New York one year more. But he decided to leave.

Aninda was looked disturbed that day after returning from office.

"What happened?" Salma asked. "Are you not well?"

Salma touched Aninda's forehead. He had no fever. So, what happened? Aninda's eyes were red. As if he lost something and disturbed terribly. Salma could not guess.

Aninda told after a few minutes, "Salma, I got a bad news today. Gopal phoned me from Kolkata."

Salma knew Gopal worked at Aninda's father's house in Kolkata. Aninda told her earlier. After death of his mother, Gopal had been taking care of his father. Gopal was middle aged and had no family. He stayed at the house as a member of the family and did all works. Joydeb Babu hired one lady cook for cooking. Joydeb Babu closed his business and was not well for last several months.

"Gopal told that my father had fallen in toilet when went to urinal," Aninda said. "He became senseless and was moved to hospital at that night. It was god's blessings that Gopal could hear the sound of his falling in the toilet. Doctors are trying to save his life."

Joydeb told Gopal not to inform Aninda. Aninda would be disturbed and would try to come. His father was senseless for almost 3 days. He was just out of danger what doctor told. Gopal told all the happenings to Aninda. Aninda could not decide what he should do.

"Don't waste time. Fly to Kolkata immediately," instant reaction came from Salma. "You must be present there. Your father would be happy."

Aninda accepted her advice. It's fact that he didn't do anything for his father. After his mother's death, his father was totally alone.

Aninda could not take immediate decision what he should do. Salma insisted him all the time to fly to Kolkata without any delay. That night Aninda and Salma could not sleep. There were many issues ahead. Aninda was in a fix. He knew that Salma had developed certain guilt feelings.

She thought that due to her, Aninda didn't keep any relation with his father. His mother died untimely. Salma blamed herself for her death. If she would not come to Aninda's life, he would certainly marry a girl as per his mother's choice and his parents would have been happy. She disturbed Aninda's life totally. Aninda's father was old and sick. Aninda was his only son. He should go to his father. Otherwise, it might be late.

Both discussed a lot. Yet Aninda could not take any decision. Aninda phoned to Gopal next day to know the current status of his father. The news was good. His father recovered a lot. He was no longer in Intensive Care Unit and shifted to general wards. Gopal himself talked to doctor who assured that improvement was great. Aninda told Gopal not to worry about cost of hospital bills. Aninda would send a draft to hospital's name within a day.

Salma was happy to hear the development. Still the issue was not solved what Aninda should do.

It was December end. Winter in New York was extremely severe. Temperature had fallen below freezing point. It was difficult to move outside and was snowing for last one week. Roads were covered with white snow. Buses were lesser in number. Metro services were also disturbed. People could not celebrate Christmas with full vigor due to bad weather. They were expecting weather would improve during New Year time. The New Year was very special that year. One century was going to end and a New Millennium 2000 was going to start. Despite bad weather, everybody was in a festive mood. It was a rare event. The world was waiting to welcome New Millennium 2000.

It was the last day of the year as well as twentieth century. Aninda returned from office early. There was no improvement in weather. It was snowing whole day. Banks and all offices would be closed on 1st and 2nd January. Incidentally, both days were fallen on Weekend days that year. Aninda returned home. Earlier he planned to go to Manhattan for dinner. He told Salma about his plan. He also told her to be ready and they would start early evening. All hotels and restaurants would be overcrowded due to New Millennium celebration.

But the weather was against his wish. Aninda was drenched with snow. Metro trains were running delayed. There was no bus at Main Street station. Aninda came by walking. It was difficult to walk even on snow. When Aninda reached home, he was exhausted and his body was full of snow. Salma laughed at seeing him. Salma wore a blue color sari. She dressed gorgeously. Salma was looked like a Queen.

Aninda forgot everything. He stared at her and lost his words completely. He discovered a new Salma, the smartest and most beautiful lady of the world. He could not believe his eyes. Salma was so beautiful.

"What are you looking?" Salma asked Aninda.

Aninda didn't answer. He came forward and could not control himself. He kissed Salma like a mad man. Aninda was feeling the warmth of Salma in his entire body. Salma surrendered fully to Aninda.

It was not possible for them to go to Manhattan for dinner. There was announcement of total shut down of all trains and bus services. The weather would be worsened at night. Aninda cancelled their dinner at Manhattan.

They would celebrate New Millennium at home. Salma was not eager to go. She wanted to stay more time with Aninda. She didn't want to leave Aninda beyond her sight.

Salma made special dishes that night. They would say goodbye to 1999 and welcomed New Millennium 2000.

It was that moment. Very special moment. It was beginning of New Millennium. Aninda bought one wine bottle for the night. Salma never saw Aninda to drink wine or any kind of alcohol. Perhaps, he bought to celebrate New Millennium. Dinner was ready. Aninda made two wine glasses for self and Salma. Salma denied to drink. Finally, she agreed due to constant request of Aninda. It was first time in her life to drink wine.

Everything was ready. Time was perfect. A new Year and Millennium would begin after one hour only. Aninda and Salma were in dinner table. Dinner was delicious. Salma made many dishes for Aninda.

"Salma, I have decided," Aninda said.

"What? You didn't tell me earlier?" Salma guessed it was certainly his decision of returning to India.

"Yes, I have taken decision yesterday. Listen carefully. I want your advice too. It is our joint decision."

"Tell, I can't wait," Salma said.

"We shall return to India. Firstly both will go to Kolkata to see my father."

"How can I go with you to your father? How will you introduce me before your father?" Salma asked.

"I told my father before coming to USA that you are also going with me," Aninda replied.

"You never told me earlier. Didn't your father ask what capacity you are taking me with you?"

"Yes, I told him the same what I told you and my bank."

"Your father accepted what you said?"

"Yes, he consented fully from his heart. He blessed you also. I didn't tell you earlier. I am sorry."

"You never told me that. I have been carrying a wrong impression all the years."

"Yesterday, I talked to my father on phone. He is now fine. He wanted to see you. He is old now. It is his last wish to see you. Please Salma, it's my request. Please go to Kolkata only one time to meet my father."

"Certainly I shall go. I shall not pardon myself if I do not fulfill his wish. Allah will not pardon me."

"Listen Salma, I have talked to my Corporate Office also. They have agreed to transfer me before complete of my tenure and post me to Kolkata at Bank's Zonal Office. They want me to report to Zonal Office, latest by end of January. I have confirmed."

"You are a good boy indeed," Salma's face became bright.

"I know I am a good boy. You don't admit. You always tell me naughty," Aninda replied promptly.

"You are naughty, not good at all. I am amending my words," Salma jumped at Aninda.

"Ok, I am not good and naughty. Accepted," Aninda continued. "In fact I want to stay with my father. I know his days are counted. After my mother's death, he is alone. Gopal always takes care. But he wants me at this time. Salma, I am giving a responsibility to you. Think if you can do."

"What is that?" Salma wanted to know.

"You will return to Nayanpur," Aninda said.

Salma's face was suddenly changed. She lost her words.

"Why? Why do you want me to go to Nayanpur?" she asked weakly.

"Salma, don't be disappointed. I know your feelings. You don't want to leave me. But it's my request."

"You don't want me to stay with you in Kolkata. It's true. What is my right? How can I stay at your house? How will you tell your friends and relatives? I am not your wife. I understand your problem. I agree to go to Nayanpur," Salma's eyes were full of tears.

"Salma, please listen to me. It is not the case. You know me. You are with me for last four years in New York. I don't care society. I don't care what other people say to me. I love you and will love up to the last breath of my life. Please don't be emotional. Please listen to me what I want to say tonight," Aninda said.

"Ok, proceed. I shall not interrupt, I swear," Salma said.

"I told you that I want to give one responsibility. Salma, I want to do something for girls in Nayanpur. I do not want that same incident would happen what happened to you and Tashlima. I did not know, meantime, how many girls became victim of human trafficking. Salma, we are ordinary people. We cannot make any change in the existing system. At least we can try. Can you understand why did I tell you to read about Muhammad Yunus and his works? Why did I suggest you to study about Self-Help Groups? It is my dream. One day you will return to Nayanpur and start forming of hundreds Self-Help groups in Nayanpur and other villages. I dream every night now. I am with you always," Aninda became emotional.

"How is it possible? It is easy to read the stories of success. You do not know Nayanpur and other villages. You do not know the attitude of the people there. They will kill me if something against their wishes happen," Salma reacted.

"It is not any work against their wishes. You will take the help of women of Nayanpur. There are hundreds of *Bewas* (widows) in your village who either lost their husbands or got *Talaq* from their husbands. You start one group with 10 or 15 members. Involve both Hindu and Muslim women. You know I opened one Savings Bank account at the People Bank when I was there. I deposited a few thousands rupees in your account that time. I told you perhaps. I sent Twenty Five lakhs to your account from New York a few days ago. You start with that money."

"Twenty Five lakhs? Are you mad? It's a huge amount."

"I know. Start drawing as per your need. Form one group and provide money to start of any new activity. You will go to Berhampore and meet the District Industries Office there and request for their help to train the women in business venture. You discuss with members and decide what would be a better activity for earnings. The Government Officials will go to Nayanpur if you arrange and pay their charges. You don't need Twenty Five lakhs immediately but I have deposited so that you will not face any monetary difficulty."

"You are taking an extreme risk. It is your hard earned money."

"What shall I do with my savings? I am gifting you. Now ok."

"I am not ready to take your gift."

"It's enough, Baby. We are diverting from the point. What I want to add that you have learnt now how to form Self-Help group. I advise you to study more during the days we are here. You will meet the officials of Block Development Office and with their help, form one Non Government Organization(NGO). They will certainly guide you how to form and what would be the rules and regulation of NGO formation. You know NGO is nothing but a Trust which will be the mother of Self-Help Groups. What I want to say, you will form groups and provide all financial support to them."

"My brain is not working. Please stop and forgive me," Salma reacted.

"Please finish me first what I want to say. You have to start. I want. You do like or not is not a matter to me. It's matter that you will do what I say," Aninda's voice was firm.

Salma was silent. After a few minutes, she said, "Ok, finish what you want to say."

"Do not wait for bank's loan. It will take longer time. Open a bank account in the name of Group. Whatever item they will make, you buy it from them and sell those things at Berhampore or any other town. You know why Self-Help groups are not getting success? The main reason is the products what the groups make, cannot be sold with good price. It is easy to make and manufacture items and products, but very difficult to sell. It is the main reason, the groups cannot survive long. You will give them money and you will buy their products. You will contact the business men in Berhampore and Islampur and will find who will buy those products. Always keep a finer margin when you will buy the items from the groups. Do not ask them to return your money. It will be rolled on."

"Can I do all what you say?" Salma was not confident.

"Yes, Salma, you will do. I am sure. Try, I am with you always. If you face any difficulty, I shall tell you what next you will do. I want you to try first. I am assuring that selling of the products will not be a problem. I shall arrange buyers from Kolkata if not sold in Islampur or Berhampore."

"My brain is not working. I will go to mad. I do not want to listen more. Please stop. If you do not want me to stay with you, I shall leave where you will never find me," Salma's voice changed.

"Salma, try to understand what I am telling. You know I have sacrificed everything only for you. I forgot my mother, father and all relatives. I can't say how I was alive when I lost you. I cannot show my mental stress what I suffered when I was sure that I shall never get you. Salma, you are my life. How can you think that I do not want you? I will be yours for ever. I have one dream only. You will fulfill my dream. I know your strength. You do not know yourself. That is your problem. I am telling, you can do what I want," Aninda's voice again became emotional.

"Ok, I shall try. But I am weak. I was born there. I know the attitude of people there. I am apprehensive that your entire savings will go to the water."

"Please don't think of money. What shall I do with the savings? Is it not your money?" Aninda said.

"You promise that you will come to Nayanpur whenever I call you," Salma wanted Aninda's promise.

Aninda was silent for the moment.

"No, Salma," he said. "I shall not go to Nayanpur. You will be weak seeing me. You feel always that I am with you. We can talk everyday on phone. Time is now changed. When I was posted at Nayanpur, there was no telephone in the entire village. Now, the villages are changed. We are going to enter a New Millennium. I am sure that Nayanpur has already got telephone facility. I am not sure if you can use mobile there. If any problem is there, come to Berhampore once in a week and talk to me," Aninda said.

Salma didn't speak. She was listening to Aninda.

"Salma, one thing you keep in mind," Aninda continued. "It is the nature of life that everything does not happen smoothly. If you see anything wrong there, tell me. I shall take care. Before starting your mission, you have to do one important work. It is to find Tashlima. I am sure she has been sold like you. I do not know where and how is she? You will contact local police station and if no good response is received, meet Superintendent of Police, Murshidabad district. You demand that you want back your sister. Tell the name of the culprits who invited man like Moslem Sheikh and sold to his hand. Open their faces. Now news agencies are strong. If needed, talk to them. I am sure, you will get result. Please do something for the girls and women who are victims of human trafficking and social injustice," Aninda said.

There was total silence in the room. Outside, there was continuous sounds of fire crackers. New Millennium and New Year started. The people despite worst weather were celebrating. It was a moment which comes every one hundred year after.

Salma cried a lot that night. Aninda consoled her all the time. Her Tears were falling on Aninda like drops of rain.

# Chapter-16

Aninda was given a warmth farewell by his colleagues. Aninda was overwhelmed and thanked one to all for their support. His colleagues came to JFK Airport also. It was truly a memorable moments. Aninda was loved by them. His soft attitude easily attracted any person who worked with him. Nobody could remember that Aninda ever spoke harsh. They would miss to see the ever smiling face of Aninda from next day.

Everybody wished Salma too. They whispered again that the pair was made for each other.

The flight landed in Delhi. They changed the flight and boarded in Kolkata flight. It was midnight when they landed in Kolkata airport.

It is said that Kolkata never sleeps. They cleared their baggage and immigration formalities. It is the city of joy. Aninda's own city where he was born and brought up. After many years he came. Aninda was literally encircled by many Taxi drivers. He laughed and told that he wanted only one Taxi. It is Kolkata which always welcomes any person with warmth. The driver put all luggage's in the dickey. In fact, he did not allow Aninda and Salma in loading their baggage in the taxi. Driver asked where he would go. Aninda told the location. Taxi rolled on the road. Aninda was surprised to see the night in Kolkata. It was a new city as if. Everything was changed. He could not recognize his own city. Salma was enjoying the beauty of Kolkata at night.

When they reached, it was about 2 a.m. Aninda knocked the door. He already talked to Gopal about their coming. Gopal opened the door. He did not sleep that night. Gopal welcomed Salma. It was first time Salma came to Aninda's house. Salma touched the feet of Gopal. Gopal blessed touching her head.

"Aninda, shall I make tea or anything? Salma Beti, will you take tea?" Gopal asked.

"Give me tea only. I have no appetite. We have finished diner at the flight," Aninda said.

"Uncle, please make tea for Aninda only. Shall I help, uncle?" Salma said.

"Beti, take rest now. You are all tired. I know it is a long journey. I am making tea for Aninda."

"How is my father?" Aninda asked.

"Your father is fine now. One full time nurse is hired. Your father can go to toilet of his own and is taking normal diet. Doctor has asked for one check up on next Monday."

Aninda and Salma were extremely happy.

Aninda was terribly tired. He went to bed.

Salma could not sleep that night. All her past memories were coming one by one. She was not sure what would be the reaction of Aninda's father seeing her. What was her relationship with Aninda? She was not his wife. In Indian society, the people did not accept that type of relationship which she had with Aninda. Aninda wanted to marry her but she refused every time. They had been staying like married couple. Aninda's colleagues in New York knew that she was Aninda's wife. It was really a sensitive situation to Salma. She was surprised how Gopal welcomed her as if she was the most lovable daughter-in-law. Salma was not sure what Aninda told about her to Gopal. Salma got up from the bed. She came out from the room.

Aninda's house was located at a prime location in Kolkata. Aninda's father was in the ground floor. Gopal also stayed at ground floor. There were several rooms in the first floor. Salma saw that all rooms were locked. It was a big house. Aninda's father constructed. He thought that his family would grow when Aninda would marry. It would never be happened.

Salma took bath early in the morning. Aninda still was in bed. She came down to the room where Aninda's father, Joydeb Babu was sleeping. The nurse was not there at that time. Gopal was also not seen. Salma was hesitant and could not decide if she entered in Joydeb Babu's room. The door was open. She was standing outside. Salma saw that Joydeb Babu woke up and tried to get up from bed. Salma could not wait. She ran to Joydeb Babu and helped him to stand. Joydeb Babu's face was full of smile like a child seeing her. Salma's heartbeat was running fast.

"Salma, you have come. I am waiting for you," Joydeb Babu said with weak voice.

Salma lost her words and could not think what should she say.

"Salma, I am old. How could you forget your old dad? I know you could not forgive me. I am now very happy. My daughter has come to my house," Joydeb told again with weak voice.

Salma requested him not to speak more. He was weak and he should not speak until well completely. Gopal by that time came to the room. He was also surprised to see Salma at that early morning.

"So Gopal, now you can go. I do not want to see your face. My daughter has come."

Gopal was happy to hear those.

"Sub, I am also waiting for this day," Gopal said. "I shall leave now."

Salma helped Joydeb to go to urinal. Joydeb was weak.

"Sub everyday told me that he will give me leave as soon as you come to this house. I am happy now," Gopal said.

Salma knew that Gopal had no family. He stayed like a family member in the house and took all care of Aninda's father.

Joydeb Babu was recovering fast. He could walk of his own strength. The check-up report was fine. Doctor was happy to see the improvement. But he was old and should take care of his health continuously. Otherwise, anything bad might happen any day.

Aninda was busy in his work. He joined at his Zonal Office. He had tremendous workloads. He returned late every day. Salma was taking full care of Joydeb Babu. There was no need of full time nurse. The members of the family were laughing after many years.

One month was gone. Aninda told Salma one day to be ready to go to Nayanpur. Salma was not ready to go so early. She wanted to stay a few weeks more. Aninda didn't agree. Salma told Joydeb Babu that she would go to Nayanpur to meet her mother and brothers. Joydeb was sad to hear that Salma would be leaving. Gopal was sad.

Joydeb wanted to say something to Salma. Aninda had gone to office. Gopal had gone for shopping. Joydeb called Salma.

"Salma, I want to say something to you. You are my daughter. Please promise me that you will keep the request of your father."

Salma bent her head. Her eyes were full of tears. She knew that within a short period of time, she had come close to Joydeb.

"Today I have one small request," Joydeb continued. "You know I am old and sick. I do not know how long I shall survive. I have serious heart problem."

"Please don't say so, Dad. You will live long. Nothing will happen to you," Salma said.

Joydeb smiled. "Please listen. Aninda is alone in this world. Please take care of him. Please promise me that you will see Aninda. We did not do justice to you. Nirmala died with lot of pain. I am happy that at last I met you before my death."

"Dad, please do not say so. Trust on me. I am taking all responsibility of Aninda. I know his age is only grown. He is still like a small child."

"You have given me a lot of relief. How many days will you stay at Nayanpur?" Joydeb asked.

Salma had no answer. She only knew that she would go to Nayanpur. She knew her works there. She didn't know when next she would come or never come. Salma was silent.

Joydeb Babu guessed something. "No problem. It's my request whenever you will get time, come here to see your old dad."

Aninda hired one cab for going to Nayanpur. Next day Salma would leave Kolkata. She would leave Aninda. Salma was sad and did not talk to Aninda. Aninda noticed that. In the dinner table, Aninda tried to break the sudden silence. Ice was not melted. Salma did not eat well in dinner table.

"Did you pack your saris, cloths and other things in suitcase?"

Salma did not answer.

"I have bought a new suitcase for you. Did you see that?"

Salma was ice silent.

"Are you not listening? I have Kept Bank passbook, checks and other papers which will be required at Nayanpur in one folder. Don't forget to take it."

Salma did not respond. Salma was determined as if she would not talk to him. Aninda was disappointed. In the bed room, Aninda again tried to break the ice with all his efforts. No outcome received. Lastly, Aninda surrendered.

"Ok, baby, don't cry. I shall talk to you every day. I enquired from our Nayanpur branch that Nayanpur has telephone facility now. Branch, Post Office have telephone. There are many people who have taken telephones at their houses. For first few days, talk from bank's phone. I told the Manager. Then take a new connection at your house. Now happy."

Salma came closer to Aninda. Aninda felt the warm breath of Salma on his chest.

"When will I see you next?" Ice was broken and Salma talked.

"Salma, I told you that I may not go to Nayanpur. You can come to Kolkata whenever you want. My father and Gopal will be happy to see you."

"Will you not be happy?" Salma asked.

Aninda didn't reply. Aninda knew it would be difficult for him to live without Salma. It was a strong bonding. Salma had become a part of his body and life.

Salma took the blessings of Joydeb Babu and Gopal. Aninda arranged everything. The car came early morning. Gopal loaded the luggage and suitcase in the car. He made lunch box for Salma. The journey was more than 6 hours. Gopal put water bottles in the car. Joydeb came to sea off Salma. Aninda told Driver about the direction to go to Nayanpur. He knew the roads and told driver to drive safe. Salma boarded in the car. She looked at Aninda. Aninda raised his hand saying good bye. Car started.

The road was not good. It was national highway but not maintained at all. Moreover, there was huge traffics on the road. The driver was not having clear knowledge of the road. He travelled first time to Berhampore. He talked to traffic police on the way to confirm the direction. It took long time to reach Berhampore. The car engine was exceptionally hot. The driver took rest at Berhampore. Salma came to Berhampore after many years. She could not remember when last she came. She knew the town well.

It was 4 p.m. when the car reached at Nayanpur. It was a different Nayanpur. Salma could not recognize. Everything was changed. There were many new houses built up both sides of the road. The road had become double lane. From Nayanpur bus stand, one new cemented road was built up. Salma was totally confused. When reached at Nayanpur, she could not identify her house. Everything was changed. Salma asked one gentleman where was the house of Javed Sheikh. The gentleman could not tell. Salma then told her brother's name. That man identified and showed the direction how to reach. Salma was confused and her brain was not working. Car finally reached at a house. It was not her little house made of mud and straw. It was a newly constructed well built concrete house. Salma was in a fix. The driver parked the car at the gate of the house. Salma entered. She was not sure if it was her brother's house. She knocked the door. One lady opened. "What do you want?" she asked Salma.

"Can you please tell me the house of Danish and Nassir?" Salma asked.

"It is their house. You have come at right place," the lady replied.

Salma thought she was dreaming.

"Where are Danish and Nassir? Can I talk?" she asked.

"They have gone to Islampur. They have business there," the lady replied

"Who are you?" Salma asked.

"I am Danish's wife."

When they were talking, two small kids came there. The lady told they were her sons.

Salma realized that she reached at correct address. The driver was waiting for unloading the baggage. Salma did not tell her introduction to that lady. She again asked, "when will Danish or Nassir come?"

"They will return at night. Many days, they stay at Islampur when there is rush in customers," the lady replied.

Salma till time did not ask about her mother. She was not sure whether her mother was alive or not. She didn't have any information.

"Can I talk to Danish's mother?" She finally asked.

"Yes, of course. Please wait for a minute. I am calling my mother-in-law. She is not well today. She is taking rest."

The lady went inside the house. Salma waited. She was happy to know that her mother was alive. She left a long breath.

After a few minutes, one old lady came. Salma looked again and again. She was Ruksana, her beloved mother. Ruksana saw Salma. She recognized seeing at a glance.

"My daughter, Salma," Ruksana shouted.

Ruksana embraced Salma with her hands. She was crying loudly.

"Sakina, my Salma came, Sakina, my Salma came. Oh Allah, you have heard my prayer."

Sakina and her two kids took Salma inside the house. Driver was waiting. Salma told the driver to unload her baggage and keep at the house. It was more than a gap of 15 years, Salma met her mother. The moment could not be described in words literally. Sakina telephoned to Danish at once to inform the news. Salma found that her brother took telephone at house. She could talk to Aninda every day.

Ruksana told one by one what happened during last 15 years.

"Your father died without any medical treatment. We had no money at all to treat Javed. Those days were terribly painful. Danish and Nassir were too young to earn. After Javed's death, one day Tahasin and Sher Ali came. That man, Moslem who married you came with them. They informed that you were sick and wanted to see Tashlima. Tashlima didn't wait for a minute. Moslem guaranteed that Tashlima would return within a few weeks after recovery of Salma. We could not distrust them. Thereafter several months were passed. Tashlima didn't return back. Danish and Nassir moved from Tahasin to Sher Ali every day. They told that they didn't get any information of Moslem. They sent letter and it was returned undelivered. They didn't know about Tashlima. Those days were truly terrible. Who would see the poor? I prayed everyday to Allah for safety of you and Tashlima." Ruksana told what was happened.

"Why did you not lodge a complaint to Police station?" Salma asked.

"Danish went to Police station to report a missing diary," Ruksana said. "The officer didn't accept. He told that he would enquire first and thereafter will accept the diary. The officer told Danish to come one week after."

"Did Danish go to file report?"

"Danish went to lodge the report next week," Ruksana continued. "The police Officer didn't accept. He told that he enquired everything about missing girl. It was not a missing case. Your sister left with your elder sister's husband. You all allowed her to go. Then it is not at all a missing case," Ruksana left a long breath. "Danish got the information that Tahasin and Sher Ali misled the Police Officer and put pressure not to accept any missing diary."

Salma could not speak. Her eyes were burning. She exactly knew what happened to Tashlima.

"One day Aninda came to our house," Ruksana said. "Allah sent him to us. He asked about you. We don't have any information. We told what happened to you and Tashlima. He gave Ten thousands rupees to Danish and Nassir and told them to start a new business with the money. He told them to send more if needed. After that Danish and Nassir opened a shop at Isalmpur. Aninda regularly sent money. Danish opened another shop for Nassir at Islampur. The business is now roaring. Danish married Sakina. He had two sons. Nassir still is not married. Aninda sent money for construction of this house. Salma, we are indebted to him. Allah sent him in right time to us. I cannot think even what would happen if Aninda did not come to us."

"Aninda gave money for business. Aninda gave money for house. He never told," Salma murmured.

"Salma, tell me where were you during this time?" Ruksana asked.

"I am tired. I shall tell everything to you. Please allow me to take some rest," Salma said.

Danish and Nassir by that time returned from Isalmpur. There was a festive occasion after long years in the house. Nobody expected that Salma would return one day.

Salma dialed to Aninda. She knew the time when Aninda would come from office. Aninda was at the other end.

"When did you reach, Salma?" Aninda asked.

Salma was holding the receiver. Didn't say anything. Aninda repeatedly said, "Hello, Hello, Salma, are you hearing?"

"Yes, I am hearing. I shall not talk to you."

"Why? I cannot remember I did anything wrong today. Of course, yesterday night, I did wrong thing whole night. But today, I didn't do. How can I do wrong thing from Kolkata?" Aninda had the habit to make everything light.

"You never told that you gave money to my brothers for start of a new business. You never told me that you gave money for house. You, you, are a liar," Salma shouted.

"I have given...who told you? Ok, they told you all. Actually, I forgot to tell. Please believe me. Salma," Aninda said.

Salma knew that it was Aninda's nature not to tell if he did help to anybody. She knew Aninda.

"When did you come from office? Did you take tea?" Salma asked.

"Everything I have taken. Now I am watching the news in TV. Salma, I am missing you," Aninda said.

"I too," Salma's voice became heavy.

# Chapter-17

Next day, Salma became busy since morning. She would go to Police Station to meet the Police Officer. Salma came to know that Tahasin was the current member of the Block *Panchayat* Committee. He was politically more influential. He had close rapport with many big leaders at Block and District level. Tahasin belonged to left party. The left party was called party for the poor who had nothing to lose. The party always fought for them. Their vision was to eradicate poverty and all evils from the society. Salma laughed. Tahasin was a front leader of that party. He was an elected member of the most powerful Block *Panchayat* Committee. He thought all the time for the poor. That man sold her and her sister to one human trafficker.

Danish and Nassir asked if they would go with her. Salma told them to go to their business. She could manage everything. Danish and Nassir could not believe their eyes if that firebrand lady was their beloved sister, Salma. Ruksana was taken aback to see her changes. She was a new Salma. Her shy and timid daughter already died and a new Salma was reborn.

Since morning, all relatives and neighbors came to meet Salma. They could not believe their eyes seeing her. They saw a smart, upright, firebrand lady. They could not find their Salma who left many years before with one unknown person from the village. Salma talked to each person and lady with respect. She was a changed lady. She saw the other side of life. She learnt from Aninda to respect every human.

Salma reached at the Police Station early morning. It was not far from Nayanpur, located at Raninagar which was in between Nayanpur and Islampur. The guard told her that Officer-In-Charge still didn't come to office. He told Salma to wait. Salma saw the name plate of the Officer-In-Charge. His name was Mr. Ajit Shome.

Mr. Shome came after half an hour. Salma entered into her chamber with permission. Officer asked her to take a chair and wanted to know the reason of her coming.

"Sir, I want to lodge a missing report of my sister."

"Your sister is missing? When did it happen?"

"Say, it happened about 12 years before," Salma replied.

"What are you talking? You are now filing report after 12 years. Are you ok, Madam," Mr. Shome asked angrily.

"Yes, I am absolutely ok and fine. I am completely normal in health wise and mental wise. My only sister was missing 12 years ago. My brother came to your police station that time. The then Officer did not accept any report of missing. Now I have come to report and I want my sister back."

"Madam, can you tell me from which village you are coming? I don't think you live in our area," Mr. Shome was curious.

"You are correct. I lived in New York for last four years and just returned to India. I have come to file a missing diary. My sister is missing for last 12 years and I want her back," Salma's words were blended with a unique firmness.

Mr. Shome was suddenly silent. He could not find what he should do. Missing diary of one young lady after 12 years, he was in dilemma.

"Officer, what are you thinking?" Salma after a few minutes asked. "Please give me your register, I shall write the report."

"Madam, give me one week time. Let me enquire at our level. We want to probe at grass root level. Give me details description of your sister, name, age, when she was missing, if any photo you have, date of missing, etc. Come after one week and I shall tell you if we can accept any missing report at this time."

"One week? No, I want to lodge missing report right now."

"I am busy. You can go," Mr. Shome was adamant.

"Ok, I am going to meet your Superintendent of Police. I shall tell what you said just now. I may go to the media also. It is now up to you if you accept the missing diary report or not," Salma told.

Mr. Shome could not find any way to avoid. He was fumbling. He got a signal within a few minutes that the lady could go to the SP. The case would go against him if it happened. It's wise to accept the missing report and the lady would be happy. It happened 12 years ago and it seemed difficult to get any trace. Mr. Shome asked his sub-ordinate to bring the register. Salma started writing the missing report. She wrote everything in details what happened to her and what happened to Tashlima. She didn't forget to write the name of Tahasin and Sher Ali Mondal. Salma brought a photo of Tashlima. It was a joint photo with her. One day they went to Islampur with Javed and that was the only photo of Tashlima she had.

"It is my sister's only photo when she was only 10 years old," Salma told Mr. Shome. "I want the photo back."

"Madam, make a few copies of this photo with only your sister from Islampur," Mr. Shome told her.

Shome's eyebrows were going up when he saw Tahasin's name.

"Is the same Tahasin who is the member of Block *Panchayat* committee?"

Salma nodded her head confirming that he was the same person.

Shome's face was changed. He was thinking a lot. It was the most sensitive case to him. He was a small person to take any action against such a big leader of the ruling party of the state. Anyway, he accepted the diary and assured Salma that he would initiate proper steps to find her missing sister. Salma was not happy. She wanted to know when did she get the progress of the missing case?

Mr. Shome could not say anything precisely. "Let me investigate. You can come next week, if you want."

Salma phoned to Aninda that night and told all what happened in police station. Aninda was happy to know.

"Salma, wait for one week and watch if anything moved or not."

"I don't think police will help at all."

"Wait and see what happens. Meantime, do the ground work of formation of groups."

Salma knew her next steps. Next day, Salma went to bank. The Manager welcomed her. Her account was renewed with fresh signature. One new passbook was given with check book. Salma saw that balance of Twenty Five lakhs in her personal account. She remembered Aninda's face. Manager requested her to tell if anything she needed. Mr. Aninda Roy phoned him and told everything of the account.

Salma had lost connection with the village. She was stranger now. She was in a fix to decide where and how to start. Sakina was local girl who could help her in her mission she thought. Salma discussed with Sakina. Salma thought that at the beginning she would form one group and started the work. If it got success, it would be easy to form more groups. First task was to gather at least 10 to 15 ladies in the village.

Sakina briefed her everything of the village scenario. There were lot of new things happened during last 15 years, new road, electricity, telephone, new school, many shops, many buses, houses, population, etc. But still Nayanpur lived in 100 years back. Sakina was sure that she could bring more than 100 distressed women from Nayanpur who were struggling every moment for their survival. Most of them either lost husbands or their husbands left them. It happened to both in Hindu and Muslim families. *Panchayat* members always were busy for their own development. The poor became poorer. Even, it was difficult to get loan from bank without strong recommendation of the ruling *Panchayat* members. The situation was truly horrible. Sakina was born and brought up in that village. She knew every dust of Nayanpur. Sakina was thrilled to know that Salma came to Nayanpur with one particular mission for helping those women. It was beyond her dream that Salma could think for them.

Salma got one strong right hand. She wanted to nurture more strong hands like Sakina. Soon she got one more Sakina. She was Parveen, a friend of Sakina. Her husband was a teacher of the Nayanpur Primary school.

The journey began. Long road ahead. Road was not smooth. Ignorance and illiteracy were one side, religious superstitious and blind belief were another side. Salma knew that. She had no school and college degree but she had total knowledge without any formal degree. She struggled to acquire it.

Every day, Salma met those poor and helpless ladies who had lost their faith and belief in life. They thought themselves curse of the society who didn't find any meaning of survival. They worked as maids at other houses. They worked at others farm as daily labors. They didn't know what to eat next day. Salma soon came to know that there were hundreds of Salma and Tashlima every year disappeared from Nayanpur and surrounding villages. The grooms came from outside and made dramas of marriage to throw dust to the eyes of the parents of helpless girls. Actually, they purchased fresh girls from villages and sold to the human flesh market in big cities and brothels. The poor villagers accepted their fate. They knew that their daughters and sisters would never return back.

The most strength Salma had that she won't think of money. It was her biggest strength. It was difficult to bring those ladies under Self-Help group umbrella. They didn't want to divert their daily life routine. Salma, Sakina and Parveen slowly grew their confidence that their daily lives and works would not be disturbed. They had to give a few hours in a day. It would be their own baby they would create. They wouldn't pay any money from their pocket. Only, they would give a few hours from their daily routine lives. 15 ladies were ready. It was a mixture of Hindus and Muslim ladies. Mostly were aged above 40 years, a few were lesser aged. It was an unique combination.

Salma saw dark in eyes to select the correct business activity. It was a real problem. No woman had any idea. Most of them did not know that there was a world beyond Nayanpur. Salma was not sure which would be the right choice of the business. She talked to Aninda. Aninda told her to meet the Officials of District Industries Office at Berhampore and also Industrial Extension Officer at Block Office. They would certainly help her.

Salma didn't forget that Mr. Shome in Police Station took one week time for enquiry of her missing sister. Just after one week, she met Mr. Shome at the Police Station. He did nothing. He said some good words only that the investigation was going on. Salma got the message from the body language of Mr. Shome. She knew that Mr. Shome had no courage to start any investigation where one powerful ruling party leader was involved. He couldn't do even if he wanted to act. It was the system and culture developed there.

What next to do? Salma was in a fix. She talked to Aninda. Aninda advised to meet Superintendent of Police of the district at Berhampore. He suggested to go after two days. Salma could meet SP as well as other Government Officials of District Industries Centre. Time was short. Salma's activity was increased. Aninda told that he had one friend posted at Police Head Quarter in Kolkata. He would request his friend to talk to SP of Murshidabad so that Salma could meet. It was a good idea. Without any reference, nothing moved. Salma already realized within a few days.

The appointment with SP was fixed on next Friday at the residence of SP. He had given 10 minutes time at nine morning. Aninda told Salma that she should not miss to meet SP. Salma went to Berhampore one day before and stayed at hotel overnight. She didn't want to take any risk of coming same day morning from Nayanpur. Buses in morning time from Nayanpur were irregular in service, she got information.

Salma reached at residence of SP before schedule meeting time. She found the address at ease. There was a big name plate in front of the gate of the house. She saw the name, Mr. Musir Alam, IPS, Superintendant of Police, Murshidabad. She met the Security Officer. She was asked to wait in the visitors room. SP called her at correct appointment time. He was a senior Officer and recently transferred to Berhampore.

Salma prepared herself before coming to meet SP. She knew she would get only 10 minutes time and she had to convince SP. Salma's voice was different that day. When she spoke, she could not believe her voice. SP was moved to hear from her. Salma without inflating anything told the episodes what happened to her and Tashlima. She told fearlessly what was the action of the local police officer when her brother first went to file missing report and also her experience a week ago. The meeting continued more than an hour. It was a heartbreaking story. SP heard before coming to Berhampore that every year hundreds of innocent village girls were trafficked and sold to big cities and red light areas. It was his live experience, he met a lady who was victim of human trafficking. SP took a detail note what Salma told. He knew the reason why the local Police Officer was dared to accept any missing report.

SP offered tea and breakfast to Salma. SP told his secretary to cancel other appointments for the day. He wanted to talk more with Salma. At the end, Salma saw SP's eyes became red. He raised his fist towards the sky. SP asked Salma to meet him at his office any time during the day and he wanted a written report from Salma with any documents, if she had. SP requested Salma not to open her mouth to the media now. The culprits would be alerted and it might be difficult for deep investigation and arrest them.

Salma was happy to see the response.

Salma returned to hotel. She wanted help from the Manager of the hotel for typing one letter. Manager was good and asked his office staff to help Salma. Salma completed the letter. It took two hours to write and type. The state was far behind of computerization. The offices still were using Type Writer. In New York, she didn't see any type writer machine anywhere.

Salma didn't waste time. She rushed to SP office. Mr. Musir Alam was in his office. Salma met Mr. Alam. She gave the application and photo of Tashlima. Mr. Alam read in between the lines of her letter.

"Sir, the photo was taken when Tashlima was 10. There may not be any similarity with her present face. We do not have any other photo. Is it ok?" Salma said.

"No problem, It will be a good help even if the face is changed. By the by, do you have telephone at your residence?" Mr.Alam asked.

"Yes Sir, I have," Salma said. She wrote the number on a piece of paper and gave to Mr.Alam.

"I am giving my both numbers, office and residence. If you want to talk, phone me before 10 morning at my residence," Mr.Alam gave a card to Salma.

Mr. Alam told that he would take care of her case. He didn't tell what action he would take. Salma was happy. At least one Government High Official heard her appeal.

Salma next visited the District Industries Office. Industrial Officer, Mr. Sudip Kar was busy in a meeting. His secretary told Salma to wait till the meeting was over. She met the Industrial Officer after meeting.

"Madam, how can I help you?" Sudip Kar asked.

"Sir, I want your help. I am, Salma Sarkar, from Nayanpur Village of Raninagar block. I want to form Self-Help Groups in my village. I have already made ground works there. I want your help in selecting viable and profitable business activities which will suit at my village."

"Good. I appreciate your efforts. I shall certainly guide you. Before discussing about business activities, I want to know one thing. Did you form one Non Government Organization(NGO)?"

"No Sir, it is not formed. What is the ground rule of NGO formation here?"

"It's simple. You want minimum 7 members and one Memorandum of Association. Then register at Block Office. Your NGO will act as a Trust which will be the umbrella of the Self-Help Group you will form."

"Sir, can I have a draft copy of Memorandum of Association, if you have any?"

"Sorry, I don't have. I am sure you will get it from Block Office. Ask them. They will give you details guidelines."

"Sir, which type of ventures will be good in my area?"

"There are many good ventures which will yield steady income. But before start of the business, train your members fully. We have expert Training team and if you want, they will go to your village to impart training to the members of the groups. But you have to pay the training cost."

"That is an unique idea," Salma appreciated.

"Madam, you will get help from our office. But remember that you have to struggle a lot to roll the ball. Once, ball is started rolling, process will be going on automatically."

"Sir, can you please tell your personal experiences?"

"I have both good and bad experiences of Self-Help groups. I am giving information of some successful groups in Murshidabad district. I have some cases of failure groups also. Study those. You will learn from them."

Sudip Kar called his secretary and asked him to give information to Salma of successful groups as well as failed groups.

She thanked a lot to the Officer. She requested for a business card and telephone number. It was a live experience to Salma. The Industrial Officer wished her a lot and assured that he would help her in any issue if Salma requested. The Officer was surprised how one lady who came from New York, would work in villages. Salma collected the list of gainful ventures and business activities of the district.

Salma talked to Aninda that night and told him what happened at SP Office and District Industrial Office. Aninda was happy to know the progress.

It happened just two weeks after. One morning, Mr. Shome and 2 Constables of local Police Station came to Salma's house. Salma welcomed Mr. Shome.

Shome's voice was highly polite.

"Good morning, Madam," Shome's voice was sugar coated.

"Good morning, Mr.Shome. What's matter? Is everything fine?" Salma greeted Shome.

Shome took a chair. "Madam, everything is not fine. I want to discuss your sister's case. Do you have time to talk?"

"Tell me what you want to discuss. I have time."

"Madam, I called Tahasin and Sher Ali at the Police Station. They could not give any information of Moslem Sheikh who married you and took Tashlima from house. It happened many years before. They told that they could not remember who was Moslem Sheikh," Shome's voice was lower suddenly.

"I expected this type of reply from Tahasin," Salma left a long breath.

"Tahasin told, being a *Panchayat* Member, every day many people come to meet him. He tries to help those as it is his duty to serve the people. The people casted their valuable votes and elected him. He has dedicated himself to the people of the *Panchayat*. He gets such type of requests of marriages often. He helps those people who have no money to arrange marriages. He takes initiative personally so that one girl of any poor family gets married. He thinks it is a social service. Again, Sher Ali Mondal could not remember at all if he had seen a person named Moslem Sheikh who came from Bihar about 15 years before."

Salma was frustrated. She was expecting that type of outcome of the investigation.

Salma asked, "Mr. Shome, what are you thinking now?"

"Madam, truly speaking, we cannot get any help from Tahasin and Sher Ali. They denied to cooperate. I want your help," Mr. Shome told.

"Tell me, Mr. Shome, what information you want from me?"

"You have written everything in details in your report to our SP. I got a copy. It is good and we got enough clues. Can you give a detail description of Moslem Sheikh and Ashadul?"

Salma thought a while. She told about Moslem and Ashadul what she could remember.

Mr. Shome told, "One information I want to give you, Madam. That Chowdhary at Ranitola Village has been identified. It is our bad luck that he died 2 years before. His sons have been interrogated by Samastipur Police Station at our request. They could not give any information of Tashlima. One son has admitted that one Hindu lady named Durga worked years before at their house. He doesn't know where is Durga now?"

"I have written in my letter that I am Durga," Salma told.

"That I know Madam. You have given detailed report of each incident. It helped us a lot. Another information, Madam, that Modern Hotel where you were brought first by Ashadul is not existing now. At the same place, one residential House complex has been built up. Samastipur Police could not find the Manager of that hotel. Madam, do you know the name of that Manager of Modern Hotel?" Officer asked.

Salma thought and told, "Sorry, Mr. Shome, Asahdul always called him as Manager. I do not know his name."

"If we can trace the man who was called Manager, the third person who was in your room that night can also be identified. Madam, please try to remember if you can give any more information which will help us to investigate of the case."

Salma closed her eyes and tried to remember of that deadly night which happened 15 years before. Salma got a flash.

"Mr. Shome, I heard one more name. Ashadul told Manager that one Badi Aunty came from Muzaffarpur. Asahdul contacted that Badi Aunty to sell me. Asahdul told..... Badi Aunty would come from Muzaffarpur. He told the name of the place. Yes, I remembered. Badi Aunty came from Chaturbhuj Sthan of Muzaffarpur."

"Thank you Madam, Thank you for this important information. Let us contact Muzaffarpur Police Station," Shome's face was bright suddenly.

Salma already told Sakina for arrangements of Tea and cookies for Mr. Shome and his Constables. Mr. Shome took tea cup.

He told with hesitation, "Madam, I have one request. Please contact me whenever you want. I am giving my residence and office phone number. Please do not report against me to SP. You know I already started investigation on the day you reported first at my office. Please Madam."

Salma smiled. She got the message why the attitude of Mr. Shome suddenly changed and he himself came to her house.

Salma told, "Ok."

Mr. Shome left and assured her to inform all the developments of the case from time to time.

Salma was busy in group formation. She went to Block Office one day and met the Block Industrial Officer. Her NGO Trust already formed and registered. Aninda guided her step by step for formation of NGO Trust. Salma studied the laws of Trust. Next she could jump to group formation. Sakina and Parveen were assisting her all the time.

Another fortnight passed. It was about 10 o'clock night. Salma just finished her dinner. Telephone rang. Salma received the phone. It was SP on the other side. SP asked her well beings first.

"Salma, are you busy tomorrow?"

"Why are you asking, Sir?

"Can you come to my office tomorrow, say around 12 noon," Alam Saheb asked.

"Yes Sir, I shall go. I have no problem."

"Ok, see you at my office tomorrow. Good night," Alam Saheb told.

Salma could not guess the reason for urgent calling of SP Saheb.

She instantly phoned to Aninda. Aninda told her to phone from Berhampore after meeting with SP.

Salma reached at SP's Office well on time next day. She didn't wait at the visitor's place. The Secretary of SP immediately told her to meet SP Saheb who was waiting for her. Salma entered and saw there were many officers in SP's room. She saw Mr. Shome there. Mr.Alam asked her to take a chair. Salma could not guess why SP called other Police Officers.

Mr. Alam asked her if she liked to have a cup of tea. Salma didn't want.

"Salma, there are certain progress of your sister's missing case," Mr. Alam said. "Please listen. One good news is that our Samastipur Police has arrested Moslem Sheikh and Ashadul. Moslem was not his real name. He has several names like Moslem, Abu, Sirajul etc. His real name is Islam Bhai. He is the king pin of the racket. They admitted that they sold you and your sister. Ashadul sold your sister to that Badi Aunty at Muzaffarpur. Muzzafarpur Police arrested that Badi Aunty from Chaturbhuj Shan. She admitted everything. She confessed the name of those culprits who were in the racket."

Salma's heart beats were running fast. She was waiting to hear his sister's whereabouts.

"Salma, one bad news…"

"What's, Sir?"

"Your sister, Tashlima is no more. She committed suicide at Chaturbhuj Sthan. SP of Muzaffarpur told us."

"What? What are you talking? I don't believe," Salma shouted intensely. She was trembling and about to fall on the ground. She could not hear anything more.

Mr. Shome rushed to her. "Salma, please be steady. We are sorry."

Salma didn't have any strength to talk. She was seeing dark in her eyes. She cried.

One Police Officer offered a glass of water to her. Salma was crying.

Fifteen minutes were passed.

"Salma, I understand your pain," Mr. Alam said. "It is fact that your sister is no more. One suicidal case was registered at Muzaffarpur Police Station exactly at the same time when your sister was taken out by Moslem alias Islam Bhai. Your sister was finally sold to Badi Aunty by Asahdul. Badi Aunty forced your sister to prostitution what information we got. Your sister committed suicide by hanging herself. The photograph of the dead body has been collected from

Muzaffarpur Police station. There is plenty of similarity with the face of the photograph you have given to me. Salma, we are sorry."

Salma still was crying. She could not control herself. Mr.Alam told other Officers not to disturb her. Let her cry.

"Salma, there is another information," Mr. Alam said. "We have arrested both Tahasin and Sher Ali Mondal today morning. You perhaps didn't get information as you started to Berhampore early morning. We are producing them to Court today. Salma, you have to come to court and help us as long as judicial proceedings will be continuing. Our department wants your help, Salma."

"OK, Sir, I shall come," Salma uttered with pain.

"Salma, the racket was powerful and it operated at Baruani, Samastipur and Muzaffarpur areas. There are many culprits involved in the racket. We have arrested only a few. The investigation is going on. I thank you personally and on behalf of our department. Due to your help, the racket is cracked," Mr. Alam thanked Salma.

Salma was still weeping. She could not speak. Mr.Alam told that Mr. Shome of the local Police station would be in touch with her as long as the Judicial case and investigation going on.

Salma had no strength to return to Nayanpur. Mr.Alam told Shome to take Salma in his car and drop her at her house at Nayanpur.

Salma cried all the way to Nayanpur. Mr. Shome consoled her like his daughter.

"Be Steady, Salma. Try to understand the situation. You shall be happy that the culprits are arrested. You and your sister will get justice now."

Salma was totally broken down. When reached, she could not speak anything. Danish and Nassir didn't go to their shop that day. All were waiting for Salma.

*Ajoy Ghosh*

Salma fell on Ruksana. "Ammi, Tashlima is no more," she could not continue any more. Salma became senseless. Ruksana, Danish and Nassir were not ready for that news. They cried loudly hearing the last news of their little Tashlima.

Many of their neighbors already came to their house. They consoled them with their words. The news was spread already that Tahasin and Sher Ali Mondal had been arrested and taken to police custody.

Sakina was taking care of Mr. Shome. Shome could not see that moment. He left telling Sakina that he would come again.

# Chapter-18

After every day, night comes. After every night, day appears. It is the life. It is going on. New day begins with new light and new hope. The pains and sufferings never stay permanently. Time comes when people try to forget the pain of loss of their nearest and dearest one. It is the reality. Time heals all pains.

It happened to Salma and her mother and brothers too. One day, they returned back to normal life. Days were going. Sakina took an important role to bring back normalcy of her family. She sat beside Salma all the time. She forced Salma to eat. She fed Ruksana. Danish and Nassir started going to their business. Neighbors were not coming everyday now. Ruksana came to normal life. Salma took more time. Aninda phoned every day. Sakina received the phone and told him the situation. After two weeks, Salma first talked to Aninda.

Lot of unfinished works were waiting. Salma only started her mission. Roads were difficult and she had to go miles before sleep. Aninda now talked to Sakina and advised her what she would do next.

By that time, a full month was gone. Salma again backed to her activity. One day Mr. Shome came to her house and gave some papers to sign. Those were affidavit and some written statements and exhibits for court proceedings. Mr.Shome requested Salma that she had to appear before court when the court proceedings would start. It was the judicial requirement as Salma was the victim as well as main witness of both cases at Berhampore and Muzaffarpur

Court. The Police Department would arrange everything for her appearance in court and Salma should not be worried at all.

One day the Pradhan of the *Panchayat*, Siraj Sheikh came to meet her. Siraj was the present Head of the Nayanpur *Panchayat*. He also belonged to Left Party. But he was a different leader. There was no similarity with Tahasin. Siraj was honest out and out and committed to the services of the *Panchayat* people. The villagers were surprised how leader like Tahasin was the member of the same Left Party where man like Siraj was a leader.

Siraj Sheikh walked in the villages bare footed. He answered the reason of his walking without shoe. When all the villagers had shoes in their feet, he would buy a pair of shoe for himself. Siraj did not marry. He devoted full time to the work of the party. He lived at Mondalpara village which was next to Nayanpur. The villagers loved Siraj from their core of hearts. He was a leader who was always available whenever there was any issue in any village of Nayanpur *Panchyat*.

"Salma, I have no words to console you," Siraj said.

Salma was silent for a while. Her eyes were full of tears.

"Siraj Bhai, my Tashlima will never come back. Please see that man like Tahasin and Sher Ali should get stringent punishment. I know Tahasin is a big leader and has connection up to the highest level of the party," Salma said.

"Salma, you will be happy to know that my party has expelled Tahasin and Sher Ali for life. Our party never supports what they did. I got the clear instructions from District Committee that our party is not going to give any support to them in Court proceedings. I have trust on legal system and I am sure they will get punishment."

"I am thankful, Siraj Bhai, for your party's action," Salma said.

"Salma, I apologize for the act of Tahasin. I talked to Pradhan of Kurshi *Panchayat* also where Sher Ali is the member. He will also come to meet and say sorry to you. It is our shame that Tahasin and Sher Ali were member of our party," Siraj said.

"It's ok, Siraj Bhai. I have heard of your works already. I have trust on you that you will not allow any incident what happened to us in your *Panchayat*. But I do not know how many girls already sold by men like Tahasin and Sher Ali."

"Salma, I am also thinking at the same line. I have just taken over the charge of *Pradhan* a few months before. Let me try. I am hopeful. By the by, I heard that you are forming Self-Help group in Nayanpur."

"Yes, Siraj Bhai, I want to work at your *Panchayat*. I want your help," Salma said.

"It's a wonderful idea. You will get all supports from me and my *Panchayat*. Please do not hesitate to ask. In fact, I am excited when I heard first of your idea."

"I was out of Nayanpur for many years. I see everything is changed now. I cannot get success in my work if I do not get your support."

Siraj again assured all helps from *Panchayat* whenever Salma requested.

First group was formed with 15 women. It was a war as if to bring the members in one fold. When the ladies found that they won't pay any amount from their own, they agreed. They were ready to offer a few hours a day for the activity. The first group formed and registered. Salma opened a Bank Account in the name of group and deposited twenty five thousand rupees in the Savings Account. 3 ladies were selected to operate the account jointly. It was difficult to identify the project. No woman had any knowledge of any business activity. It was fact, most of them never saw any place beyond Nayanpur and its surrounding villages.

Salma talked to Aninda and told him to suggest a viable project which they would start. Aninda was in Nayanpur for several years. He knew that the main crop of that area was rice and second main crop was jute. In West Bengal, jute was grown only in a few districts and

Murshidabad district was leading in jute crop. There was a growing demand in cities of jute made products and other handicrafts. There were many export companies in Kolkata who regularly exported jute made products to Europe and America. It should be a perfect choice if the ladies were trained in making jute made products like family bags, purse, hand bags, hats, toys, dolls and other handicrafts. Aninda knew that being a local grown product, raw jute would be available at cheap rate. District Industries Centre had experts who could train the members how to make those items. Aninda advised to start that business and he would take care of marketing side in Kolkata of their products.

He told Salma to contact DIC at the earliest time and requested for training. DIC people would suggest what type of knitting machines, tools and other ingredients required for making jute made handicrafts products.

Salma went to DIC and met Sudip Kar. He agreed to send his Training Officer to Nayanpur. Salma was ready to pay their travelling and training expenses.

DIC Training Officer came to Nayanpur and imparted practical training to all members of the group. The members were excited. DIC Officer gave a list to Salma of knitting and other small machines as well as other raw materials viz. colors, threads, buttons, chains, plastic handles, materials for decoration, etc. which were plenty available at Berhampore. The main item, raw jute was available at Nayanpur and the rate was cheap. DIC Officer advised to buy sufficient raw jute directly from the farmers in the village and store. Salma calculated the requirement of raw jute for 6 months roughly in consultation with the DIC Officer. She got entire technical support of the item making activities which she also learnt. DIC Officer stayed at Nayanpur for one whole week and assured to support whenever Salma would call him.

Sakina and Parveen were instrumental in the process. Salma procured everything from Nayanpur and Berhampore. She was so excited that she forgot to eat and sleep on time. It was a challenge to her. Aninda everyday followed up the progress.

Salma kept all items in one room at her house. The raw jutes were kept in one member's house. Salma told the ladies to work from their own house and Sakina and Parveen would deliver the jute and other raw materials to their houses. One feeling was growing that it was their own business and the profit would be shared by all members. The capital had been given by Salma initially and they would pay back the capital over the years to Salma from their profit. Aninda firmly told Salma that if the feelings of ownership was not grown among the ladies, they would not devote wholeheartedly. They must feel that it was their own business and Salma only gave capital and other raw materials. They would get the profits whatever they would earn. It would be their extra earnings and their normal day to day work would not be affected at all. Only a few hours a day would be given by them.

The ladies were excited too. Salma after one week again called that DIC Training Officer to Nayanpur to supervise the progress and quality of works. The Officer came and gave advice to the members and rectified the errors they did. It was the process of beginning and the ladies were not having any past knowledge. They did series of mistakes and Salma helped them to correct those properly.

Salma maintained a register where she kept records of all ladies works. The finished items were stored at Salma's house. Salma thought to take an office on rent when more groups would be formed.

The day came when the first consignment was ready for sale. Salma told Aninda. Aninda already contacted one company in Kolkata who did the business of handicrafts items. The company also exported the items abroad. Aninda told Salma to deliver the items to one transporter at Berhampore. The items were bagged nicely in one large gunny bag and leveled as per direction of Aninda. Nassir one day carried the packet by local bus to Berhampore and delivered to that transporter.

Aninda kept constant touch with all process. The first consignment reached one day to Kolkata. He was happy to see the items. Being the first made items by the ladies with no experiences, there were defects in the products. But those were really good as told by the buyer, Mr. Suraj Prakash. Aninda was in constant touch with Mr. Suraj Prakash. Aninda assured him to take all care in the next lots. An unexpected price was offered by Suraj Prakash. Aninda could not think that the prices of those jute made handicrafts would fetch such good price. He congratulated Salma and told her to congratulate all members of the groups.

Aninda collected the check from Suraj Prakash and mailed to Salma. The check was given to the group's name. It was their beyond expectation that they would get such good amount by selling their items. Salma deposited the check to bank.

Salma kept all income and expenses recorded in her book. Every rupee was important to her. The ladies had no knowledge of income and expenses. They could only give their labor. Salma involved Sakina and Parveen in the accounting matters. Sakina and Parveen had school level education and they were trained by Salma how to record all income and expenses items and profit and loss.

Salma told that the first consignment fetched good profit but it didn't mean that all their next consignments would fetch profits. Salma drew money from the account when the check was collected and distributed a certain percentage of profit to all ladies. It was their beyond dreams. They were so happy to get the money in hand that many of them could not control their tears. The helpless and ill-fated poor ladies never dreamt that they would earn that much of money in their life. A new morning came to their life as if.

The quality of 2nd consignment was better than the first. The ladies corrected their mistakes and made an all out efforts to make the handicrafts perfectly. The DIC Officer at the request of Salma regularly visited and trained the ladies.

4 consignments were ready by the next 3 months and those consignments sold at good rates. Salma contacted the transporter who agreed to pick up the consignment from Nayanpur. It would save time and money.

Salma's bird eyes was to form 2nd group. The first group was her first baby and she learnt a lot how to manage the baby. She got confidence. Sakina and Parveen were given the share of profit and they were excited to form next group.

Salma one day met Siraj Sheikh. She requested for one small house on rent for her office and store. Siraj had one extra house at Nayanpur where *Panchayat* office was opened many years before. The new *Panchayat* Office had been built and the old office had been abandoned. The house needed lot of repair works but it had several rooms and located near the bus stand. Salma was happy to see the house. Salma requested a lesser rent for the house. Siraj agreed.

Salma started repairing works of the house. It was old and damaged house. Salma made total change within a month. She applied for electricity connection. She made backyard of the house as storage purpose and took 3 rooms for office. She bought a few furniture and one day opened the house for her office and storage. Henceforth, the members could also work at the office if they had any issue to work in their own house. Salma arranged everything.

Salma phoned to Aninda that night. The last 6 months, Salma forgot everything. She didn't eat on time, she spent sleepless every night. Ruksana was worried about her health.

Aninda guessed that Salma needed rest otherwise she would fall sick. Last 6 months, they didn't meet. Aninda told Salma to come to Kolkata for a week. Salma could not say no to Aninda.

Before leaving, Salma told Sakina and Parveen to manage the works in her absence. She had to go to Kolkata. Parveen's face was changed and her eyes were twinkling.

"Didi, who approached first to go to Kolkata, Anindada or you?" she was kidding.

Sakina sat at other side as if she didn't hear anything. But her face was full of different smile. Salma behaved as if she didn't like to discuss in any issue of Aninda. But she was extremely happy that she would see Aninda after 6 months.

Aninda was present at Sealdah Station to receive Salma.

"I have doubt. Are You Salma or a different lady?" Aninda asked on first seeing.

In fact, Salma's health had gone down like anything. Aninda knew the cause. Last 6 months, she worked almost 24 hours a day. She didn't eat on time and slept a few hours at night. She didn't take minimum care of her health. Salma also wanted a short break.

Salma didn't talk. Aninda tried to break the ice throughout the way to home.

"You forgot me totally," Salma finally talked.

Aninda left a long breath and said, "If I could open and show my heart, you will see your name is written there."

Joydeb Babu and Gopal were extremely happy to see Salma. They were waiting for Salma.

Aninda made an appointment with his house Physician for Salma. The Doctor advised to take rest for at least two weeks. Aninda didn't allow Salma to return to Nayanpur. Salma phoned to Sakina that she would stay in Kolkata for one more week. Sakina wished for happy staying and enjoy vacation.

Salma took complete rest. She spent time talking to Joydeb Babu and Gopal. Days were like dream to her. Aninda returned from office early.

Two week were over. Salma would return to Nayanpur next day.

That night, Aninda said, "Salma, I want to say a few things. The progress of your group is good. Now you have to form more groups. Keep in your mind that all groups would not work at the same manner like your first baby. You will focus to form groups in other villages also. Keep in constant touch with the *Pradhan* and you will be safe from village politics. Go to *Pradhan's* office once in a week or fortnight. I got information that Siraj Sheikh is a committed leader. Unlike other *Panchayat* members and leaders, he focuses on developmental activities and encourages good works. I am sure you will get good help from him."

"I meet Siraj Bhai at least once in a week. He is truly helpful," Salma appreciated Siraj Sheikh.

"Another thing, now you have only one group and I am sure that you will form 3 or 4 more groups in the next 6 months," Aninda said. "You are managing entire accounting matters with yourself. Time will come when you have to hire one good Accountant for accounting works. It is not possible to look into entire areas. Sakina and Parveen have limitations. They will help in collecting of members and other works. When there will be 5 or 6 groups, you have to maintain full records of income and expenses of each group. Otherwise, you will not come to know what is the actual profit or loss."

"I am also thinking at the same line. I am managing now. But when there will be more groups, I have to give more time in management and marketing areas. I shall keep your advice in mind. Let me find a good Accountant."

"Another request. It's not request. Take it as my order. It's most important and urgent. I am certain that you will not let me down," Aninda's voice was changed and Salma's eyes were bigger in size.

"What?"

Aninda took a cigarette from the packet and lighted it. He inhaled the smoke and closed his eyes. He was silent for a few minutes. Salma was impatient.

"I don't like it. You stopped suddenly. Tell me what is your urgent and important order."

Aninda still closed his eyes and he looked very serious.

"Marry one young boy and start family right now," Aninda said.

"You, you, I will kill you," Salma jumped to Aninda.

Aninda took her closest to his heart.

After returning from Kolkata, Salma was busy as usual. She got two weeks rest and started with new energy and vigor.

Parveen asked, "Didi, what medicine you have bought in Kolkata which is giving you such energy?"

Sakina answered the name of medicine, "Anindavita Ex".

Salma put a gentle kick on her chick.

2nd group was formed soon. Salma thought she would form at least 5 groups in Nayanpur and then moved to other villages. Her workloads were increased more. The first group was sending consignments regularly. The group's capital would be returned back within one year, Salma worked out. Salma discussed with Sudip Kar about viable project for her 2nd group. He suggested for seasonal fruit preservation and processing activity. The soil of the area was super fertile and there were many orchards of mangos, banana, papaya and other fruits. It would be a viable activity if they bought seasonal fruits locally and made products like jam, jelly, squash etc. Salma appreciated the suggestion and the second group was trained in that line. There were steady availability of seasonal fruits though out the year. The area was famous for good quality of tomatoes. The rate was cheap.

Aninda searched for a new buyer for preserved food products. Aninda advised to find buyers from Berhampore and other towns too. Salma contacted a few agencies in Berhampore who agreed to buy. Aninda also contacted one good buyer in Kolkata. Salma worked like war footing and arranged training and buying machines and tools. She opened bank Account in the name of her second group. Sakina's and Parveen's work also increased. They gathered new members for the second group. It was terribly difficult to make them convinced. But since that first group got good success, the ladies were of their own interest agreed to join the groups. They had to give a few hours in a day and Salma didn't ask for any fees or contribution from their pocket.

The second group started their operation. It was making preserved food products. Sudip Kar advised to take maximum care in making to avoid health related problems.

The response of the products was lukewarm and Salma could not sell the first consignment fully. The Kolkata buyer returned the consignment as he was not happy with the bottling and packaging. Salma tried to sell the products at Berhampore. But she could not be able to sell the entire lot. She went to other big towns, Krishnagar and Ranaghat. Finally she was able to sell all bottles at reduced price. There was no profit and Salma suffered loss. Aninda told earlier that she should not expect profit in all her ventures and all the time. It was the part of business.

She learnt from her failure. Aninda advised her to change the bottles and leveling. It was the era of modern marketing. The item which would be sold must contain attractive leveling. Salma changed the bottles and made attractive packaging in the next consignment.

Selling of each product depended on the marketing technique. There were series of food products of reputed brands in the market and they advertised in media and newspapers widely for their products. It was not possible for Salma to spend money for marketing and advertisement to compete with those brands. Salma decided to sell the food products in small towns. She got success as the prices of her products were much lesser as comparison with the branded products. She struggled a lot and finally got success. Her second group was running with profit.

Salma had to give more time in marketing. She had to travel almost daily. Sakina and Parveen had been looking after entire works in Nayanpur. Salma wanted more hands like Sakina and Parveen.

2 groups were running successfully and the members were getting good share of profit each month. It encouraged other ladies in the village to form groups. It was easier to form groups. Earlier, Salma, Sakina and Parveen approached woman to woman to join group. It happened finally that ladies were coming forward and forming groups. Salma got 2 hands more. They were friends of Parveen and Sakina. They were also house wives and younger in ages.

With the end of year, total 4 groups were formed. Each group was making different products. Salma thought that she needed a full time Manager who would manage the accounting and Banking matters. Every night, Salma talked to Aninda. Aninda putting pressure on her for hiring a full time person for accounting and banking matters and other office works. Every week, Officers from DIC were visiting Nayanpur and they stayed at Nayanpur for days. Salma had to organize everything. She also felt the need of one hand.

—⁓⁓∘◦◖◗◦◖◗◦∘⁓⁓—

"Madam, we have reached at Barasat. Will you take a cup of tea?"Nitish Babu asks.

Salma opens her eyes. It is dark around already. The car has stopped at Barasat market on the highway. Barasat is the gateway to Kolkata. There are tremendous traffics on the road. It is evening time and the office persons are returning from their works. The distance from Barasat to Kolkata is not more than 20 miles. Pintu wants rest. Salma gets down from the car. Nitish Babu asks Pintu to wait in the car. He will bring tea and cookies on his return.

"Madam, there is a good tea shop. We can go there," Nitish Babu says.

Salma follows Nitish Babu to the Tea shop. The shop is full of customers. The television is on. There is one cricket match live telecast going on. Many customers are watching the cricket.

Nitish Babu asks one person in the shop, "do you have any special table for distinguished customers?"

"Yes Sir, please go to upstairs and it is made for VIP customers," that person tells.

Salma follows Nitish babu to upstairs. She likes the place. There is less noise and only a few customers are there.

"Madam, will you take anything more with tea?" Nitish Babu asks.

Salma asks for two pieces *samosa*. She does not feel hungry. Tea comes with *samosa*. Nitish Babu tells one boy to serve tea and *samosa* to Pintu at the car. Nitish Babu pays the bill.

Salma is now feeling tired. It is a long journey. The road is not good at all. It is taking more time due to bad road conditions.

Pintu is ready and the car engine starts.

———

Salma remembered that day. She was finding one Accountant. One day she went to local school to meet the Head Master. She had a plan to donate books for poor students who could not buy books. It was the beginning of new year. Salma wanted to donate books to 2 poor students in each class. It was a great idea and Aninda suggested her. She was talking to the Head Master. The Head Master was so pleased to hear the proposal that he could not find words to thank Salma. He immediately called one Office Staff to give the names of the poor students.

Salma first saw Nitish Babu. He was the then time a part time Clerk in the School. Salma liked his approach. Nitish Babu was submissive and polite. He spoke little. The Head Master introduced Salma with Nitish Babu. Nitish Babu lived at Durgapur village which was the next village of Nayanpur. Nitish Babu within 10 minutes prepared a list what Salma wanted. His hand writing was good and Salma appreciated his work.

Salma asked about his family. Nitish Babu was married and having two daughters. His age would be around 40. He passed Higher Secondary from the same school and due to his financial hardship, could not study at college. He got that Part time clerical job in the school. His pay was less and that too his job was not secured. He got the job at the mercy of the Head Master who liked him. But the Secretary of the school didn't like him and the Secretary wanted to hire another person in his place.

Salma before leaving called Nitish Babu."If you don't mind, can you please come to my office tomorrow when you will get a chance?"

"Yes, Madam, I shall meet at your office after my school duty is over tomorrow. Is it ok?"

Nitish Babu came next day early morning. He was eager to hear why Salma wanted to talk. He could not wait till time his office duty was over. Salma was planning to go to Office. Salma talked to Nitish Babu. Exactly, she wanted such type of down to earth person. Salma liked his attitude.

Salma instantly offered the job of Accountant and she told the amount of his pay. It was like a dream to Nitish Babu. He knew that his job at the school would go any day. He was literally tensed what he would do if he lost the school job. Salma offered him almost double what he was getting from the school. Nitish Babu was overwhelmed and his eyes were full of tears.

That was the beginning and soon, Salma was satisfied with his efficiency. He was really a hard working guy and was managing all the accounting works honestly. Salma got a relief and she was focusing on group formation, marketing and other areas only. Yet, she never forgot to check the accounting works of Nitish Babu always.

Salma focused on formation of groups at other villages. Nitish Babu gave her information of new members of other villages. Salma identified one lady in each village who would be the volunteer to collect the members. The *Pradhan*, Siraj Sheikh helped her to identify the volunteers.

By that time, the success stories of the groups were spread to all the villages in Nayanpur *Panchayat*. It was a regular topic of discussion. More and more groups were formed. Activities were increased a lot. Salma had to go to Berhampore and other towns for contacting new buyers for marketing of the products. The DIC people always advised her about the new projects and ventures.

There were 25 groups formed in the Nayanpur *Panchayat*. Barring a few groups, all groups were earning good profit margin. Salma took the challenge to make all the groups viable and profitable.

The success stories reached to the Block Office one day. Siraj Sheikh appreciated the works of Salma to Block Development Officer and he requested him to see in his eyes what activities Salma was doing in Nayanpur *Panchayat*.

It was the formation day of 25th Group. Salma invited Siraj Sheikh to be present on that day.

"Salma, if you want, I can invite our Block Development Officer, Mr.Debasis Mondal. I want to show your works to the head of our Block," Siraj asked her consent.

"Siraj Bhai, I want to work silently."

"I know, Salma, you do not want any publicity. But local Government Office should know what you are doing. It's time to tell them that you are working independently without any monetary help from any corner and how hundreds of poor and helpless ladies of our area are benefited."

"Siraj Bhai, what shall I tell you? Please invite if you like. But BDO is very busy always. Will he come to such a small function?"

"I am going to Block Office tomorrow and shall personally request him to come. I think he will not turn down my request so far I know him."

Debasis Mondal, BDO came on the day of formation of 25th Group. Siraj introduced Salma with him. Siraj already told him about Salma's works. Mr.Mondal met the members of the groups too. He was highly excited to see their works. He appreciated openly to Salma and encouraged to form more and more groups.

"Government is always with such activities. It's the time to form such type of women groups which will facilitate women empowerment, Mr. Mondal stressed. "That might be the road of success for women in rural India who are living a stressful life."

Salma requested for their support in coming days. She told her stressful past how she was a victim of human trafficking and her journey to come at the present stage. Salma didn't forget to mention the saddest incident happened to her only sister, Tashlima.

In her groups, there are many women who were victim of social abuses and human trafficking. There was no bar of age and religion. Any women, married, unmarried, widow could join the group.

BDO reiterated that he would inform the District and State Administration so that Salma's works were adequately highlighted in the higher forums. It was a dream to Salma that her works finally recognized by the Government authority. Salma was satisfied and thought, at least she had crossed one big mile stone.

That evening, one bad news came. She was not prepared. Gopal telephoned from Kolkata. Joydeb Babu was no more. He left his last breath. It happened suddenly. Aninda was in office. Gopal called the doctor. Joydeb Babu had died before the doctor came. Gopal requested Salma to come to Kolkata as early as possible. Aninda had broken down totally. The body already brought to the funeral place for last ritual.

Salma cried like a child. She could not control herself. Joydeb Babu was like her father. Salma had no time to wait. She wanted to go to Kolkata at that moment. Danish arranged one car to go to Berhampore. Danish came to Berhampore Rail station and he also wanted to go with Salma to Kolkata. Salma told him not to go. She could manage everything. The train was on time. Salma reached at Aninda's house at early morning next day. Gopal was waiting for her. Aninda sat on the ground. He returned at late night after completing funeral. He was totally broken down. Salma sat his side. Aninda could not control himself. He cried loudly to see Salma.

The days were painful to them. Aninda could not believe that his father was no more. When he left office, his father was totally fine. He talked before going to office. When Gopal phoned him, Aninda could not believe that his father was no more. The neighbors and relatives were coming to their house to console and pay respect. Salma looked after everything like daughter-in-law of the house. She took all loads of works on her shoulder.

After two days, Aninda was back to normal slowly. Salma was managing all the sides. Gopal told that the *Sharad* ceremony would be observed after 10 days as per Hindu practice. There were lot of activities to follow. Aninda's mental condition was not well and it was not good to ask him to arrange for *Sharad* ceremony. Lot of works were needed to do. Salma was hesitant to involve herself in all those Hindu rituals. She told that to Gopal and asked his advice.

"Salma, I know you have hesitation," Gopal said. "My late master, Joydeb Babu and myself have accepted you as our daughter. I am permitting you to do all *Sharad* related works. You are our daughter and daughter has same religion."

Salma was happy indeed. She started to do all *Sharad* related works with Gopal. She informed the progress to Aninda every time. Aninda got tremendous relief.

Those days were busy. Time was short and there were lot of works. It was new to Salma. Every time, she consulted with Gopal. She worked almost 24 hours in a day. Aninda went one day to invite his office colleagues and relatives. Salma took entire load of works. She with the help of Gopal made a beautiful arrangement which was praised by all guests and relatives. She forgot her religion. She became an ideal Hindu wife.

One day, Gopal told her, "Salma, religion was created by man. God created man. He didn't create religion. Man created Hindu, Muslim, Christen etc. God will be happy when he will see that his creation has forgotten religion."

Everything was done perfectly under supervision of Salma. Gopal was happy. He was old and worried how to manage all sides. He knew Aninda could not do all the works. When Aninda's mother died, Joydeb Babu did entire works of *Sharad*. Aninda didn't touch a single item.

Two weeks were over. All works were done. Aninda had joined Office. The family again backed to normal life. Salma wanted to stay a few weeks more. Aninda didn't agree. He knew that every day was important for Salma. She had just started her mission. There were miles to go. Salma took permission from Gopal. Gopal told her to come at least for a few days in every month. Salma asked Aninda, "when shall I come to Kolkata permanently?"

Aninda was silent. Lastly told, "when time will come, I will go to Nayanpur to bring you permanently."

# Chapter-19

Everybody was waiting for Salma at Nayanpur. There was no movement of work during her absence. Salma knew that. She didn't blame to anybody. She devoted her entire time to work. The most difficulty Salma was facing that was selling of the products which were made by the groups. It was becoming difficult day by day. There was tremendous competition in market. The buyers were not agreed easily. The customers preferred branded items. Who would buy the non branded products?

Salma was in fix. She could not get any good way to market the products effectively. Most of the products were preserved food items. It was not possible to store them indefinite period. The products could not be sold if those were expired. There was no issue for non food products. She could wait if not sold immediately. She talked to Aninda. Aninda told her to open a retail shop at Berhampore and other towns. He advised to open the retail shops on franchise basis involving the local shoppers at that town. Slowly, market would be created and the customers would prefer to buy. He also advised to give a good margin to those franchises so that they would get more interest to sell her products.

Meantime, Aninda contacted a few more new companies in Kolkata and adjacent areas for sale of the products. Salma made a plan and worked on war footing basis. She received lukewarm response initially, later on she was able to open franchises at most of the important towns in Murshidabad and Nadia district. Salma had to visit almost daily to those towns. It was not possible for her to return everyday to Nayanpur. She took a small apartment on rent at Berhampore for her staying and made cooking arrangements there. She talked to Nitish Babu everyday and followed up the progress when she was not in Nayanpur. She instructed Sakina, Parveen and other volunteers every day. She provided mobile phones to them.

Salma got results. The items were getting response in the market. The customers liked those products. Those were cheap as compared to branded items and quality was good.

Salma came to Nayanpur after one month. She was so busy that she could not manage a day even to come to Nayanpur. Already 50 Groups were formed and most of the villages in Nayanpur *Panchayat* areas were covered. Salma targeted to other *Panchayat* areas. She started opening of groups there too. Nitish Babu's workload had been increased tremendously. Salma hired 4 new staffs at the office. Sakina and Parveen worked around the clock.

Salma wanted to form groups in other blocks of the district. But it was difficult to manage those groups from Nayanpur.

Nitish Babu one day said, "Madam, it's now time to open an office at Berhampore. Being the district head quarter, you can supervise the groups from Berhampore well. It is not possible to monitor from Nayanpur. The group leaders will come to meet you regularly. You have to visit their places. Nayanpur is located at one corner and there is no hotel. Where will the volunteers and group leaders stay? Please keep my suggestion in mind."

Salma was also thinking at the same line. She wanted to open a new office at Berhampore to spread her works to all the blocks of the district. She got a good market cap and the problems of selling the products were not intense as happened initially. It was the time to move to Berhampore for wide spread of groups to all areas of Murshidabad district.

"Nitish Babu, if I open a new office at Berhampore, who will run that office? Is it possible for you to move to Berhampore?" Salma asked.

"Madam, I am ready to move. I have no issue at all. I am sure my wife will also agree to move. My two daughters are married already. If you want, I can move."

"Let me think, Nitish Babu. I have got your response. Now, I have to find a house where I can open the office."

"Madam, you can take one office on rent at Berhampore. I am sure you will get if you contact any real estate broker. Rents are expensive in Berhampore main town. But if you go a mile away from Berhampore towards Khagra Ghat Station, you will get at cheap rate. Roads are good there and the town is now extending to that area."

"It's good idea. I shall contact real estate brokers. Where will you stay with your wife?"

"I can rent any small house nearby office. Initially, I can stay at one room of the office with my wife if you permit."

Salma appreciated his advice again. She contacted a few real estate brokers at Berhampore. Soon she got one house. It was old but good for residence and office purpose, located only one mile from Berhampore. Rent was reasonable.

Salma moved to her new house at Berhampore. She asked Ruksana to stay with her at Berhampore. Ruksana didn't agree. She didn't want to leave her husband's house. Sakina and Parveen were sad. Salma told them that she would visit Nayanpur at least once in a week. She gave more works to them.

Salma moved to Berhampore. She liked the house. It was located near the river Ganga. The house was old but had good spaces for residential as well as office. Nitish Babu and his wife helped her a lot to move and arranged there. Salma hired one senior person for Nayanpur office in place of Nitish Babu. The office of Nayanpur was working as usual. Salma focused to spread her net work to other Blocks also. She was in constant touch with Sudip Kar of DIC and other Government Officers. The District Collector knew her personally by that time.

In her office at Berhampore, she hired 4 new staffs for work. She was able to form another 50 groups at various villages of Murshidabad districts. Soon, she had covered all Blocks in the districts. The days were hectic to Salma. The office was very busy. Hundreds groups were working. Salma personally was looking each group and met the members regularly. She called the Group leaders and volunteers at her Berhampore office whenever needed. Salma hired 2 fresh guys for looking after the marketing activities. There was meeting and visit every day. Salma hired one cook and one maid for working at her house. Once she was a cook and maid. The day came when she hired cook and maid for her work.

Salma bought one laptop for her use where she maintained all information and records. It was difficult to keep everything in memory. She moved one corner to other everyday with her laptop. She opened more franchisees and hired more young boys and girls for marketing. There were about 20 staffs at her office.

Every night, she talked to Aninda and told her the progress. Aninda at the end of talk that night told, "Salma, I booked a car for you which will be delivered to you within a day or two."

Aninda knew that it was becoming difficult for Salma to travel everyday hundreds of miles by bus and train. She was aging and she needed a car for travel.

"I don't have any problem to travel. I am not facing any difficulty in travelling by bus and train. I do not like unnecessary expenses for any comforts." Salma didn't agree to use the car.

"Salma, it's not question of comforts. It's a question of time management. You can manage lot of time if you own a car. I have already booked and the dealer will deliver to you this weekend."

Aninda didn't listen to her. The car was delivered to her house. Nitish Babu appointed Pintu as driver.

Days were flying, months were running and years were passing. Long ten years were gone. Salma had 500 groups working in Murshidabad district. She had been invited by the Distinct Collector of Nadia and other districts to form groups in their districts also. Salma was a well known figure in the district and her works already reached to State head quarter also.

Salma didn't feel tired any time. She was working at the same pace when she started the first group. She was happy that more than 5000 helpless women had stood on their own feet. They had said goodbye to their most painful and distressful past.

It is the life. Dark does not continue long. New dawn arises one day.

It was during Durga Puja time. She declared one week holiday. Salma decided to go to Kolkata. Last she went, it was about 6 months before. She nowadays didn't find time to go to Kolkata and take rest. Aninda never asked her to come to Kolkata.

Aninda as usual came to Sealdah station to receive Salma. The night train reached at early morning. Aninda was waiting at the station. Salma forgot her tiredness totally when she saw ever smiling face of Aninda.

"Good Morning, Madam," Aninda said. "Are you ok? Any problem in journey?"

Salma smiled. Aninda recent time addressed her saying "Madam". Aninda had same childish nature. His age was increased but not the nature.

Gopal was too old. Still he was managing everything. Gopal was extremely happy to see her after a long gap. Gopal literally wept. He repeatedly request her to settle permanently there. Aninda's hair became white totally.

Salma after reaching was busy in kitchen. The day was Sunday. The house became joyful again after many months. Salma made many dishes in lunch. Gopal went to market early and bought fresh fish. Salma made fish items and other curries. Aninda enjoyed the lunch after many months.

After lunch, Salma cleaned everything. Aninda was waiting for her. Aninda was reading one newspaper.

"Why are you standing there, Madam? Will you not come to me?" seeing Salma, he said.

"No, I do not like an old man," Salma replied.

"I am old in age but still more young than any man of twenties. Do you want to see?" Aninda said.

Salma scared and started to leave, "No, please pardon me. I do not want to see."

"There are certain things which do not require your permission. I do not care if you agree or not," Aninda laughed.

Salma knew that it was Aninda's turn and she had to surrender to him totally. Salma also was waiting for that moment.

Salma stayed one full week with Aninda. One night, Salma told Aninda to come to Berhampore to stay a few days with her at her house. Aninda didn't see her house at Berhampore. Salma bought the house a year ago and remodeled it totally. She was not tenant now but owner of the house. She also bought a vacant land for gardening which was adjacent to her house. It was about one acre land including the house. Several rooms were built up. Her office had got a new look. It was fully computerized with new furniture. Nowadays, the big Governments Officials also were visiting to her office. Salma made two rooms for guests who would come from distant places. She wanted to spread her net work to other districts also. Aninda gave consent and told her to go ahead. Still, Aninda didn't tell when Salma would come to Kolkata permanently. Salma would wait till Aninda called her.

Salma returned to Berhampore after one Week. She had new plans to start. She wanted to spread her work to other districts. She travelled to Maldah and Nadia districts which were bordered districts of Murshidabad. She made detail ground work there. She got help from the district administration. Soon, she opened first group in each district. She had plan to open more groups in those districts and opened a office there.

Salma was out of Berhampore for making ground work for about one month. When she returned, one day she got a phone call from Superintendant of Police's office. She went there. The new Superintendant of Police was Mr. Jahar Sen. Salma met him earlier and Mr. Sen knew her well. The works of Salma was a regular news in district daily news papers. Even her stories were published in newspapers and magazines from Kolkata. A few days before, one leading TV News Channel from National Capital, Delhi came to her house and took her interview. Her interview was telecasted.

Mr. Sen told Salma the news for which Salma was waiting for years. Tahasin and Sher Ali Mondal finally got sentence for 7 years in jail. Badi Aunty, Moslem Sheikh alias Islam Bhai and Ashadul earlier got 12 years jail punishment from Muzaffarpur court. Salma was happy to hear the final punishment given to Tahasin and Sher Ali Mondal. At least one strong message would spread. Mr. Sen was also an admirer of Salma. He offered cup of tea and introduced with all office staffs. It was a great honor to Salma.

Salma went to Nayanpur to her mother whenever got any free time. She could not look day to day activity of all her groups. Sakina and Parveen had taken all charges of the groups in Nayanpur *Panchayat*. The staffs at Nayanpur office was good and they were in constant touch with Nitish Babu daily. Salma visited the Nayanpur Office also. The staffs were happy to see her after long time.

Salma went to meet the members of her first group. The group was still working. 4 old members died already and new members were inducted at their places. Salma was surprised to see their family. They got a new life. They could not control themselves when saw Salma. They got a new life and it was possible only due to Salma. Salma stayed a few days with her mother.

Sakina and Parveen gave her a detail report of all the groups. 4 groups of Char Gopinathpur had some problems. The members misused the funds and stopped working. Salma knew it was not possible to expect desired results from each group. Aninda taught that. She was not angry. She had at least 25 groups who were not working good and there were reports of misuse of funds and cheating. Salma accepted that.

Salma instructed Sakina to stop work of those groups and taken away the raw materials from them. Time would come when the members would realize their mistakes and come back to the fold. She didn't punish any member even if she got serious report against some of the groups. It was her strategy to make the group idle. When they would realize their mistakes, they would come forward. She saw the darkest phase of life. She had no word of punishment in her dictionary.

Ruksana was not well nowadays. Sakina's sons were grown up. They were studying at local school. Nassir didn't marry. Danish had opened one more shop at Islampur. Both brothers were highly busy with their business. Salma spent hours time with Ruksana.

Sakina asked about Aninda's health. Salma was also worried about Aninda nowadays. Aninda was aging and he was total careless all the time. He never cared of his health at all. He should check up his health and follow the doctor's advice. Salma was unmindful when she remembered Aninda.

Salma on her return from Nayanpur next day got one call from the District Collector Office. District Collector wanted to see her at his office urgently. Salma could not guess the reason. She took Nitish Babu with her and went to District Collector office.

District Collector was waiting for her. Salma was called to his chamber. District Collector told that the Honorable Chief Minister, Manasi Mukherjee would be visiting Berhampore in the next week. She would address a public rally at the college ground and before her meeting, she would attend Review Meeting of the performances of the district. The Honorable Chief Minister desired to meet Salma on that day. District Collector had been asked by Chief Minister's office to fix an appointment. Salma was surprised.

"Sir, I am very ordinary. I am really hesitant to meet," she said.

"Madam, now your name has gone not only to the State Capital, but also to the National Capital," the District Collector said. "Chief Minister heard the stories of your groups and works. She personally wants to meet you."

"Sir, I want to work silently. I do not like to be focused."

"Madam, we are proud that you are working for this district. I personally want you to meet our Chief Minister. I know, you want to spread your work to other districts and it is the greatest opportunity you are getting to present your plan before her. I am sure you will get all supports. Please come."

"Ok, Sir, I shall come. What time?" Salma asked.

"She will meet you between 12 to 1 p.m. at Circuit House. One car will go to your office to pick up."

"I can come of my own. Why are you taking pain to send car for me?" Salma said.

"It is not taking pain. It is my duty to pick up from your house. Please do not say no."

Salma thanked District Collector for inviting her.

Salma phoned to Aninda and told her schedule of meeting with the Chief Minister. Aninda was kidding that Salma had become a VIP and she had no time to talk to the small man like Aninda. Salma remembered that she didn't talk to Aninda last night. Actually she was in Nayanpur and there was poor connectivity of mobile yesterday night. Salma declared a strong punishment to Aninda for his unparliamentarily talk. Aninda wanted to hear which punishment had been awarded to him. Salma told her to wait for a few weeks. She would go to Kolkata next month.

The news that Salma was invited to meet with the Chief Minister was spread. Nitish Babu and all the office staffs were happy to hear the news. The groups also got the news. It was their feeling that time had come to recognize the works of Salma Madam.

It was a big day for Salma. Car picked her on time. Salma reached to the Circuit House for the first time. All high Government Officials and Party leaders gathered there. The Circuit House was almost full. Salma saw the District Collector and Superintendant of Police there. District Collector took her to one room and asked to wait for a few minutes. The Chief Minister was busy with review meeting. Salma saw there were many persons waiting to meet with the Chief Minister. Everybody brought flowers or special gift packets. Salma came with empty hands. She was suddenly ashamed. Actually it was her first time in life to meet such person. She was not having any previous experience. She wore a very simple sari and did not do any make up. Still Salma was looked exceptionally bright.

After a few minutes, one gentleman came to Salma and told her to go to Chief Minister chamber. Chief Minister called off meeting to meet her. All the guests who were waiting there before were surprised how Chief Minister called that ordinary lady who just came.

The Chief Minister was alone there. Salma's heartbeats were going fast. She greeted Chief Minister with folded hands. Chief Minister stood up to welcome her. Salma saw Chief Minister of the state first time. The Chief Minister was also in a very simple dress. Salma saw her photo in newspapers and TV channels. It was first time, she saw her close. Chief Minister asked her to sit on the nearest chair close to her.

"Salma, I heard everything of your works," the Chief Minister said. "My District Collector and Superintendant of Police told me everything. I am proud, Salma, of your work. I want you to organize more and more Self-Help groups not only in Murshidabad but also all districts in our state. You will get all supports from the administration."

Salma lost her words. Her voices were weak. She thanked to Chief Minister with a few words.

"Salma, I want to know your story fully. How did you start? Please tell me from the beginning. I have already called off the meeting. Nobody will come to us. Feel free and I am eager to listen your story," the Chief Minister said.

Salma was silent. She could not find where to start. It was a long journey, darkest past, and a god who saved her. Salma was remembering everything what happened to her. Was it a story or real fife? Salma began to tell her journey. Her voice became heavy when she was telling her darkest phase of life. Yes, she was sold repeatedly like an animal in market.

When finished, the Chief Minister's eyes were full of tears. She could not believe it happened to Salma. It was a cruel fact. Salma forgot time. She got a complete relief after saying to the Chief Minister. The Chief Minister listened patiently. Salma could not control herself when finished. She cried before the Chief Minister. She forgot everything.

"Salma, I understand your pain. I am also a woman," the Chief Minister touched her shoulder and said.

The Chief Minister told her to join the lunch with her. She wanted to spend more time with Salma. In the dining table, Chief Minister introduced Salma with all her officials who came from State Capital, Kolkata. The Chief Minister introduced Salma before all as "Bengal Lady with a lamp".

Salma could not eat properly. She was ashamed fully in front of all high officials. The Chief Minister invited Salma to her Kolkata Office and requested to keep in touch always.

The day was memorable to Salma. Salma phoned to Aninda after her meeting was over. She told each and every word of Chief Minister. Salma's voice was again heavy and chocked. She cried over phone. Aninda congratulated Salma. Salma wanted to see Aninda right now.

Salma got fresh energy after the meeting. She wanted to form more Self-Help Groups in Nadia and Maldah districts. Again she knew that the formation of groups needed longer time. Selection for proper projects were the most important to get success. There were series of activities linked to group. If there was any laxity or lapses, the ultimate objective would die. She believed the principle of slow and steady win the race.

Salma spent more time to those two districts. She didn't select any Volunteer unless she herself was fully satisfied. She knew that once the machine rolled over in those district, the ball would roll automatically. She had good knowledge of her own district, but her knowledge was limited about those two new districts. She always tried to avoid the village politics and leaders whose market reports were not good. She did enough ground work before taking any decision.

Salma's hard work yielded results one day. She owned 25 new groups in each of two districts.

After one month, she returned to Berhampore. Salma was terribly tired. Last one month, she could not talk to Aninda properly due to poor connection of phone line in remote villages of Nadia and Maldah districts.

It was almost midnight when Salma returned to Berhampore. She was not feeling well. Salma could not get Aninda in his mobile. She thought that Aninda had gone to sleep that time. She should not disturb Aninda. It was good to talk at the morning, she thought.

Salma went to bed. She saw Aninda's face when closed her eyes. Salma wanted to go to Kolkata within a day. She didn't see Aninda long time.

# Chapter-20

Mobile was ringing continuously. Salma was too tired to open her eyes. She saw there were 3 miscalls. It was from home telephone number of Aninda. Salma got up instantly as if she got an electric shock. She saw outside the window. Morning's first light was entering into the windows. She could not guess what's the matter. Aninda always used his mobile. Only Gopal phoned from that land line.

Salma was sweating. She immediately called back to that number. Gopal received the phone. He was literally crying. Gopal could not speak properly. Salma repeatedly asked what happened. Gopal spoke only a few broken words, "Aninda is not well. Come urgently." The phone got disconnected.

Salma dialed Aninda's mobile. It was ringing and went to voice message. Salma's brain was not working. She saw dark all over.

She called Nitish Babu at that very time. She could not guess what happened to Aninda. But she knew that she had to go to Kolkata immediately and there was no time to think any more. Nitish Babu came within 5 minutes. Salma told Nitish Babu to inform Pintu. She would go to Kolkata right now. She also told Nitish Babu to go with her.

Nitish Babu guessed something serious. He asked softly what's the matter. Salma lost her words. She told with broken words. Aninda was not well. Nitish Babu got the message. He ran from the place and went to Pintu's room. Pintu already got up. Nitish Babu told his wife that he had to go to Kolkata right now. Nitish Babu was ready. Pintu parked the car in front of the gate. Salma came down from her room. She was looked totally disturbed and was literally crying. Car stated. Nitish Babu didn't forget to take the check book and cash money.

Salma asked Pintu to drive as fast as possible. It was early morning time and there was no traffic on the highway. Pintu pushed pressure on accelerator and the car moved in the air as if. Salma's brain was not working. She tried to talk to Gopal. Land phone was ringing. Gopal didn't respond. Aninda's mobile was going to voice message constantly.

Salma was broken down totally. Nitish Babu was continuously requesting to be steady. Nothing wrong happened. Everything was fine. When car reached at Ranaghat, Salma got one call from an unknown number.

"May I talk to Salma Sarkar?" one lady on the other side said.

"Yes, I am Salma Sarkar. May I know who are you calling?"

"Madam, I am calling from Atlas Hospital. One patient, Mr. Aninda Roy has been admitted to our hospital. Can you come please?" the lady said.

Salma all of a sudden saw dark all around.

"How is Aninda?" her voice was chocked.

"Madam, he has been moved to ICU. Doctors are attending the patient. One Mr. Gopal Saha gave your number and requested to inform you."

"I am on the way. Please tell me the correct location of your hospital," Salma asked.

The lady told the location. It was located near the Eastern Bypass of Kolkata. Salma heard the name of the hospital earlier. It was famous for heart treatment.

Salma gave direction to Pintu how to reach the hospital. Her eyes were full of tears suddenly.

The car reached at 12 noon. Salma ran from the car. When entered in the Main Hall, she saw Gopal waiting there. Salma rushed to Gopal. Gopal was devastated totally and could not tell properly. He told Salma to talk to Doctor. Aninda was shifted to ICU, Cabin number B-12. Salma didn't waste a single second. She was running almost. It was located at the 3rd floor. Salma reached there within a minute. She entered inside the cabin without taking any permission.

She saw Aninda lying on a complete white bed. One doctor and one nurse were there. Aninda's eyes were closed. Doctor, seeing her inside the cabin, asked to wait outside.

Salma didn't leave. She stood like a statue. After a few minutes, Doctor told her to go outside and he wanted to say something. Nurse also came out with the doctor.

"Are you Salma?" the nurse asked.

"Yes, I am Salma."

"Actually, the patient told this name when brought to the hospital. He told to phone you. We are waiting for you, Madam," the nurse said.

"Doc, how is Aninda?"

"I can't say correctly at this time. We have to wait. We are trying our best. The patient is slowly responding to the treatment," the doctor said.

"What happened Doc?" Salma asked.

"It was a sudden Cardiac Arrest. The patient brought here late. We have started treatment immediately he brought here. We have done tests and are waiting for the reports now. You can wait at the Visitor's lounge."

Salma was not satisfied with those words of the doctor. She was repeatedly asking when Aninda would be recovered. The doctor knew the mental condition of patient's relatives in such time.

"I cannot say good or bad before 48 hours," he replied softly. "Please remain in touch with the attending nurse who will tell the progress from time to time." The doctor left to attend other patients.

Meantime, Gopal and Nitish Babu reached there.

"Sister, may I stay at patient's Cabin?" Salma asked the nurse.

"No, Madam, it is not permitted. I am sorry." Nurse replied. "Madam, Mr. Roy when brought to the cabin, has given me one envelope and told your name to give." The nurse gave a yellow color envelope to Salma.

"Uncle, what exactly happened?" Salma asked Gopal.

Gopal got back to his normalcy seeing Salma. Gopal narrated that it was late night time. He didn't see the time. He was sleeping in his room. He heard that somebody knocked the door. Gopal opened and saw Aninda. Aninda told him to call a car. He wanted to go to hospital. He was not feeling well. Gopal phoned for a car. It was odd time and he contacted one at last. Car came and Aninda told the driver to go to Atlas Hospital.

"Aninda could not speak at all. His body was full of sweat as if he was drenched in water. Aninda told me to stay at house and phoned you. I lost your number and got it lastly. I came to hospital after phoned to you," Gopal added.

"Did you inform Aninda's office?"

"Today is Sunday. Office is closed. I do not have any phone number of his office, Salma," Gopal replied.

"Ok, uncle, I shall inform them. Please eat something now and wait at the Lounge. You have not taken any food since morning," Salma told.

"Madam, you also please eat something. There is one canteen at the ground floor," Nithis Babu requested.

"I am waiting here. I have no appetite now. Please go and take lunch, Nithis Babu. Please take Pintu also to the canteen," Salma said.

Salma didn't agree to eat. She told them that she would wait outside Aninda's cabin. She would not move from the place for a single minute.

Gopal and Nitish Babu left. Salma sat on the floor near the door of the cabin.

Salma opened the envelope. She saw a letter written by Aninda inside and other papers. Salma read the letter.

"My dear Sweet Heart Salma,

I am not well. I didn't tell you that last month, I had severe pain on chest. I went to one Doctor. He did lot of tests and told me that there are blocks in heart. He advised me to undergo Bypass surgery early. He gave me medicines and told me for operation without any delay. After that, I didn't feel any pain. You know my nature. I forgot his advice.

Yesterday, I had pain again since morning. I was not well. I left office early. I thought that I shall be ok if I take rest. At least nothing fatal will happen immediately. I was feeling better during evening time. Gopal asked me if he would call a doctor. I didn't want. I was not hungry and told Gopal to give me only a cup of coffee. No dinner.

I slept early. After a few hours, I again had severe pain in chest. I could not breath properly. It was 12 night. I thought to go to hospital morning time. I didn't want to disturb you. I thought to write a letter to you before going to hospital. I know that your love will not allow me to die. Still, I do not take any chance.

I want to say one secret thing which I didn't tell you. Please forgive me.

It happened in Delhi before our repatriation to New York. Can you remember, one day we both went to one office and I told you to sign on one register and other documents there? I also signed on the same register and documents. I told you that the certificate of that office was required for passport and visa. Actually, it was our marriage papers. Yes, Salma, I lied you on that day. The office was Marriage Register Office and the document you and I signed was our Marriage Registration certificate. Salma we were married that day. I managed everything earlier and requested my two friends for witness. I managed everything so secretly that you could not doubt anything. I know that you would never agree to the marriage.

I apologize again and again for telling lie to you. You went to New York as my wife. In passport and Visa, your name was written as wife of Aninda Roy. I knew that you would never ask me to see those papers.

You will see our Marriage Certificate in this envelope. You are my wife, Salma.

I told to my father about our marriage and requested him not to divulge before you. Perhaps, my father told Gopal.

Salma, I kept all my bank deposits certificate and accounts in my almirah. Gopal knew where is the key. I have nominated your name in all my deposits and accounts. My house will be your house.

If anything bad happens, please do not cry. Do your works. You will always feel that I am standing behind you.

One more thing, please take care of Gopal. He came to our house when I was born. He stayed in our house as a family member. He had no family and no relative. Please give me words that you will take care of him. He is very old.

Don't cry, please. It's my order. Smile please, my sweet heart.

yours and yours

Aninda"

Salma could not control. She had broken down. Stream of tears was flowing from her eyes. Salma was crying.

Doctors and nurses were entering in to the cabin and coming out all the time. Salma was waiting outside. Nurses and doctors repeated the same word, "wait"

Salma waited day and night like a stone piece. Nitish Babu and Gopal tried their level best to make her agree to eat something. Salma didn't move from the place.

It was early morning next day. East side was becoming clear and somebody painted red color on the sky. Sun yet to start his daily work.

The doctor and nurse came out from the cabin. Doctor's face was different.

"I am sorry," he uttered a few words. He left.

Salma lost control of her body. She was falling. The nurse took hold in her arms.

"We are sorry, Madam," she also repeated the same.

Salma entered in the cabin. Aninda was sleeping. He would never get up. He would never talk to Salma. His face was full of smile. As if, he would call, "Salma, why are you standing there? Come to me. Come close to my heart."

Salma didn't cry.

"I shall never forgive you. Why did you leave me?" Salma fell on Aninda's body.

"Madam, who will receive the body?" doctor came again and asked.

Salma was calm now.

"I shall receive the body. I am his wife," she said.

# Chapter-21

*Where the end is the beginning!*

"Madam, we have reached. Please get down," Nitish Babu says.

Salma opens eyes. The car has stopped at the gate of Aninda's house. Gopal comes to open the gate. Salma gets down from the car. She touches the feet of Gopal and asks, "How are you uncle?"

"I am fine, Salma. When did you start today?" Gopal asks.

"We started at morning. Road is not good, Uncle. It takes long time today."

"Take rest. You look tired," Gopal says.

Pintu has parked the car into the garage. All enter in the house. Nitish Babu came here several times. He knows everything. Gopal also knows why Salma has come. The Chief Minister will confer one award on Salma next day.

Salma doesn't want to eat that night. She wants to cry whole night in Aninda's bed room. She now comes once in a month. She herself now maintains Aninda's room. She has been doing for last 3 years after death of Aninda. It is their room where Salma left all her happiness and joys. She is alone, very alone now.

Gopal comes. He is too old now to walk steadily. Gopal walks with the help of one stick. Earlier, Salma requested Gopal several times to go to Berhampore and stay with her there. Gopal didn't want to leave the house. Salma comes to Kolkata once in a month now due to her Gopal uncle.

It is a big gathering arranged at the City Hall. Salma reaches on time. She is welcomed by the volunteers there and asks to sit at the front row. One chair is kept for her. There are 10 more distinguished persons also invited by the Chief Minister to confer *Bengal Ratna* award on their exemplary works in their own fields. The Chief Minister comes to the dais. All other Ministers also come along with her.

The Chief Minister starts addressing and introduces the distinguished persons who have been selected for *Bengal Ratna* award. The Chief Minister in her address repeats 3 times of Salma's name and her contribution to the society. She decorates Salma as *"Bengal Lady with Lamp"* whose aim is to remove dark from the families of helpless and ill-fated women in villages. The Chief Minister calls the awardees one by one. Salma is called to the dais and the Chief Minister presents one Buddha Statue to her hand as award. She also gives one check of two lakh rupees.

Salma is literally encircled by the press reporters. They all want to know her feelings. They are asking questions after questions to her. Salma couldn't speak. Her eyes are full of tears.

The Chief Minister sees that. She comes from the dais.

"Please do not ask any question to her," the Chief Minister tells the reporters. "You will get answer of all your questions from her tears."

**END**